W9-AEP-969

Lazar Malkin Enters Heaven

Also by Steve Stern

The Moon and Ruben Shein

Isaac and the Undertaker's Daughter

for children

Mickey and the Golem

Lazar Malkin Enters Heaven

Stories by
Steve Stern

Viking

For my Violet—
who else?

VIKING
Viking Penguin Inc., 40 West 23rd Street,
New York, New York 10010, U.S.A.
Penguin Books Ltd, Harmondsworth,
Middlesex, England
Penguin Books Australia Ltd, Ringwood,
Victoria, Australia
Penguin Books Canada Limited, 2801 John Street,
Markham, Ontario, Canada L3R 1B4
Penguin Books (N.Z.) Ltd, 182–190 Wairau Road,
Auckland 10, New Zealand

First published in 1986 by Viking Penguin Inc.
Published simultaneously in Canada

Page 250 constitutes a continuation of this copyright page.

LIBRARY OF CONGRESS CATALOGING IN PUBLICATION DATA
Stern, Steve, 1947–
Lazar Malkin enters heaven.
1. Jews—Fiction. I. Title.
PS3569.T414L3 1987 813′.54 86-40264
ISBN 0-670-81379-6

Printed in the United States of America by
R. R. Donnelley & Sons Company, Harrisonburg, Virginia
Set in Sabon
Designed by Beth Tondreau

Contents

Moishe the Just

It was the summer we spent on the roof, spying on our neighbors across the street. There was Ivan Salky, Harold Panitz, the late Nathan Siripkin, and me. We would kneel on the sticky tarpaper, our chins propped on top of a low parapet encrusted with bird droppings. In this way we watched the clumsy progress of the courtship of Billy Rubin and the shoemaker's daughter. We saw, like a puppet play in silhouette, Old Man Crow beating his wife behind drawn shades. Through their open windows we saw the noisy family Pinkus gesticulating over their hysterical evening meal. We saw Eddie Kid Katz sparring with shadows and the amply endowed Widow Taubenblatt in her bath, but even with her we got bored.

"What if Billy Rubin went for her tush? What if Kid Katz got decked by his own shadow?" Nathan would needle us in a constant catechism. It was his never-ending campaign to infect us with his cockeyed fantasies.

But we had already begun to grow out of them. Didn't we know better than anyone that our neighborhood held no particular secrets? What people did in the privacy of their apartments at night was not so different from their antics in the street by day. Old Man Crow abused his wife outside their haberdashery; the Pinkuses, behind their lunch counter, were hysterical. The Widow Taubenblatt, although not naked, struck distinctly suggestive poses at her cash register. So when, at the close of day, they entered their rooms and the windows above North Main Street shed light on their private lives, there were no surprises. And even Nathan Siripkin's more modest speculations couldn't lead us to expect them.

"What if Moishe Purim was a *lamed vovnik*?" asked Nathan one sweltering evening toward the end of June. By then the novelty of our espionage had nearly worn off. Ivan and Harold and I were hardly paying attention to the predictable performances of our neighbors. Instead we worried about the future; we sniffed the breeze that blew in off the river. Like a whiff of what was coming, it smelled fishy.

But Nathan still had the gift of recalling us from our distraction and suckering us into his own. Despite ourselves we were curious—as Nathan must have calculated—to find out exactly what a lamed vovnik was.

"You know," said Nathan offhandedly, as if we only needed reminding, "like a saint. There's always thirty-six of them living secretly in different places. They're the excuse God gives himself not to blow us the hell out of the universe."

We were a little slow to take his meaning. Cheder boys all, we were nevertheless reluctant learners, content with no more than a nodding acquaintance with our exotic heritage. What interested us in those lean years was free enterprise. At the risk of a rap from the ruler of Rabbi Fishbein, we stole glances out the dirty windows of the Talmud Torah class. We worried that other kids were staking claim to the corners we sold papers on; they were peddling our bottles to the bootleggers down on Beale Street.

Among us only Nathan Siripkin still had time for the old superstitions, which he was not above exploiting for his own ends. That night, for instance, by way of recalling our errant attention, he went so far as to propose that the lowly Moishe was one of God's elect.

"Name me one person in the Pinch that's holier," he challenged, his eyeglasses glinting moonlight, head nodding like an overripe melon on the scrawny stalk of his neck. And we had to admit that if destitution and monotonous ritual observance were the measure, Moishe was certainly holy.

Of all the neighbors that we spied on, his activities were the most forgettable. Each dusk, with a homecoming kiss to the doorpost, he climbed six flights of stairs to his junk-cluttered room. He switched on an unshaded bulb and, shedding the bulk of his person, unpeeled himself of two or three overcoats. Anointing his hands at a grimy sink, he sat down to his packing crate and praised the Lord for a mostly imaginary repast of kosher leavings. Then, with his party cap of a yarmelke perched precariously atop his mottled head, he swayed for hours over an open scripture. Repeatedly he buried the hatchet of his face in its crumb-strewn pages, so that it looked as if he were bobbing for wisdom. Though Nathan had often made cruder suggestions as to what he might be about.

But now he was taking another tack.

For years Nathan Siripkin had appointed himself the task of keeping us amused. It was his compulsion. Spunky for such a nebbish, he could ferret out whatever squalor and romance our neighborhood had to offer. He'd introduced us, always with his air of a proprietor, to the disreputable goings-on upstairs at the Green Owl Café. He'd led us into the sewers (catacombs, he called them) beneath North Main Street, which were given over to a refuge for forgotten men. And whenever it looked like the neighborhood might be depleted of spectacle, Nathan replenished it from his own fanciful reserves.

At his instigation we'd been trespassers, truants, and now peeping-toms. But lately, waking up to the fact that there was life outside the Pinch, we had begun to develop an immunity to his big ideas.

To salvage what was left of his influence, Nathan made an effort to outdo himself. He provided us with the cross-sectioned lives of our neighbors, taking it personally when our interests flagged. Given the extremes he went to to hold our attention, you'd have thought that their lives depended on our watching to give them significance. But none of Nathan's embroideries was making much of an impression anymore.

Then he presented the theory that Moishe Purim was one of those for whose sake God neglected to destroy the world, and suddenly we were all ears.

Not exactly a luftmensch—like so many that wandered North Main Street in those days—old Moishe had barely visible means of support. His own dilapidated beast of burden, he pulled a rattling wooden cart with rubber tires around the Pinch. In it he collected scrap metal, which he sold to Blockman's junkyard; he took in castoff garments, kitchen utensils, broken clocks and gramophones, which he hocked for peanuts over at Kaplan's loans. With his perpetually bemused expression, his rheumy eyes rolled up under his heavy lids, he was oblivious to traffic and streetcars and barking dogs. He never solicited, though our parents, when they heard his jingling approach, took him the unwanted bits of their past. These he dutifully hauled away.

"It's like," Nathan once commented (he was big on pestilence and disasters), "the way people in the plague used to bring out their dead." But that was before he was committed to the idea that old Moishe was a saint.

I don't know why we were so susceptible. After all, we were practical kids whose first allegiance was to the power of the almighty buck. Maybe it was the times, which, besides being tough, were also a little scary. The news from abroad—our parents never tired of telling us—was bleak. Relations were beginning to get lost. And if momzers like Father Coughlin were any indication, what was happening there might happen here. So maybe we were primed for giving our cagey suspicions a rest. In any case, at Nathan Siripkin's invitation, we began to follow Moishe around the Pinch.

At first we told ourselves that we were only humoring Nathan—but then we were taken in by the old contagion. School was out and we were working in our families' shops; we were hawking papers, delivering piecework, selling policy. But we stole time to meet in the afternoons. It was then that Nathan attempted to bear out in broad daylight what he'd concluded during our evenings on the roof.

"Have a look," he charged us, waving in the direction of the old man like he was shaking him out of his unbuttoned sleeve. "He's got one foot in this world and one foot in the other."

"Looks to me like he's got both feet in the gutter," said Ivan Salky. That was the cue to elbow each other and hoot at Nathan's expense—which we did. But playing it safe, we kept our hilarity to a minimum.

"So why don't we ask him if he's a lamed whatsit already?" Harold Panitz, whose flair for the obvious could always be counted on, wanted to know.

Nathan did his famous slow burn. He spent a moment in suffering our boorishness bravely, then took the opportunity to reveal to us the paradoxical nature of the just man.

"Because, putz, if a lamed vovnik suspects that he's holy, he ain't holy anymore. It's a secret . . ."

"Between us and the Lord," I threw in irreverently, trying to one-up Nathan's presumptions. Because I was smart (I read books), Nathan sometimes treated me like I was his protégé. This of course made me stick even closer to the others. Now he gave me one of his meaningful glances, as if we both understood what a mouthful I'd said.

He was such a pisher, Nathan Siripkin, with his outsized head of copper curls boiling out of his overheated brain. Behind his back we took great pleasure in mocking him: we supposed that he was from Mars, that his swollen brain would one day burst through the walls of his skull. Then all hell would break loose; a carnival of demented creatures would run amok through the streets of the Pinch. But for all of our mutinous jokes, we remained more or less his grudging disciples. We were intrigued that, in the face of so much pressing reality, Nathan continued to treat his fabrications with such high seriousness.

Despite all the commotion of North Main Street, he put a finger to his lips whenever we were shadowing Moishe. This was doubly irrelevant since Moishe was so obviously indifferent to his surroundings. Streetcars would clang, hook-and-ladders peel out of the Number 4 station, and the old man would appear in their dust, serenely trudging. Elevators bearing piano crates and porters would rise up out of the pavement as Moishe passed over. Children might stampede, pigeons pelt the rim of his hat, paint buckets graze his shoulders as they toppled off of scaffolds. And demons, as Nathan assured us, might pull his beard and tug at the wisps of his hair. But nothing could distract the junk collector from his self-appointed rounds.

"That's what they're like," Nathan had whispered, beckoning us into a doorway for the confidence. "They walk around in a trance all day while God looks out for them."

We had to admit that the old kocker turned out to be more interesting than we'd bargained for. For the hour or so that we tailed him in the afternoons, we were fascinated. We were under the impression, unspoken of course, that so long as we were riding the junk collector's coattails, we were also preserved from harm. What with the world going to hell in a handbag, it was nice to think that our neighborhood was still, so to speak, safe for democracy. Nothing threatened us anymore: not Rabbi Fishbein's ruler or the bullying Mackerel Gang, not the butcher's rotten temper or the promise of high water or the voices from the radio prophesying war. Whatever perils lurked along the length of North Main Street parted like the Red Sea for Moishe, and for us as we crept stealthily behind him.

Naturally Nathan assumed full credit for the sense of well-being that Moishe had lulled us into.

"You have to understand," he explained in his most aggravating tone of condescension, "he's in direct communication with the Lord. Break that connection and he's just like you and me."

Then we chafed a little at the implication that we were like Nathan. It made us prickly and uncomfortable. Ivan Salky, lowering the bill of his cap, was the first among us to utter a word of dissent.

"All right," he said, swallowing hard to get it out, "so the old geek don't know how to get out of the rain. He's too feeble-minded to understand he's a bum. So nu?"

And as Ivan remained unstruck by lightning, the spell was lifted. Harold Panitz and I were encouraged to second and third our discontent. So Moishe ignored traffic signals, walked on freshly poured cement, lived on crumbs and Hebrew characters. He was a strange one, there was no denying it; but a saint? Show us some solid evidence.

There was a satisfaction we always took in turning on Nathan, even if it meant we were the victims of our own rebellion. Sure, we'd gotten a kick out of following Moishe, and yes, there was something about him that made us feel at peace with the world. But we were ready to forfeit it all in an instant for the sake of putting Nathan on the spot.

"Okay, okay," he protested, "I get your drift." Making his martyr's face, he pressed the palms of his hands to his temples as if to still the metronome of his head, which continued its nodding. Apparently for his own benefit he recited an axiom—this by way of gathering his wits.

"You don't judge a holy man by what he does so much as by what he don't do. Now what don't he do?" There was a pause during which we looked at one another while Nathan's brain went into labor. Eventually, releasing his temples, he gave birth to this assumption:

"He don't get led into temptation, that's what!"

Then it became a question of what temptation to place before Moishe, by virtue of his resistance to which he would prove he was holy.

Impatient as he was with our insubordination, Nathan Siripkin could never pass up a chance to be devious. Quickly forgetting to feel persecuted, he got down to business. He summarily ruled out the lesser vices, deeming it unlikely that, say, a barbecued spare rib dangled in front of Moishe's nose would offer him any genuine allure. By the same token, it was hard to image him being drawn into a crap game or a policy scam. How could he be seduced by what he probably couldn't even identify? And as for placing some item of value in his path, the lifting of which would make him a thief, what would he notice that wasn't dropped directly into his cart? No, what was called for was a kind of temptation that even Moishe could not ignore.

Had we offered any assistance, Nathan would have received it as interfering with the intricate workings of his mind. Which was fine with us. It wasn't so much that we lacked imagination, though why should we tax our own when we could rely upon his? And anyway, we didn't like to lose an opportunity of watching him warm to inspiration—the way he would wad up his face, yank his corkscrewing hair like he was trying to unstopper ideas. In a while his features would resolve themselves into an insipid grin; a forefinger would shoot up eureka-wise. Then he would reveal some half-baked prescription, just as now he announced what might have been a watchword:

"Anastasia!"

Ivan Salky, Harold Panitz, and I exchanged glances to the effect that we were not in the slightest surprised.

Anastasia Tomashefsky, with her greasy hair and her thick body as shapeless as a laundry bag, was most of what we knew about the charms of the opposite sex. Where the Widow Taubenblatt was our tantalizing but unattainable ideal, Anastasia could be had for the price of a potato knish. True, we had not had much of her, but the odd glimpse of raw pink nipple, the casually exposed dirty underwear, had been enough to frighten us out of wanting more. Although she was a discovery of Nathan's, even he became squeamish when it came to taking advantage of what she offered. Though we fortified ourselves with boasts of our wicked intentions, we blenched at the critical moments, remembering rumors of the disfiguring diseases that might ensue.

But on Moishe's account we took heart. We were disinterested parties engaging her services for the sake of a bold experiment. It cost us three danishes, a pound of chopped liver, and considerable time lost in persuasion.

"You want me to what? In front of who?" Anastasia kept asking, not so much shocked as bewildered by what we proposed. We snickered into our sleeves as Nathan, juggling invisible grapefruits, mimed a demonstration of what we had in mind. In the end Anastasia, who was nothing if not a good sport, joined in the general hilarity.

"The old fart'll have a heart attack!" she squealed in unwholesome abandon—giving some of us cause for second thoughts. But we knew that Nathan had already been goaded beyond the point of no return.

After dinner we convened as usual on the roof. Through a collapsible spyglass that Nathan had managed to get out of hock for the occasion, we took turns in sighting old Moishe bent over his book. He was one floor above us and a street width away, but seeing him like that—tobacco-colored in the weathered telescope lens—was like putting an eye to his keyhole. But where on the one hand he seemed so close, on the other he seemed even farther away, in a remoter place and time. It was a sensation that kept us interested for a while, then began to tire us out. But just when we'd practically given up believing that the appointment would be kept, Moishe got up to answer the door.

Who knows what we expected to happen? For all our predictions about his jumping into her arms and worse, I don't think we really imagined that Moishe would ever succumb to temptation. But what we weren't prepared for was the offhand regard with which he greeted Anastasia at the door.

She stood there in her hoisted brassiere, her blouse held professionally open, like a gonif might open his coat to display his wares. Though we couldn't see Moishe's expression, it couldn't have been so different from the blinking complacency he wore when he turned around. Then he crept away from her as if she might have been walking in her sleep and he was taking pains not to wake her up. (While for her part Anastasia stole a peek at her drooping boobies, like she had to make sure that they were still there.) From his cot the old man removed a mouse-gray blanket and padded back to the doorway. He draped the blanket over Anastasia's nakedness the way you put a shade over a lamp that's too bright. Then, ever so gently, he closed the door in her face.

It was the proper way for a saint to behave; of that we were all agreed. Like Nathan had said: You know them by what they don't do. But who couldn't help feeling disappointed that nothing unspeakable had taken place? Already we were grousing, what a wet blanket was Moishe, what a shnook—when Nathan, in a theatrically maritime stance, spectacles on his forehead, spyglass to his eye, told us, "Shah! Pipe down." We turned back toward his window in time to see the old man blowing dust from a plum-colored bottle of wine.

Uncorking the bottle between his bony knees, he raised it hastily, plugging his lips like he was staunching a wound. We held our breaths watching him drink but had to breathe again before he stopped; and Nathan assured us that the bottle was nearly empty when he put it down. Then, as the spirits began to move him, he commenced what, for want of another word, must be called a dance. He danced with his knees bent stiffly, his fleshless arms stretching out of his ragged sleeves. His fingers snapped, whiskers furled, while his head lolled from side to side, as if he were being electrocuted in slow motion.

"He's nuts!" blurted Harold Panitz, but this time we echoed Nathan in saying shut up. Then we astonished ourselves a little, since what was there to be quiet for? Unless we were listening for the same music that Moishe must have thought he heard.

In a window beneath him Billy Rubin was tentatively putting an arm around his sweetheart, who promptly removed it, and in another window the Pinkuses were slinging food. Behind a butter-yellow shade Old Man Crow was lifting a vase to brain his wife. Kid Katz was cranking out deep-knee bends, and the widow, in her unfastened dressing gown, was gazing into a mirror. They were doing what they always did, though it all took place tonight—or so you might have concluded—by the grace of Moishe's doddering dance. He could have been their puppeteer.

We remained transfixed until the old goat's unending contortions began eventually to wear us down. Enough was enough, we complained; such monkeyshines were unnatural in a man of his age. And one by one we left the roof, all but Nathan, who kept his spyglass trained exclusively on Moishe.

The next night, in the absence of any further drama (Moishe fell typically asleep over his book), we were full of contentiousness again. So he hadn't tried to shtup Anastasia, we said—so what? With a body like hers, it didn't take a saint to resist. And anyway, what had his lunatic dance been all about? Was it right that a just man—one of the thirty-six pillars of the civilized world, as Nathan was fond of saying—should get drunk and hop about all alone in his room?

Unprepared for our attack, Nathan Siripkin fell uncharacteristically into sulking, which antagonized us all the more. At one point, his spectacles fogging, head nodding woodpeckerishly, he seemed actually to be in pain.

"You guys got no faith!" he accused, prompting us to look at one another in consternation. What was this foreign currency that we were suddenly supposed to possess? Where could you spend it around here? It was unlike Nathan to stoop to such tactics by way of shirking the burden of proof.

After a while, however, he began to come around. "All

right, okay" —he dismissed the problem with a wave— "so we'll tempt him again. We'll swipe some muggles from Nutty Iskowitz or we'll . . ." We could see he was clutching at straws.

Then it was Ivan Salky who brought Nathan up short. "Enough temptation," he stated flatly, leading with his lantern jaw. "What we want is a miracle." He turned to Harold Panitz and me for confirmation, and we uniformly wagged our heads. Though we hadn't known it until that moment when Ivan became our spokesman, nothing short of a miracle would ever convince us of Moishe's sanctity.

Nathan eyed us in acute exasperation. "Schmucks."

"If he's really what you say, he can do a miracle," said I, feeling my oats, ignoring the glance I got from Nathan of utter betrayal.

"Of course he can do a miracle," sighed Nathan, as if it went without saying. "Only he just don't know that he can."

"Oh, neat, oh, very convenient." We mugged and rolled our eyes. We were back to the business of knowing the holy man by what he didn't do.

Then popeyed Harold Panitz tugged at Nathan's sleeve and asked an inspired question.

"Can he die?"

Ivan Salky and I lit up at the astuteness of this; we slapped Harold's back in hearty congratulation. Death was surely the thing by which, if it turned out he wasn't prey to it in the ordinary sense, Moishe could be proven a saint.

Cornered, Nathan had to confess it was so: a lamed vovnik never passed on until God himself decided it was time. "Then He takes them up to paradise alive." But this was a phenomenon you might have to wait an eternity to see, and we didn't have that kind of patience. We were confident that Nathan, calling upon his wily devices, could settle the matter more instantly.

"Prove it now!" we insisted, as proud of our ultimatum as we were frightened at having delivered it. Because we saw how Nathan Siripkin, stilling his head in the vise of his forefinger and thumb, had already begun to consider. Already he was plotting how to place the poor junk collector's life in jeopardy.

It was a little chilling the way Nathan put himself through his paces. Traditionally, by the time he'd converted us to his current obsession, he was carried away by something new. We might just be getting the hang of finding the loose change beneath the bleachers at the Phoenix boxing arena when Nathan would talk us into, say, volunteering for the hypnotist at the Idle Hour talent night. In his fickleness he was always one step ahead of us.

So you'd have thought that we'd been contrary enough over Moishe for Nathan to take the hint. As a variety of entertainment—who should know better than him?—the old man had had his day. But this one Nathan refused to give up gracefully; he hung onto his fixed idea about the junk collector as if it were a matter of life and death.

At night on the roof, lounging against the dusty skylight, we listened to him presenting designs for what he'd begun to call his "saint trap." But this wasn't the old Nathan Siripkin, full of infectious mischief and crackpot illusions. Something about him had changed. Not only did he seem to have bought his own spiel, but he'd become fanatically single-minded in his scheming. In fact he might have been as determined to disprove the junkman's authenticity as to prove it.

At first he invoked what he knew to be the classical fates of saints—goyishe saints, that is, since the Jewish ones were immortal. There was stoning, of course, immolation, crucifixion, and so on, though none of these were up-to-date enough for his purposes. Still he continued to lean toward the apocalyptic. He was sold for a while on the notion that the earth might be made to open up beneath Moishe. Bridges could collapse, freight elevators might plummet down bottomless shafts. And as the town was situated on a famous fault line, giant fissures might be caused to erupt along the surface of North Main Street.

When we reasoned that the technical know how for such assassinations was beyond our modest means, Nathan shifted without ceremony to an alternate vision.

"How about we drop a live wire in his bathtub?" he submitted. His bones would be illumined through his ashen skin, and he would dance again at his own transfiguration.

Rather than do him the courtesy of egging him on, we pressed him to consider more conservative measures. It was how we attempted to call his bluff. Since when, we wondered, did Moishe ever take a bath? And who knew (in response to Nathan's next proposal that we poison the old man's wine) when he might be moved to drink again?

At one point Harold Panitz, aiming for the heart of the matter, said, "Why don't we just hit the old buzzard over the head?" But Nathan only laughed him to scorn. It was just the kind of guileless suggestion you might expect from the unsophisticated Harold.

Then Nathan thought a little longer. He was stalling, of course, and he knew that we knew. Having failed to back us off with his loftier ideas, he was forced to come down to earth. He went through all the motions, bludgeoning his brow with the heel of his hand, and after a time his forefinger shot up like a perennial sprout.

"I got it!" he announced, davening from the neck up only. "We'll drop some big weight on his head."

• • •

Climbing up the fire escape outside of Moishe's building, we were supposed to pass for a party of honest workmen. Though if called upon to do so, even Nathan would have been hard pressed to account for all our paraphernalia. There were the ropes, for instance, and the beltful of tools in which Nathan was festooned, so that he clanked like Marley's ghost. Then came the armload of boards against which Harold Panitz appeared to be fighting a losing battle. Not to mention the anvil that Ivan Salky and I—stopping every few steps to gasp for breath and look over our shoulders—reluctantly lugged.

To spur us on, Nathan kept comparing us to an expedition up a mountain, but that only made the ascent seem more punishing.

He'd campaigned for a millstone, which was supposed to signify the weight of the world's woe, or something of that order. But for the sake of expediency (and in lieu of a vault, his second choice), he'd conceded to the more available anvil, which we stole from Harold's father's tinsmithy. It was a scored and misshapen hunk of iron, about which Nathan wasn't happy until he'd dignified it with a mythological status: "It's like the one they pulled the sword out of in King Arthur." Though he sounded a little less than convinced.

From his girdle of tools Nathan had drawn forth a crowbar with a mighty flourish. It proved unnecessary, however, as Moishe's window, the corner one overlooking Auction Street, was already open. Then it seemed natural enough that we should be standing inside his room. Hadn't it been for us like some kind of stage? So now we were a crew come to rearrange the props between acts. But after a few moments the atmosphere began to oppress us. We lowered our heads in the presence of his makeshift table, his fractured cot, the orphaned steam irons and mixers, the broken clocks with their arms in a semaphore of all hours. There was the fetor of fish and stale pee, odors dense as ghosts that were trying to crowd us out of the room.

"Right," chirped Nathan, rubbing his hands, still refusing to take the hint, "let's get to work." But he was no less lumpish than the rest of us. For all of his big ideas, he hadn't a clue about how to proceed with rigging his booby trap. It was up to Ivan Salky, the handyman's son, to take the initiative.

Standing on a crate precariously balanced in the lap of a listing chair, he hammered a pair of pulleys into the ceiling. Cracks spread out in the plaster like fossilized lightning. Then Ivan threaded ropes through the pulleys, making a kind of cat's cradle. He took the plank, into which I'd been busily boring a hole, and secured it among the ropes like the seat of a swing. He knotted some twine, passed it through the plank and over his network of ropes, then looped it around the dangling light cord. Climbing down, he began to test his contraption, switching the light off and on—which caused the swing to dip in a mechanical approximation of Nathan's perpetual nod.

It only remained to mount the anvil in place. This we accomplished, after a couple of abortive efforts, through the offices of a tottering human totem pole. With the anvil in its cradle, the totem pole collapsed, and we picked ourselves up to admire our handiwork. Sinister device that it was, it hung in the center of that seedy room as conspicuously as a chandelier. No one but the heedless Moishe could have failed to see it immediately upon walking in.

Then Nathan Siripkin pronounced his verdict: "Rube Goldberg meets Edgar Allan Poe." Apparently he was satisfied.

We'd been expecting him at any moment to relent. Having played along with him until now, we were ready for him to admit that the joke had gone far enough. But Nathan continued to make a good show of it. Diabolical architect of Moishe's execution, he still professed a faith in miracles. And if he saw any contradiction, it wasn't obvious; not unless you considered his grinding teeth, his feverish hopping about, as evidence.

He was orchestrating exactly how the saint trap ought to be sprung.

"He'll pull the cord like this," said Nathan, teasing us with a tug at thin air, "and the anvil will fall. But it'll never touch a hair on his head." And for a second you could almost see it: the anvil suspended and radiant, balanced on the pinnacle of the junkman's paper yarmelke.

Then Harold Panitz, whose skepticism was sometimes in question, asked, "So what if God decides it's his time?"

Nathan shrugged if off with the cavalier assurance that trumpets would blow, angels descend. He grinned skittishly in the face of our lack of conviction, taking us to task. "Don't bother me with technicalities. Besides, in times as screwy as these, do you think that God can spare a single lamed vovnik?"

It was the only occasion in anyone's recollection that Nathan Siripkin had stooped to acknowledge the times.

That night, around dusk, by prior arrangement, Ivan and Harold and I met on the roof before Nathan arrived. In the west the setting sun, like a broken yolk, was running an angry red all over the sky, spilling into the river. Somewhere in the east, beyond the ocean, a storm—as our parents liked to remind us—was brewing. And there we were on a roof above our crummy neighborhood, feeling particularly exposed to the elements, like we might be marooned. Ivan Salky pulled the bill of his cap down nearly to the bridge of his nose, and Harold Panitz kept looking like, Who knows, maybe Nathan could be right.

But we were wise to Nathan Siripkin; we understood how this had turned into a contest of wills. This whole elaborate plot was for our benefit; it was intended to scare us into subscribing to his latest, crowning mishegoss. No doubt Nathan assumed that any moment now we would lose our nerve, but we were one step ahead of him. We were resolved that come what may we would let him play his hand through to the bitter end.

Then the skylight slid open and Nathan emerged with his hands in his pockets, his head barely nodding, whistling a tune. Gone was his jumping-bean agitation of the afternoon. Not that we were fooled for a minute by his confidence—which was maybe the point. Maybe he wanted us to think he didn't require our endorsement to believe that something was true.

Our hearts sank as he cautioned us not to do precisely what we'd sworn, despite him, not to do: "Nobody but nobody tries to warn him, see?"

Having put it to us so bluntly, he felt obliged to reiterate: If we tipped off Moishe to the danger, everything would have to come out. He would learn what the trap was for; he would know who he was, and as a consequence he wouldn't be who he was anymore. It was the same old screwball logic that he had hooked us with in the first place. Only tonight it seemed like another kind of a trap, one in which Nathan himself was already caught. And he was crazy if he expected us to join him.

Still, we waited in our typical genuflection on the bubbling tarpaper, passing the spyglass back and forth. We chewed jawbreakers, mopped sweat from our foreheads, and avoided each other's eyes.

Then ("Moishe ahoy") we spotted him pushing his cart along North Main Street, weaving a path between the five-globed streetlamps and the sparks from the trolley cars. He left his cart in an alley beside his building, then entered the vestibule, where he would climb the six flights of stairs up to his room. He would climb the stairs at a weary trudge, pausing perhaps on every landing, cautioning his heart to stop rattling the cage of his brittle ribs. Minutes would elapse before he reached the top. There was plenty of time, if we shook a leg, to divert him from what was in store.

Then the time had run out and we looked to Nathan as if he might forgodsakes turn back the clock. But Nathan wasn't there.

He must have dived headlong through the skylight, ridden banisters down to the street, then shot up the fire escape on the other side. He must have bolted through the window just in time to intercept the junkman's fate. In any case, when the light came on in Moishe's room, I saw through the spy-glass, which I'd wrestled out of Harold's hands, the old man stumbling backward. I saw Nathan, who must have shoved him, crumpling under the fallen anvil, dropping out of the golden frame of the lens.

Lowering the glass, I saw how everything had spilled out through the crack in Nathan Siripkin's size nine head: the old man with outstretched arms and upturned face, dancing his grief; the klutzy kid stealing a kiss and getting a slap from a skinny girl; a couple of families giving each other hell; a palooka delivering a Sunday punch to phantoms; a lonely woman in her bath.

At the inquest we held onto a hope against all odds, that old Moishe was deaf and dumb. But when it all came out, how we'd tried to prove that the junk collector was one of the holy thirty-six, he opened his mouth. Gesturing shame with a pair of crooked forefingers, he spoke in an accent thick as sour cream.

"Bed, bed boychikls. Somebody better potch dere tushies."

When he saw that no one but himself was laughing, he suddenly appeared perplexed. His amused expression sagged like a sack whose bottom drops out in the rain. It was an expression that we were certain had echoes; it was repeated maybe thirty-five times, until every other lamed vovnik wherever he might be had lost his innocence too.

That was something that Nathan had neglected to tell us, a piece of the legend we figured out for ourselves. When you exposed one just man, you as good as exposed the lot. We understood this better after the storm finally broke in Europe. At the same time the swollen river overflowed the Pinch. North Main Street was under water, and the high ground was awash with homeless families and bedraggled animals. For those of us who were able to read the signs, we knew that it was the beginning of the end of the world.

Lazar Malkin Enters Heaven

My father-in-law, Lazar Malkin, may he rest in peace, refused to die. This was in keeping with his lifelong stubbornness. Of course there were those who said that he'd passed away already and come back again, as if death were another of his so-called peddling trips, from which he always returned with a sackful of crazy gifts.

There were those in our neighborhood who joked that he'd been dead for years before his end. And there was more than a little truth in this. Hadn't he been declared clinically kaput not once but twice on the operating table? Over the years they'd extracted more of his internal organs than it seemed possible to do without. And what with his wooden leg, his empty left eye socket concealed by a gabardine patch, his missing teeth and sparse white hair, there was hardly enough of old Lazar left in this world to constitute a human being.

"Papa," my wife, Sophie, once asked him, just after the first of his miraculous recoveries, "what was it like to be dead?" She was sometimes untactful, my Sophie, and in this she took after her father—whose child she was by one of his unholy alliances. (Typically obstinate, he had always refused to marry.)

Lazar had looked at her with his good eye, which, despite

being set in a face like last week's roast, was usually wet and amused.

"Why ask me?" he wondered, refusing to take the question seriously. "Ask Alabaster the cobbler, who ain't left his shop in fifty years. He makes shoes, you'd think he's building coffins. Ask Petrofsky whose lunch counter serves nobody but ghosts. Ask Gruber the shammes or Milstein the tinsmith. Ask your husband, who is as good as wearing his sewing machine around his neck . . ."

I protested that he was being unfair, though we both knew that he wasn't. The neighborhood, which was called the Pinch, had been dead since the War. Life and business had moved east, leaving us with our shops falling down around our ears. Myself and the others, we kidded ourselves that North Main Street would come back. Our children would come back again. The ready-made industry, we kept insisting, was just a passing fancy; people would return to quality. So who needed luftmenschen like Lazar to remind us that we were deceived?

"The Pinch ain't the world," he would inform us, before setting off on one of his mysterious peddling expeditions. He would haul himself into the cab of his corroded relic of a truck piled with shmattes and tools got on credit from a local wholesale outfit. Then he would sputter off in some random direction for points unknown.

Weeks later he would return, his pockets as empty as the bed of his truck. But he always brought back souvenirs in his burlap sack, which he prized like the kid in the story who swapped a cow for a handful of beans.

"I want you to have this," he would say to Mr. Alabaster or Gruber or Schloss or myself. Then he would give us a harp made out of a crocodile's tail; he would give us a Negro's toe, a root that looked like a little man, a contraption called a go-devil, a singletree, the uses of which he had no idea. "This will make you wise," he told us. "This will make you amorous. This came from Itta Bena and this from Nankipoo"—as if they were places as far away as China, which for all we knew they were.

"Don't thank me," he would say, like he thought we might be speechless with gratitude. Then he would borrow a few bucks and limp away to whatever hole in the wall he was staying in.

Most of my neighbors got rid of Lazar's fetishes and elixirs, complaining that it made them nervous to have them around. I was likewise inclined, but in deference to my wife I kept them. Rather than leave them lying around the apartment, however, I tossed them into the storage shed behind my shop.

No one knew how old Lazar really was, though it was generally agreed that he was far past the age when it was still dignified to be alive. None of us, after all, was a spring chicken anymore. We were worn out from the years of trying to supplement our pensions with the occasional alteration or the sale of a pair of shoelaces. If our time should be near, nobody was complaining. Funerals were anyhow the most festive occasions we had in the Pinch. We would make a day of it, traveling in a long entourage out to the cemetery, then back to North Main for a feast at the home of the bereaved. You might say that death was very popular in our neighborhood. So it aggravated us that Lazar, who preceded us by a whole generation, should persist in hanging around.

He made certain that most of what we knew about him was hearsay. It was his nature to be mysterious. Even Sophie, his daughter by one of his several scandals, knew only the rumors. As to the many versions of his past, she would tell me to take my pick. "I would rather not, if you don't mind," I said. The idea of Lazar Malkin as a figure of romance was a little more than I could handle. But that never stopped Sophie from regaling me by telling stories of her father the way another woman might sing to herself.

He lost his eye as a young man, when he refused to get out of the way of a rampaging Cossack in his village of Podolsk. Walking away from Kamchatka, where he'd been sent for refusing to be drafted into the army of the Czar, the frostbite turned to gangrene and he lost his leg. Or was it the other way around? He was dismembered by a Cossack, snowblinded in one eye for good? . . . What did it matter? The only moral I got out of the tales of Lazar's mishegoss was that every time he refused to do what was sensible, there was a little less of him left to refuse with.

It puzzled me that Sophie could continue to have such affection for the old kocker. Hadn't he ruined her mother, among others, at a time when women did not go so willingly to their ruin? Of course, the living proofs of his wickedness were gone now. His old mistresses had long since passed on, and it was assumed there were no offspring other than Sophie. Though sometimes I was haunted by the thought of the surrounding countryside populated by the children of Lazar Malkin.

So what was the attraction? Did the ladies think he was some pirate with his eye patch and clunking artificial leg? That one I still find hard to swallow. Or maybe they thought that with him it didn't count. Because he refused to settle down to any particular life, it was as if he had no legitimate life at all. None worth considering in any case. And I cursed myself for the time I took to think about him, an old fool responsible for making my wife a bastard—though who could think of Sophie in such a light?

• • •

"You're a sick man, Lazar," I told him, meaning in more ways than one. "See a doctor."

"I never felt better, I'll dance on your grave," he insisted, asking me incidentally did I have a little change to spare.

I admit that this did not sit well with me, the idea of his hobbling a jig on my headstone. Lie down already and die, I thought, God forgive me. But from the way he'd been lingering in the neighborhood lately, postponing his journeys, it was apparent to whoever noticed that something was wrong. His unshaven face was the gray of dirty sheets, and his wizened stick of a frame was shrinking visibly. His odor, no longer merely the ripe stench of the unwashed, had about it a musty smell of decay. Despite my imploring, he refused to see a physician, though it wasn't like he hadn't been in the hospital before. (Didn't I have a bundle of his unpaid bills to prove it?) So maybe this time he knew that for what he had there wasn't a cure.

When I didn't see him for a while, I supposed that, regardless of the pain he was in, he had gone off on another of his peddling trips.

"Your father needs a doctor," I informed Sophie over dinner one night.

"He won't go," she said, wagging her chins like what can you do with such a man. "So I invited him to come stay with us."

She offered me more kreplach, as if my wide-open mouth meant that I must still be hungry. I was thinking of the times he'd sat at our table in the vile, moth-eaten overcoat he wore in all seasons. I was thinking of the dubious mementos he left us with.

"Don't worry," said my good wife, "he won't stay in the apartment . . ."

"Thank God."

". . . But he asked if he could have the shed out back."

"I won't have it!" I shouted, putting my foot down. "I won't have him making a flophouse out of my storehouse."

"Julius," said Sophie in her watch-your-blood-pressure tone of voice, "he's been out there a week already."

I went down to the little brick shed behind the shop. The truth was that I seldom used it—only to dump the odd bolt of material and the broken sewing machines that I was too attached to to throw away. And Lazar's gifts. Though I could see through the window that an oil lamp was burning beneath a halo of mosquitoes, there was no answer to my knock. Entering anyway, I saw cobwebs, mouse droppings, the usual junk—but no Lazar.

Then I was aware of him propped in a chair in a corner, his burlap sack and a few greasy dishes at his feet. It took me so long to notice because I was not used to seeing him sit still. Always he was hopping from his real leg to his phony, being a nuisance, telling us we ought to get out and see more of the world. Now with his leg unhitched and lying across some skeins of mildewed cloth, I could have mistaken him for one of my discarded manikins.

"Lazar," I said, "in hospitals they at least have beds."

"Who sleeps?" he wanted to know, his voice straining up from his hollow chest. This was as much as admitting his frailty. Shocked out of my aggravation, I proceeded to worry.

"You can't live in here," I told him, thinking that no one would confuse this with living. "Pardon my saying so, but it stinks like Gehinom." I had observed the coffee tin he was using for a slop jar.

"A couple of days," he managed in a pathetic attempt to recover his native chutzpah, "and I'll be back on my feet again. I'll hit the road." When he coughed, there was dust, like when you beat a rug.

I looked over at one of the feet that he hoped to be back on and groaned. It might have been another of his curiosities, taking its place alongside of the boar's tusk and the cypress knee.

"Lazar," I implored, astonished at my presumption, "go to heaven already. Your organs and limbs are waiting there for a happy reunion. What do you want to hang around this miserable place anyway?" I made a gesture intended to take in more than the shed, which included the whole of the dilapidated Pinch with its empty shops and abandoned synagogue. Then I understood that for Lazar my gesture had included even more. It took in the high roads to Iuka and Yazoo City, where the shwartzers swapped him moonshine for a yard of calico.

"Heaven," he said in a whisper that was half a shout, turning his head to spit on the floor. "Heaven is wasted on the dead. Anyway, I like it here."

Feeling that my aggravation had returned, I started to leave.

"Julius," he called to me, reaching into the sack at his feet, extracting with his withered fingers I don't know what—some disgusting composition of feathers and bones and hair. "Julius," he wheezed in all sincerity, "I have something for you."

What can you do with such a man?

I went back the following afternoon with Dr. Seligman. Lazar told the doctor don't touch him, and the doctor shrugged like he didn't need to dirty his hands.

"Malkin," he said, "this isn't becoming. You can't borrow time the way you borrow gelt."

Seligman was something of a neighborhood philosopher. Outside the shed he assured me that the old man was past worrying about. "If he thinks he can play hide-and-go-seek with death, then let him. It doesn't hurt anybody but himself." He had such a way of putting things, Seligman.

"But Doc," I said, still not comforted, "it ain't in *your* backyard that he's playing his farkokte game."

It didn't help, now that the word was out, that my so-called friends and neighbors treated me like I was confining old Lazar against his will. For years they'd wished him out of their hair, and now they behaved as if they actually missed him. Nothing was the same since he failed to turn up at odd hours in their shops, leaving them with some ugly doll made from corn husks or a rabbit's foot.

"You think I like it," I asked them, "that the old fortz won't get it over with?" Then they looked at me like it wasn't nice to take his name in vain.

Meanwhile Sophie continued to carry her noodle puddings and bowls of chicken broth out to the shed. She was furtive in this activity, as if she was harboring an outlaw, and sometimes I thought she enjoyed the intrigue. More often than not, however, she brought back her plates with the food untouched.

I still looked in on him every couple of days, though it made me nauseous. It spoiled my constitution, the sight of him practically decomposing.

"You're sitting shivah for yourself, that's what," I accused him, holding my nose. When he bothered to communicate, it was only in grunts.

I complained to Sophie: "I was worried a flophouse, but charnel house is more like it."

"Shah!" she said, like it mattered whether the old so-and-so could hear us. "Soon he'll be himself again."

I couldn't believe my ears.

"Petrofsky," I confided at his lunch counter the next day, "my wife's as crazy as Lazar. She thinks he's going to get well."

"So why you got to bury him before his time?"

Petrofsky wasn't the only one to express this sentiment. It was contagious. Alabaster, Ridblatt, Schloss, they were all in the act, all of them suddenly defenders of my undying father-in-law. If I so much as opened my mouth to kvetch about the old man, they told me hush up, they spat against the evil eye. "But only yesterday you said it's unnatural he should live so long," I protested.

"Doc," I told Seligman in the office where he sat in front of a standing skeleton, "the whole street's gone crazy. They think that maybe a one-legged corpse can dance again."

The doctor looked a little nervous himself, like somebody might be listening. He took off his nickel-rimmed spectacles to speak.

"Maybe they think that if the angel of death can pass over Lazar, he can pass over the whole neighborhood."

"Forgive me, Doctor, but you're crazy too. Since when is everyone so excited to preserve our picturesque community? And anyway, wouldn't your angel look first in an open grave, which after all is what the Pinch has become." Then I was angry with myself for having stooped to speaking in riddles too.

But in the end I began to succumb to the general contagion. I was afraid for Lazar, I told myself, though—who was I kidding?—like the rest, I was afraid for myself.

"Sophie," I confessed to my wife, who had been treating me like a stranger lately, "I wish that old Lazar was out peddling again." Without him out wandering in the boondocks beyond our neighborhood, returning with his cockamamie gifts, it was like there wasn't a "beyond" anymore. The Pinch, for better or worse, was all there was. This I tried to explain to my Sophie, who squeezed my hand like I was her Julius again.

• • •

Each time I looked in on him, it was harder to distinguish the immobile Lazar from the rest of the dust and drek. I described this to Seligman, expecting medical opinion, and got only that it put him in mind of the story of the golem—dormant and moldering in a synagogue attic these six hundred years.

Then there was a new development. There were bits of cloth sticking out of the old man's nostrils and ears, and he refused to open his mouth at all.

"It's to keep his soul from escaping," Sophie told me, mussing my hair as if any ninny could see that. I groaned and rested my head in my hands, trying not to imagine what other orifices he might have plugged up.

After that I didn't visit him anymore. I learned to ignore Sophie, with her kerchief over her face against the smell, going to and fro with the food he refused to eat. I was satisfied it was impossible that he should still be alive, which fact made it easier to forget about him for periods of time.

This was also the tack that my friends and neighbors seemed to be taking. On the subject of Lazar Malkin we had all become deaf and dumb. It was like he was a secret we shared, holding our breaths lest someone should find us out.

Meanwhile on North Main Street it was business (or lack of same) as usual.

Of course I wasn't sleeping so well. In the middle of the night I remembered that, among the items and artifacts stored away in my shed, there was my still breathing father-in-law. This always gave an unpleasant jolt to my system. Then I would get out of bed and make what I called my cocktail—some antacid and a shpritz of soda water. It was summer and the rooms above the shop were an oven, so I would go out to the open back porch for air. I would sip my medicine, looking down at the yard and the shed—where Lazar's lamp had not been kindled for a while.

On one such night, however, I observed that the lamp was burning again. What's more, I detected movement through the little window. Who knew but some miracle had taken place and Lazar was up again? Shivering despite the heat, I grabbed my bathrobe and went down to investigate.

I tiptoed out to the shed, pressed my nose against the filthy windowpane, and told myself that I didn't see what I saw. But while I bit the heel of my hand to keep from crying out loud, he wouldn't go away—the stoop-shouldered man in his middle years, his face sad and creased like the seat of someone's baggy pants. He was wearing a rumpled blue serge suit, its coat a few sizes large to accommodate the hump on his back. Because it fidgeted and twitched, I thought at first that the hump must be alive; then I understood that it was a hidden pair of wings.

So this was he, Malach ha-Mavet, the Angel of Death. I admit to being somewhat disappointed. Such a sight should have been forbidden me, it should have struck me blind and left me gibbering in awe. But all I could feel for the angel's presence was my profoundest sympathy. The poor shnook, he obviously had his work cut out for him. From the way he massaged his temples with the tips of his fingers, his complexion a little bilious (from the smell?), I guessed that he'd been at it for a while. He looked like he'd come a long way expecting more cooperation than this.

"For the last time, Malkin," I could hear him saying, his tone quite similar in its aggravation to the one I'd used with Lazar myself, "are you or aren't you going to give up the ghost?"

In his corner old Lazar was nothing, a heap of dust, his moldy overcoat and eye patch the only indications that he was supposed to resemble a man.

"What are you playing, you ain't at home?" the angel went on. "You're at home. So who do you think you're fooling?"

But no matter how much the angel sighed like he didn't have all night, like the jig was already up, Lazar Malkin kept mum. For this I gave thanks and wondered how, in my moment of weakness, I had been on the side of the angel.

"Awright, awright," the angel was saying, bending his head to squeeze the bridge of his nose. The flame of the lamp leaped with every tired syllable he uttered. "So it ain't vested in me, the authority to take from you what you won't give. So what. I got my orders to bring you back. And if you don't come dead, I take you alive."

There was a stirring in Lazar's corner. Keep still, you fool, I wanted to say. But bony fingers had already emerged from his coatsleeves; they were snatching the plugs of cloth from his ears. The angel leaned forward as if Lazar had spoken, but I could hear nothing—oh, maybe a squeak like a rusty hinge. Then I heard it again.

"Nu?" was what Lazar had said.

The angel began to repeat the part about taking him back, but before he could finish, Lazar interrupted.

"Take me where?"

"Where else?" said the angel. "To paradise, of course."

There was a tremor in the corner which produced a commotion of moths.

"Don't make me laugh," the old man replied, actually coughing the distant relation of a chortle. "There ain't no such place."

The angel: "I beg your pardon?"

"You heard me," said Lazar, his voice became amazingly clear.

"Okay," said the angel, trying hard not to seem offended. "We're even. In paradise they'll never believe you're for real."

Where he got the strength then I don't know—unless it was born from the pain that he'd kept to himself all those weeks—but Lazar began to get up. Spider webs came apart and bugs abandoned him like he was sprouting out of the ground. Risen to his foot, he cried out,

"There ain't no world but this!"

The flame leaped, the windowpane rattled.

This was apparently the final straw. The angel shook his melancholy head, mourning the loss of his patience. He removed his coat, revealing a sweat-stained shirt and a pitiful pair of wings no larger than a chicken's.

"Understand, this is not my style," he protested, folding his coat, approaching what was left of my father-in-law.

Lazar dropped back into the chair, which collapsed beneath him. When the angel attempted to pull him erect, he struggled. I worried a moment that the old man might crumble to pieces in the angel's embrace. But he was substantial enough to shriek bloody murder, and not too proud to offer bribes: "I got for you a nice feather headdress . . ."

He flopped about and kicked as the angel stuffed him head first into his own empty burlap peddler's sack.

Then the worldweary angel manhandled Lazar—whose muffled voice was still trying to bargain from inside his sack—across the cluttered shed. And hefting his armload, the angel of death battered open the back door, then carried his burden, still kicking, over the threshold.

I threw up the window sash and opened my mouth to shout. But I never found my tongue. Because that was when, before the door slammed behind them, I got a glimpse of kingdom come.

It looked exactly like the yard in back of the shop, only—how should I explain it?—sensitive. It was the same brick wall with glass embedded on top, the same ashes and rusty tin cans, but they were tender and ticklish to look at. Intimate like (excuse me) flesh beneath underwear. For the split second that the door stayed open, I felt that I was turned inside-out, and what I saw was glowing under my skin in place of my kishkes and heart.

Wiping my eyes, I hurried into the shed and opened the back door. What met me was a wall, some ashes and cans, some unruly weeds and vines, the rear of the derelict coffee factory, the rotten wooden porches of the tenements of our dreary neighborhood. Then I remembered—slapping my forehead, stepping gingerly into the yard—that the shed had never had a back door.

Climbing the stairs to our apartment, I had to laugh out loud.

"Sophie!" I shouted to my wife—who, without waking, told me where to find the bicarbonate of soda. "Sophie," I cried, "set a place at the table for your father. He'll be coming back with God only knows what souvenirs."

The Gramophone

Arnold Siripkin broke the thermometer and dropped tears of quicksilver into the boiling cauldron.

"This here is azoth from the sorcerers of Babylon," he intoned, pushing his thick spectacles up onto the hump of his nose. "Now Stymie Cohen," he commanded, indicating that someone should shove forward a sullen boy who was lost in the contemplation of the swimming mercury. The boy was resentful.

"This here's whatever you said," he sulked, tossing a sea-green marble into the gurgling tub.

"An eye of newt!" said Arnold, losing patience. "Now Dumbo Klotwog." A fat kid with enormous ears began giggling unhealthily.

"This is what you said is snake venom," he wheezed, emptying a bottle of rusty liquid into the tub, "but what is really the Sloan's Liniment what my mama rubs on my fadder's . . ." A sharp glance from Arnold, and Dumbo subsided into a chortling fit.

Then it was Phoebe Schutz's turn to utter an incantation, prompted by Arnold, as she squeezed the tube of pimple ointment which she'd stolen from her big sister's drawer. Other contributions were submitted from the rest of the kids assembled in that blind alley between the pharmacy and the kosher butcher. Into the cauldron they consigned such items of personal fetish as mothballs, suet, blackstrap molasses, a pair of dentures, a photograph of Itzhak Perlman, a wishbone, a pubic hair, noodle pudding, a potted hibiscus, shaving cream which Arnold insisted was foam from the mouth of a madman. When all of the sacred ingredients had been added, Arnold left off stirring the broth with his boat oar and lifted his eyes to heaven. This was a gesture borrowed from Rabbi Fishbein, under whom Arnold was currently studying for bar mitzvah. His Adam's apple was prominent, and his tuft of coarse red hair a burning bush atop his forehead. It was difficult to tell whether the bush had set fire to the orange October sky or vice versa, but suddenly it was dusk.

"Nathan!" Arnold's voice echoed in the alley. "Bring forth the candidate for resurrection."

Nathan, Arnold's younger brother, had been watching the proceedings with rapt fascination from outside the circle of children. Summoned, he came forward smiling stupidly, holding a dead tabby cat.

"We gotta go home in a minute," he said sheepishly, as Arnold snatched the cat away from him by its stiff tail.

"This cat was once a priest of Moloch . . ." he began, examining the tire tread across the animal's greasy fur.

As he listened to his big brother recite the history of the cat's reincarnations, Nathan was full of pride. Though he had no feeling for the solemnity of such occasions, he believed implicitly in his brother's wisdom. If Arnold said that the tin washtub, mounted on a folding cot over a fire fed by gutted theater seats, was in fact the magic cauldron of Judah Maccabee, then it must be true. For Arnold had read it in a book with snuff-colored pages which he claimed was older than God. It told how the ancient Jews had flung the bodies of their dead warriors into such a cauldron, how the warriors had leaped forth with vacant eyes to fight again.

Arnold let go of the cat's tail, and it plopped into the vat of seething debris.

"Let us pray," he exhorted, inclining his head. Nathan closed his eyes tightly, while the other children, exchanging elbows in ribs and trying not to laugh, watched him. The fire about which they huddled took the edge off the chilly evening and augmented the atmosphere of conspiracy.

"Behold!" shouted Arnold, and Nathan opened his eyes in time to see a cat somersault through the air, land on all fours, and sprint out of the alley. It made no difference that the cat was a tortoiseshell, unlike the original tabby, or that Dumbo Klotwog, wheezing dangerously, had just risen from where he was crouched behind the washtub. These things did not interfere with Nathan's wonder. Arnold had proclaimed that the holy resurrection was accomplished, and Nathan, applauding with wide-open mouth, was convinced.

The other kids howled themselves dizzy over Nathan's gullibility. "Nathan's a nudnik!" "Nathan don't know nuttin!" "Nathan's so naive," this from Phoebe Schutz. But eventually, when they were sore from derision, a kind of reverence set in. They gathered closer round the cauldron and peered into the churning swill, a little spellbound as they listened to Arnold droning something about the soup primeval.

His little brother was such a willing dupe. His only recreation lay in observing his older brother and anticipating his next project. At night he sat vigil in their bedroom while Arnold dragged moldering tomes from the Front Street library into bed with him, where he read them by flashlight beneath the sheets. Not content to let his world remain cramped between cloth bindings, Arnold felt compelled to set it loose upon the neighborhood. On these occasions Nathan, his brother's loyal famulus, would practically volunteer himself for bait.

There was the time after Arnold had read the volume on the Spanish Inquisition, whose pages had crumbled like dead leaves and earned him a substantial library fine. He had convinced Nathan that it was in his best interests to be strappadoed. In a derelict factory the children bound Nathan's hands behind him and hoisted him to the ceiling with a winch, while Arnold, his parka hood pulled over his head, appealed to the dangling Nathan to abjure his false faith. Nathan's general good humor was impaired by the near dislocation of his arms. His small frame flinched like a marionette, and his outsized pink head lolled grotesquely. The children shuddered as he spat out words that Arnold had put in his mouth: "I will not be forsworn!"

Then Arnold read *Tales of the Prague Ghetto* and led a few friends by candlelight up into the loft of the old Market Street synagogue. There Nathan had been waiting patiently for several hours in the dark, standing where Arnold had planted him amid a pile of siddurs. The candle discovered his tiny eyes and his body, naked save for his underpants, dusted in talcum powder. Hebrew letters were scrawled in charcoal across his forehead.

"Behold the golem!" cried Arnold. When the boys in Arnold's party were recovered from their fright, they took their indignation out on Nathan. They knocked him over and kicked him until he soiled himself, then left him where Arnold said he would lie forgotten for another seven hundred years.

Lately Arnold had turned to mythology—ritual murder, premature burial, magic cauldrons, and the like. Today his victim was merely an alley cat; tomorrow he might be more ambitious. To be honest, Nathan had reservations about being hurled into boiling muck from which he would emerge a zombie. Still, if his older brother should expect it, Nathan would not let him down.

Arnold and Nathan lived in an apartment above a dry-goods store on North Main Street with their widowed mother and their grandmother, who was dying in an alcove off the parlor.

"This is the living room," Arnold was fond of saying, standing outside the alcove curtain, pointing, "and this is the dying room."

There was an unstable Negro nurse named Frieda, who attended the old woman on weekdays while Mrs. Siripkin worked in a millinery shop. Each afternoon the nurse departed, and an hour elapsed before Mrs. Siripkin returned home, removing her shoes and complaining that she was so goddam tired. During that hour the boys were required to look after their grandmother, whom Nathan called Memaw and Arnold called whatever should happen to enter his head.

She was little more than a death rattle in a flannel nightgown. She had a pair of rheumy eyes which drooled from a ruined face that was as populous with silver hairs as the top of her head. In sleep her mouth, which was toothless and surrounded by a pink stain of borscht, made a sucking motion like a baby or a fish. She seldom spoke, except to say Oy or Gott or, on days of unnatural vitality, Oy Gott, while being washed behind her floral curtain. When Nurse Frieda, who belonged to a fanatical religious cult, promised her that soon she would be in the bosom of Jesus, she said "God forbid." Occasionally she farted with the sound of a playing card fastened to a bicycle spoke. Her only diversion, before Arnold broke it, had been the antique gramophone that she had brought with her from Cracow.

Watching his grandmother die was for each of the boys a separate and unique experience. Nathan retained a fondness for his Memaw, who with her borscht breath and Yiddish lullabies had been the companion of his infancy. She had played him her gramophone, cranking the handle slowly and savoring her old record of Strauss waltzes that sounded as if the orchestra were treading upon their instruments. She had called him Moishe Kapoyr and given him pennies, while the neighborhood labeled him Nathan the Noodle for his ponderous head. Where his brother had his unquestioning allegiance, his grandmother had his affection. When she slipped on a herring and broke her hip—the broken hip in the Siripkin family was a traditional prelude to death—Nathan sat at her bedside with the gramophone. Moribund, she was sacred to him, like an old toy.

Arnold, on the other hand, delighted in the old woman's dying. He studied her slow passage and took advantage of her decrepitude to perform what he called experiments. These were conventional enough at the outset. He might tickle her nose with a feather as she slept, or dip her hand in warm water until her bladder let go. Becoming intrepid, he might hold a mirror beneath her hirsute nostrils, place coins on her eyelids, speak to her from behind an armchair as Jehovah. Discarding all scruple, he might wave his callow member at her saying, "Hey, Medusa, looka my shmuck." After which the invalid hissed Gevalt! and spat up her cottage cheese. And recently Arnold had broken his grandmother's gramophone.

Nathan told himself that his brother had not done it on purpose. Still, it was hard to explain how Arnold, in stumbling, had managed to fall so mightily, to crack the turntable and mangle the copper speaker so thoroughly.

"It was an accident," Arnold protested, grinning with gapped teeth as he removed himself from the wreckage. Later that evening the grandmother, through whimpering and Yiddish gutter slang, was able to communicate to her daughter the crime of her momzer son.

"I'm so goddam tired," complained Mrs. Siripkin, massaging her instep, while Arnold suggested that the old lady was maybe confusing him with the Czar.

In any case Nathan had salvaged the record of Strauss, and he knew of a local pawnshop in whose window there was a similar gramophone. He was certain that his brother, with his greater allowance, would buy it to replace the other. Nevertheless, his feelings were hurt. Though he said nothing, he felt it unworthy of his brother to stoop to abusing the helpless Memaw. Such pranks did not become his native dignity. Still, it made Nathan sick to doubt his older brother. Arnold knows best, he thought, presenting himself for further proofs of loyalty. Besides, Nathan's own persecution might distract his brother from tormenting the dying woman.

Arnold held several unflattering theories concerning his grandmother: that her veins were full of glue, that her bowels would not move, that she was becoming a fossil for which the museum might offer a tidy sum. On a hopeful note he'd asserted that she was a hermaphrodite soothsayer, and, abandoning that, that she was a man.

"She don't wear pants," ventured Nathan, not wishing to gainsay his brother's authority. But Arnold pointed out that she had no particularly distinguishing female characteristics and that her whiskers argued in favor of masculinity. Nathan conceded the truth in this, though it bothered him profoundly.

On the evening of the cauldron the boys arrived home after sunset. Nurse Frieda, looking forward to leaving, had neglected to close the alcove curtain while holding the grandmother over her bedpan. The invalid, saying Oy and Oy, had hoisted her nightgown above her hips. Amber water trickled from the cobwebs between her legs; it tattooed in the pan like a tin drum. Hearing the boys enter, Nurse Frieda drew the curtain. In a moment she emerged, mopping her brow and saying goodnight, adding: "Soon dat ol' woman gots to be washed in de blood o' de lamm."

"Why don't you try disinfectant," said Arnold, disappointed at the revelation of his grandmother's true sex. But as the nurse left, he saw that Nathan, still fascinated, continued to stare at the faded curtain across the alcove.

Then Arnold had parted the curtain again. The old woman, exhausted from the effort of her pee, was snoring despondently. The air around her bed smelled of buttermilk and gas. Crooking a finger toward his brother, Arnold told him come here, and Nathan dutifully complied. He obediently bent his bloated head, so that Arnold could grab it by the curls and shove it toward the hem of the grandmother's gown.

"I'm gonna introduce ya to the jaws of hell!" declared Arnold, losing enthusiasm in mid-threat, because Nathan didn't really seem to mind. Hell was just another aspect of the education with which his big brother was providing him.

The invalid drowsily opened her eyes, then shut them again, preferring nightmares. Exasperated, Arnold let go of Nathan and stamped into the kitchen. Nathan scarcely had time to speculate on the mysteries to which he'd nearly been initiated when his brother returned, carrying a bowl of viscous, mouse-gray gruel. It was customary for Arnold to feed his grandmother a little something before his mama arrived. Holding the bowl aloft with one hand, he reached with the other into the pocket of his baggy trousers and produced a test tube full of violet food coloring.

"The spinal fluid of a loup garou," he pronounced, "mixed

with ratsbane to make the victim claw out her kishkas and eat her own tongue. When she's stiff we can throw her in the cauldron."

He uncorked the vial with his teeth and prepared to pour it into the gruel, when Nathan did the implausible. Charging forward, he intercepted the test tube and swallowed the alleged poison. Stunned, Arnold spat out the cork.

"Whadja do that for?" he gasped.

"I'm sorry," said Nathan, bewildered by his own temerity. Arnold's features contorted as though outrage were a pie in his face.

"It won't work on you anyway," he muttered. "You're too dumb to die."

Nathan stood for a moment reflectively, while Arnold spooned the ropy mess into his grandmother's mouth, smeared it over her cheeks and chin. Downcast, Nathan went to bed. It was not that he doubted his older brother or that the tasteless poison had made him nauseous in the least. It was just that he wanted—no offense toward Arnold—to be murdered in place of his Memaw.

So he closed his eyes and thought of a skeleton in a black robe swinging a long-handled scythe. He lay corpselike until suppertime, when his weary mother came in and, seeing him in his posture of sham rigor mortis, said, "This I don't need." She brought him a frozen dinner which he refused to acknowledge, brought him a laxative in a bottle called a McSomething's Cocktail. Unable to stir him, she left the room, saying, "I got headaches enough without this."

Nathan kept his eyes closed and thought of angels. Eventually he dozed and awoke hours later to the frustrating fact that he was still alive. Sitting up, he spoke to the adjacent bed.

"Arnold," he said to the light beneath the sheet. At these

times Nathan felt he was talking to a ghost.

"I'm immersed in the study of hermetic lore," snapped Arnold.

"When you gonna buy Memaw another phonograph?"

"I'm saving my dough for *The Cabbala Unveiled*, edition of nineteen aught six, top shelf on the left hand wall of Kaplan's in Apple Street," said Arnold. "And anyway, we can throw the old witch in the cauldron tomorrow."

Something quietly falling to pieces inside him, Nathan began to sob.

Nathan continued sobbing through the night, and in the morning he said that his heart was sore and he wished he could spit it up. Mrs. Siripkin said that he had no fever and was just malingering and should be in school. She needed this, she decided, like a hole in the head, and then she went to work. Nathan felt a little better.

He spent the day spying on Nurse Frieda as she read her Bible and administered morphine to Memaw. At one point he called her ("Psst, psst.") to his bedroom door from behind which he whispered, "Don't let her out of your sight."

"You crazy," said the nurse, returning to her Scriptures and her sardines and crackers.

Toward the middle of the afternoon Nathan's restlessness got the better of him. Satisfied that his Memaw was resting comfortably, he cautioned the nurse once again to be vigilant and left the flat. At the top of Market Street, among kids who were returning from school, he could make out the indigo parka that belonged to his big brother Arnold. He was doubtless on his way to stoke the cauldron.

Nathan ducked down a windy side street and ran three blocks to Novack's pawnshop. The large front window of the shop was frosted in swirls of cleaning wax. Nathan stood on the pavement panting, watching a rag inside the glass wipe a circle whose diameter spread to the width of the window. Items materialized: toasters and radios, clocks and guitars, a consumptive pawnbroker, a gramophone with a speaker like a giant tiger lily. Impervious to the pawnbroker, who signaled him first to come in and then to get lost, Nathan coveted the gramophone for an entire half hour.

Then he wandered for an indefinite time, talking with an imaginary Arnold.

"I know where there's a phonograph," he would say.

"So tell me," demanded the make-believe Arnold, "and I will buy it for the Memaw to make her happy."

It was nearly dusk when Nathan arrived at the alley. A couple of kids were still tending the fire, while Arnold and his trio of lieutenants, bored from a surfeit of magic, reclined in the theater seats that were not yet kindling. There were a few token jeers which ebbed to indifference at Nathan's approach. Dumbo Klotwog was occupied in using Phoebe Schutz's pigtail for a moustache. Phoebe was eavesdropping on Arnold, who was suggesting to Stymie Cohen that the birthmark on his cheek was cancer. No one noticed that Nathan sought an audience with his brother until he was tugging at Arnold's coat sleeve.

"Don't soil the material," said Arnold, turning back around to Stymie who was begging for a cure.

"Arnold," said Nathan, but Arnold was busy prescribing a spider swallowed whole in maple syrup. "Arnold," a little louder, but his brother was recommending an albatross talisman.

Nathan persisted. "I know where a phonograph is."

This earned him a halfhearted reply. "So what? I told you already we gonna throw the old lady in the cauldron."

Nathan shook his head, too excited by his brother's words

to note that his voice carried little conviction. He understood only one alternative.

"Throw me," he urged, "not Memaw. Throw me in the cauldron."

Suddenly interested, Arnold arched an eyebrow and gave Nathan his full attention.

"We can't throw you in the cauldron."

"Why cantcha?" It had seemed such a simple solution. But Arnold was frowning as if Nathan were of insufficient quality to share a washtub with superior refuse.

He was right, of course; Arnold was always right. And Nathan was surprised to find that he didn't care. All he wanted was to die in the cauldron for Memaw, and it was too bad if he couldn't be reborn from the steaming sludge for Arnold. He was glad, as he lurched toward the fire, to be depriving his big brother of a zombie.

He had one foot on the folding cot and one foot poised over the smoldering washtub, when the pair of stokers grabbed him. Punishing his presumption, they pulled him onto the cobblestones and pressed his face into an oily puddle. Dumbo Klotwog waddled over and, brandishing the wooden boat oar like a white hunter, planted a heavy brogue on the small of Nathan's back. Arnold rose slowly from his seat, his eyeglasses full of the setting sun. Officially, he raised the hood of his parka so that his hatchet-thin face was framed in fur. As he spoke, he swayed like a cantor, his voice breaking frequently in its first throes of puberty.

"We gonna steal her corpse outta the mortuary. We gonna roll her in a carpet and bring her to the alley. Then we gonna throw her in the pot without no clothes on. We gonna boil her old knish in the sauce of resurrection. We gonna cook her till she comes alive again, till she walks around at midnight with her false teeth chatterin' like some kinda maneatin' clam."

Because he could not hold his ears, Nathan flapped his head from side to side and said Shutup. "Shutup shutup shutup!" he shouted, until the word was as empty of meaning as a prayer in a foreign tongue. Thus he was unable to hear his older brother, who was cataloguing where and on whom they would set loose the undead grandmother. In the mikveh, the courthouse, the school cafeteria; on the junkman, the rabbi, the congregation of the Church of the Holy Communion, cousin Myra's wedding. "And we'll serve up the soup at Passover," he finished. Then, remarking that Nathan, too, was silent, he began again.

"We gonna put her in the pot," he taunted, "where it's as dark as her old you-know-what." Pleased with his impromptu rhyme, he repeated it with more concision.

"In the pot where it's dark as her you-know-what."

The other kids took up the chant. "In the pot . . ."

Nathan closed his eyes and was someplace mysterious and warm. He was dreaming, and in the dream he was not Nathan but a Jewish warrior, come to avenge his dishonored grandmother. The warrior was tranquil, despite the fat boy who was sitting on his spine and the surrounding litany: ". . . dark as her you-know-what." Nathan knew that it would be dangerous to open his eyes, but he was lonely in his dream, and he missed his brother.

He was not yet shed of his tranquillity when he started to scream. It was a sound which escaped him like a pent-up genie from a cracked urn. Everything happened in the space of that scream. His captors spread out to give him more room. Dumbo Klotwog rolled from his back in fright, relinquishing the oar which Nathan, springing to his feet, took up and swung above his pomegranate of a head. Arnold had just enough time to ask himself the first half of a rhetorical question: "Who does the little shlemiel think he is?" He omitted the second half, which went: "Samson with the jawbone of an ass?" because his curiosity had been terminated by the edge of the oar, which caught him at the base of his neck. His spectacles flew off and his head, before he folded onto the cobbles, was cocked to one side, as if he were listening to music.

Arnold's friends and disciples evacuated the alley, calling for their mothers and stumbling over those who had fallen. Some of the fallen crawled on their knees rather than stop to pick themselves up. Then Nathan was alone with his brother, whose face was coming to resemble the blue of his parka. His meaty lips were, as always, bemused, but his eyes, green and bulging, contained an unlikely innocence. Dead, Arnold inspired in his younger brother something that went deeper than respect. And Nathan embraced him like a long-lost friend; he lifted him beneath the armpits and hauled him toward the fire. With a passionate effort, he raised Arnold so that his knees rested on the folding cot and his chest lay on the rim of the washtub. Then it was a simple matter to heave him—quickly, before his trousers ignited—into the vintage broth. The displaced liquid sloshed over the side of the tub, sizzling in the flames, and Arnold, still hooded, lay curled in the murky soup like a baby with a caul.

Nathan stood back and made a wish, then, settling himself in a damp theater seat, waited for the wish to come true.

The old woman, forsakenly snoring in her alcove, was awakened when Nurse Frieda, shrieking over her open Scriptures, fell face forward out of her chair in a swoon. Opening her yellow, sleep-filled eyes, she saw her grandson Nathan before her, beaming with his surplus of sympathy. Behind him stood the meshuggener brother in his soaking-wet parka to which shards of glass were still clinging. His narrow face, trimmed in a halo of ratty fur, was tallowy and distended; it was the face of a potato or a misshapen moon. His stench was more acrid than burning grease. In one arm he was holding an old-fashioned gramophone whose handle he turned with methodical slowness. The recording of Strauss crackled from the speaker, as if the orchestra were all eating toast. The grandmother endeavored to smile at her grandchildren. Nathan, he was her shany kin, and Arnold she forgave for his mischief. How could she not when the tilt of his head said that he too was enjoying the waltz? The old woman rattled a sigh and floated a mottled hand in time to the music. For a moment she was unsure if she were in heaven or in the park in Cracow, young again, with a pair of suitors, under an umbrella in the rain.

The Lord and Morton Gruber

Morton Gruber, czar of a string of lucrative coin-operated laundries, gave his wife a perfunctory peck and got out of bed. With a brain still thickly encrusted with dreams—a recurring one in particular in which he was force-fed leaden slugs—he padded downstairs to the kitchen. Crossing freshly waxed tiles to an island with a copper roof, he lit a gas burner on the stainless-steel range. As he was reaching for the kettle, the flame shot up and a voice called out his name.

"MORTON GRUBER."

The kettle slipped out of his hand and clattered noisily over the tiles. From the upstairs bedroom came the voice of his wife shouting, "Morty, what have you done?"

"Nothing," replied Morton. "Go back to sleep." But he was talking not so much to his wife as to the unruly flame.

Again the flame spouted up in a fierce red column, piercing the copper hood and scorching the ceiling.

"MORTON GRUBER, THIS IS THE LORD."

Morton folded his vulnerable belly into the monogrammed silk of his bathrobe and backed toward a window, glancing out over manicured lawns as if for help.

"It's God, Morty," repeated the flame, modulating itself to a milder blue blaze, "and you're going to be my prophet."

Groaning aloud, Morton rolled his eyes in an appeal to heaven: "Who needs this?" He caught sight of the blackened spot on the ceiling. "This we don't need, no way. Thanks but no thanks." For a man whose livelihood depended on the precision of manufactured appliances, this kind of thing was unacceptable. It was more than the law allowed.

As the flame was burning evenly now, Morton took courage. "It never happened," he assured himself, studiously avoiding the ceiling with his puffy eyes. "I wasn't awake yet, that's all." He wagged his broad face this way and that, pounded his temple with the heel of his hand, dislodging clusters of dreams like old snow. "Now I'm awake, all right, okay. I don't hear nothing."

The flame danced and Morton flung himself back up against the window, cracking a pane.

"DON'T FIGHT IT, GRUBER."

Careless of his blood pressure, Morton felt his hackles rising—that such an unnatural occurrence should take place in his home. My home, he reflected, with its gracefully appointed fixtures, its scrubbed and polished surfaces, its mortgage paid off a decade ago. Then squaring off with the range, he mocked in defiance, " 'Don't fight it, Gruber.' " This he repeated until it came to him: "You sound like me."

"I am you, in a sense," from the burner, spitting sparks as if a throat were being cleared, "but let's not get into that. The thing is, I want you to . . ."

But at that point Morton had clapped his hands over his ears and fled the room.

Back upstairs he hid his head beneath a pillow, his well-padded rump in the air. "Lolly," he spoke into pastel satin sheets, "what would you say if I told you that I just heard the voice of the Lord?"

Still drowsing, Morton's wife lifted her sleeping visor and uttered a soft interrogative grunt. Morton emerged from under the pillow, his sparse hair in bedeviled tufts, and restated his question with an unmuffled tongue.

Lolly opened her eyes far enough to admit the sight of her agitated husband, then shut them again. "See a doctor," was her automatic reply, and completing the reflex, "You're overworked."

She and Morton both knew of course that this was not the case. In the past few years, since their wayward son Jason had finally begun to take an interest in the business, Morton had found himself in a state of semi-retirement. He still went to the office, shuffled papers, and made supervisory noises. But most of his time was spent on the phone to his former partner, who countered his chronic boasting with endless reminiscences.

Catnapping again, Lolly surfaced enough to inquire, "So what did He say?"

"Who?" wondered Morton, still hugging his pillow, already wishing he'd kept his mouth shut.

"You know, the Lord."

Morton gave his wife an incredulous frown. What did she mean by dignifying what he was trying his best to discredit in his mind? He was ready to bite off her head when he heard it again, the voice like his own, rattling the long-settled foundation.

"GRUBERRR."

Morton's jowls flapped as his head swiveled left and right, searching among the haremlike furnishings for a sign.

"What do you think, I need props?" the voice resounded. "I don't need props. Listen, putz, YOU'RE IT."

"I'm it?" echoed Morton in a whisper. He looked to Lolly to maybe tell him otherwise; but, with her eyes still closed, she gave no indication of having heard a thing.

Then an irresistible impulse to protest swelled within him: Who was lord of this particular manor anyway? But on second thought, he'd better, for Lolly's sake, spare her a potential scene. Curbing his temper, and with a humility that went against his nature, Morton asked the draperied walls, "Why me?"

"There was a lottery in heaven and you won," came the voice, sardonically. "What's the difference? I'm the Lord and you're my prophet. Now get off your tush and spread the word."

Morton's jaw sagged into receding chins, his eyes shifting warily. "Um," he tendered, still humble, "begging Your pardon, but what is the word?"

Said the voice: "What else, shmendrick? DOOM."

Finding it suddenly difficult to breathe, Morton tugged at the lapels of his pajamas, bursting buttons and baring his hairy chest. He was on his knees in the middle of the canopied bed, his clenched fists raised in supplication.

"Get off my back, why dontcha!" he railed. "Can't You see I'm a happy man?"

At this Lolly sat up and, remarking her husband's condition, let out a piercing scream. She wrapped her arms about his sweating torso as if to drag him back down to earth.

"Oh, Morty!" she moaned, tears filling the parched cracks in her cold cream. "Morty," trying to rock him against her breast, "you're having a breakdown."

"That's it," cried Morton, clutching at a final straw. "I'm nuts!" But who would believe it of such a solid citizen as he?

"I'm crazy," Morton confessed to the elegant doctor seated behind his barge-sized desk, a wreath of degrees on the wall above his head.

The doctor nodded un-hmm, collapsing the cathedral roof of his fingers. He cast down his impassive eyes and made a note on the pad in his lap, then lifted his eyes back over the rims of his glasses. It was an expression that said to Morton, What else is new?

"I hear voices," Morton hastened to add, but was forced to qualify, "Well, actually, *a* voice."

The doctor nodded again with a hint of vigor, arched a brow. Encouraged, Morton practically grinned as he delivered the goods.

"The voice says it's the Lord."

When the doctor nodded with apparent satisfaction and made another note, Morton relaxed. He locked his hands behind his head, leaned back in his chair, and prepared himself to hear the verdict. But the doctor's pen was still poised above his pad, implying that Morton should go on. His quizzical look seemed to say through sealed lips, This is not an audition.

Morton awarded himself high marks in interpreting the doctor's body language, but was it for this that he'd come? Quiz him about his potty training, the ancient history of his love life, anything. At these prices, was it too much to ask that the shrink should occasionally open his mouth?

In the continuing silence Morton determined to prove that two could play at this game—though not for long. Never a patient man—for him a clock was as good as a taxi meter—it was Morton who eventually broke the deadlock. Testily he got to his feet.

"The talk I don't need, I get free of charge," he snapped. "But when I pay, what do I get but . . ." Here he pantomimed the doctor's note-taking. "I might as well be talking to myself."

Jotting down another note, the doctor spoke, easily abandoning whatever principle had kept him mum. "So, Mr. Gruber, what else does this voice of yours say?"

Morton was disappointed on a couple of counts: first, that

the doctor did not have an exotic foreign accent; and second, that his question, where originality was concerned, was not much improvement over Lolly's. Rather than answer, he chose to stand and glower.

The doctor stroked his beard like a pet, considering, then directed Morton's attention to a leather-upholstered chaise lounge.

"Would you perhaps like to lie down?"

Morton knitted his brow, suspicious of appeasement. Then he relented, thinking he had maybe been a bit too temperamental. Moreover, it was true that he always thought better on his back.

"Why not?" He shrugged. "God forbid I shouldn't get my money's worth."

Lying on the couch, Morton twined his fingers over the mound of his stomach and felt talkative.

"It comes to me from out of the blue, the voice, and tells me I'm it—a prophet, y'know. Me, Morton Gruber." He chuckled at the absurdity of it. "The only profit I understand is the kind that puts bread on the table, if you take my meaning." Then he wheezed in outright amusement over his joke.

Having removed himself to a chair at the head of the chaise, the doctor crossed his legs and flipped a page of the erstwhile notepad in his lap. "And how long," he matter-of-factly inquired, "has this delusion of yours persisted?"

"What delusion?" replied Morton, suddenly on his guard again. "My voice is real." Then he allowed himself to gloat over the way he'd outfoxed the doc.

To admit that he believed in the voice, this was smart; it would get him labeled certifiably farmisht. Then the doctor would have no recourse but to prescribe a nice sanatorium in the country. There Morton would sit in the sun, pampered and spoonfed by young nurses. He would play dominoes with contented lunatics between naps. In a couple of weeks, refreshed from his holiday, he'd come home a new man. And that, he presumed, would be that.

Still, there was something unkosher here; he needed to think. But behind him the doctor, who naturally couldn't keep quiet when you wanted him to, was speaking even as he scribbled.

"Mr. Gruber, would you consider yourself a religious man?"

"Eh?" said Morton, taken unaware. "I ain't no fanatic, if that's what you mean." He and his family were members of the reform synagogue, nu? Like everyone else, he was hedging his bets against the afterlife. So what was this headshrinker getting at anyway?

"Then would you say that this delusion . . ." continued the doctor, when Morton interrupted.

"There's that word again." He sat up and growled. "Didn't I tell you already? It ain't a delusion!"

Now he thought he understood what was bothering him. It was the doctor's insinuating tone he resented; but more than that, it was the nasty way he had of taking Morton's voice in vain. Again Morton was on his feet.

"My voice is real," he reiterated, not without a touch of pride. "And there's nothing wrong with me that a little letting off steam wouldn't cure."

As he stomped out of the office, he thanked the doctor very much and told him what he could do with his bill.

Stepping out of the elevator into the columned foyer of the doctor's building, Morton was staggered off balance by the public address.

"THE LORD PAGING MORTON GRUBER" reverberated about the marble walls.

He froze to the spot, jostled by passersby whose faces showed no particular signs of alarm. Nevertheless, feeling conspicuous, Morton looked around for someplace to hide. He ducked into a phone booth, folded the door shut, and gazed out as if from inside a block of ice. The phone rang and, though he knew better, he lifted the receiver slowly to his ear.

"Gruber," said the hearty voice that rightfully belonged to himself, "God here."

"Gimme a break, willya?" cried Morton, then shuddered to the marrow as he remembered Whom he was supposed to be talking to.

Taking advantage of his subsequent speechlessness, the voice was carrying on, "Now, sonny boy, leave us not mince words . . . " when Morton, struck by a technicality (or a doubt, if you will), found the sudden nerve to break in.

"I thought You said You didn't need props."

"Who needs?" replied the voice. "But it makes a nice effect, don't you think?" Then back to business. "Anyhow, I'm talking DOOM here, Gruber. Not just your nickel-and-dime decline-and-fall stuff, but apocalypse, kiddo—a big bang-up finish like the big bang I started with . . . "

Morton experimentally replaced the receiver, while the voice continued loud and clear. There was a moment when he was certain that ulcers were spawning in his intestines; his pulse was outrunning the capacity of his tired blood to keep up. So this was what it was like to talk to God, he reflected. It was enough to make you nostalgic for a little heartburn.

" . . . Now what I want," pursued the Lord, "is that you should get off the pot, then sit down and write Me a book . . . "

Slow down a minute, Morton had it in mind to say. A book? What did a book have to do with wandering around collaring strangers, with kvetching and making a general nuisance in the marketplace? Wasn't that, after all, what prophets did? Kvetching, Morton thought he might know something about. But a book?

" . . . A sort of scripture, y'know; like a new testament . . . " the Lord was proposing, as Morton picked up the receiver again. It was a pointless gesture, but it made him feel slightly more comfortable.

"Excuse me."

" . . . It's the age-old story with a newfangled twist . . . "

"Beg pardon," Morton found himself respectfully submitting, albeit he was no expert in such things, "but ain't you got a new testament already?"

The Lord sounded frankly peeved. "Two thousand years old is new?"

"It still sells, don't it?" Morton interjected with reverence.

"So do rabbits' feet, but whodoyaknow that's lucky anymore?"

Morton wasn't sure that he saw the connection; he wondered if it were possible for God to blaspheme.

"The point is, Gruber, that the thing has got to be written," insisted the Lord. It was the tone that Morton so often used, usually to no avail, when arguing with his wife and son.

The shoe on the other foot for a change, he let slip a single obstinate syllable: "Why?" And heartened, as one good word called for another, "Why a book if we're all doomed anyway?"

Pleased with himself, Morton rested his case. He thought he already knew the answer: This doom business was all a joke, right?—just to frighten everybody back into line. But with the lengthening silence on the other end, Morton's momentary confidence dwindled. It occurred to him that his question might have stumped the Lord, and while not a praying man, he prayed that it hadn't.

Finally came the considered reply, confirming the worst: "To tell you the God's honest truth, I don't know." And a weary afterthought, "Something to do with the triumph of the spirit and all that."

Such an admission of something less than omniscience made Morton sick at heart. It pulled the rug out, though he couldn't say why; made him swallow hard and wipe his bullet-sweating brow.

Lord, he rehearsed subvocally until he could find his tongue. "Lord," he hoarsely appealed.

"Yeah, Morty." At least they were back on a first-name basis.

"Lord, you're scaring the pants offa me."

Then he hung up the phone and beat it out of the booth.

Safe in his office Morton collected his fugitive wits and wondered what made him think he was safe. Had these paneled walls been soundproofed against the meddlesome voice of You-Know-Who? Still, he couldn't help feeling that here he was in his own domain; that at least among his ledgers and due bills, his antique adding machine, the company calendars decades out of date, he was, relatively speaking, the boss.

The offices of the Suds-O-Mat Self-Service Laundries were situated in a meticulously landscaped suburban plaza a mile or so from Morton's own neighborhood. It was where, at the pushy behest of his progressive son Jason, Morton had finally agreed to move the seat of their operations. It was an exodus he'd postponed for years, clinging to his former premises on the rundown North Main Street where Morton had grown up. To his son's accusation that sentiment alone had kept him in that seedy building, Morton replied that it was only for the sake of cheap rent. There was not, he contended, a sentimental bone in his body.

"So why," Jason had needled him with the zeal of a recent convert to free enterprise, "why did you bring your old office with you, right down to the original dust?"

It was the kind of disrespectful remark that kept Morton constantly put out with his only son. Where did he get off questioning (as Morton saw it) his father's authority, especially now when that authority was little more than token? Wasn't it enough that Jason was lately regarded as the driving force behind the business, while Morton was reduced to a well-pensioned figurehead?

Without Morton's foresight there would have been no business. If he hadn't had such faith in the future over a quarter of a century ago, they might still be back in steam-cleaning with his ex-partner Louie Gold; though Gold wasn't complaining. Blithely, if at a constant loss, he operated the laundry that he and Morton had begun in their youth. Despite Morton's hooting derision he hung onto it with a curator's loyalty to the past. He lived above it with his wife, while around him the neighborhood collapsed into vacant lots and weeds.

He even had the nerve to patronize Morton, his success notwithstanding, as if Morton were a prodigal who would eventually return to the fold.

"I'm making money hand over toches," Morton would boast during the phone calls which were a daily ritual since he'd emigrated from North Main. "Only yesterday my real estate investments . . . " But Louie would interrupt in the wistful tone which suggested that Morton's priorities were not straight.

"Guess who dropped in" or "passed away" or "Remember the time we cut cheder with Anastasia Tomashefsky?" he might say, as if memories, not money, were the standard currency.

"Wake up, Louie!" Morton was frequently compelled to shout, real life being such a far cry from the past. But not today. Today he didn't feel like shouting. Having had it on good authority that there was no future, it seemed to Morton more urgent than ever to tap his repository of memories.

"Louie," he greeted cheerlessly, the telephone having become for him a loathsome instrument.

"Morty," hailed Louie, "how's the weather out there in paradise?"

"Louie," Morton tried again edgewise, but his old friend was already off and running.

"Hey, Morty, you'll never guess who dropped by. Remember Hyman Nieman, old Numb Nuts Nieman? The time he was swimming in the river? He swam nearly across and said, 'I can't make it,' then turned around and swam back again."

Impatient as he was to get a word in, Morton savored the recollection. A sweet mental laxative, it set loose an image of himself as a boy on the levee, hopping from bare foot to foot on the hot cobblestones. The image purged, Morton was instantly restored to a worried late middle age.

"Louie, will you stop?" he pleaded. "I got tsores."

There was a courteous silence momentarily overruled by curiosity. "What's the matter, Morty?"

But Morton's clenched jaw refused to release what he held on the tip of his tongue. Maybe he was being a little too hasty. Here he'd been designated the Lord's confidant, and what did he do but broadcast it all over town. Already Lolly knew (which meant that her canasta club knew, and so on); then there was Dr. Whatsit, and now he was spilling the beans to Louie. But wasn't that what a prophet did?

A voice which was not *the* voice seemed to prompt him: Save it for the book. Only what did Morton know from books? The last one he'd read was *Forever Amber* in 1948, and then he'd skipped all but the raciest parts. He was very perplexed.

"Morty, speak to me. It's Louie, your pal."

"Louie," said Morton with uncustomary sincerity, "we've always leveled with each other, right?"

"Right."

"You don't still hold a grudge 'cause I left you for the coin-ops?"

"Water under the bridge."

"Louie."

"What, Morty?"

But divine revelation no longer seemed to be the most pressing subject at hand. "Louie, do you think I'm a happy man?"

"Happy," Louie considered. "What's happy? You live in a palace, drive a car as long as my debit column. Ain't that happy?"

"Louie, you didn't answer my question."

A ponderous sigh at the other end. "You ain't *un*happy, though I wouldn't exactly call you happy. Comfortable, that's what you are."

Morton had to smirk over Louie's attempt at diplomacy. "Not today I ain't," he confessed.

"So what are you today, Morty?"

"I'm scared."

"Morty, Morty," warbled Louie, "come down to the laundry. We'll walk around the old neighborhood. Y'know, sometimes I think I can still smell Mrs. Ridblatt baking challah—"

Thinking he could smell it too, Morton violently blew his nose.

"Louie, will you shut up with the ghosts already? What is it with you and ghosts? Maybe you're one of them, Louie. You're a ghost too."

In the lull of Louie's sulking, Morton attempted an apology, but his ex-partner shouted him down.

"If what you are is living, then I'd rather be a ghost. I can't help you, Gruber. Go and see a rabbi." After which a clunk and a dial tone.

"So?" asked Lolly for the third or fourth time, following Morton around the house as he searched for his cigars. "So?" she repeated, as he settled with an oy into a reclining armchair. Then Jason, whom she'd alerted to his father's freakish condition, burst in in time to lend his two cents' worth.

Toying with the remote control, which in turn flashed random lives across the television screen, Morton prolonged his family's suspense.

"So?" he mocked them under his breath. "So what?"

"So what did the doctor say?"

Advancing the serial images before they could capture his interest, Morton heaved the hybrid of a shrug and a sigh. "I'm beyond doctors, Lolly," he asserted with a suggestion of vanity. "For what I got, who knows? Maybe it's time to call in the rabbi."

Lolly slapped her forehead and made her "Can-You-believe-this" face at the ceiling. Out of the corner of his eye Morton registered her expression: Boy, did she have the wrong supreme being.

"It's all right, Mama," said Jason, taking charge. A veteran no-account who had lately contracted ambition, he was resplendent with self-esteem, his gold chain glinting at his open throat. "Papa," he said, inclining his coiffured head to signify that the moment of reckoning had arrived, "don't you think it's time you threw in the towel?"

Morton turned in his chair, about to breathe fire. But rather than play any further into his family's hands, he checked himself. He raised the volume and continued to switch the channels, his attention arrested for a split second by the image of Charlton Heston on Sinai.

Still he was sensitive to the sound of his wife and son in commiseration, muttering an exchange that might have been a kaddish. Swiveling toward them in annoyance, Morton barked, "I'll get some advice from the rabbi tomorrow. He'll fix me up, you'll see." Then he waved his hand indicating that the subject was formally closed.

Jason, who would have to have the last word, mumbled in phony deference, "He has spoken."

Born out of his conversation with Louie, visiting the rabbi was a whim which had ripened into a conviction. At first Morton hadn't known he was serious himself. In this resolve he hesitated long enough to mourn the man he'd been only days before. For him, for the old Morton Gruber, such superstitious bunkum would have been beneath contempt.

Nor did the atmosphere of the opulent new synagogue, diamond-in-the-roughly situated among the pines, help to dispel Morton's doubts. The rabbi's office, give or take a few Jewish artifacts—the spice box, the shofar mounted on a plaque like a leaping bass—was practically interchangeable with the shrink's. The rabbi himself was youthful and nattily dressed, his hands folded patiently atop his barge-sized desk, the bouquet of his after-shave suffusing the room.

Completely unruffled by his congregant's pronouncements, he spoke to Morton the way an adult speaks man-to-man to a child. Breezily he dismissed Morton's experience as unfashionable.

"Sometimes," he averred, removing his tinted glasses, "we personify the conscience and call it the word of God. I've done this myself. But you know, Morton"—who for some reason resented the intimate use of his given name—"word-of-mouth prophecy is a thing of the past. It belongs to the infancy of our faith. Today the Lord uses far subtler means of communicating His will . . . "

But Morton had already given up listening. He half suspected that the rabbi was in cahoots with his son to hasten his obsolescence. Why couldn't he get it through anyone's head that what was happening to him was the one and only real thing? His spine curved like a question mark under the terrible onus of his familiarity with the absolute.

Upon hearing the phrase "aural hallucination" released like a ring of smoke from the rabbi's mouth, Morton got up to take his leave. He thanked the rabbi politely (for nothing) and showed himself to the door.

On his way out, however, he followed an impulse to duck into the lavish sanctuary. He saw the carpeted altar backed by a sumptuous tapestry depicting the usual miracles, and upon the altar an old man in a baggy black suit. Morton recognized him as the doddering Rabbi Fishbein, the former spiritual leader of Temple Emanuel. But that was before the synagogue had moved from its original location downtown just off of North Main Street. A kind of rabbi emeritus now, he was something of an embarrassment to the congregation, having delegated to himself in senility the tasks of a beadle. Puttering about in his stockinged feet, he dusted the standing candelabra, arranged the flowers.

As uncomfortable with the rabbi's Old Country habits as anyone else, Morton found himself today unaccountably drawn to the motheaten old man. With his ashen complexion fraying into his unkempt whiskers, his yarmelke like a listing cupola, he looked perfectly benign, even holy; though what did Morton know from holy? Nevertheless Morton, a schnorrer, not a chooser, thought it was maybe worth a try. Maybe this scarecrow Fishbein knew just the right mumbo jumbo to get Morton out of his predicament.

Adopting the humility that was becoming second nature to him lately, Morton shambled to the foot of the altar and cleared his throat.

"Rabbi," he submitted, "God won't leave me alone."

The old man paused, dabbing his forehead thoughtfully with the dustcloth. Without the least alteration of his generally bemused features, he looked down at Morton. It was a look that might at any moment break into a radiant piety, and Morton, bending his psoriatic scalp, would be there to receive its curative benefits.

But when the old rabbi spoke, his eyes flared like gas flames, and his whiskers stood out from the gale of his words. His voice was the voice that was borrowed from Morton, His wonders to perform.

"So, Morty, consider yourself a lucky boy."

Unprepared for this meanest of the Lord's parlor tricks, Morton practically retched, swatting the air as he backed away. He puffed on unsteady legs up the aisle, hounded by the voice which shook the scrolls in their ark and guttered the Everlasting Light.

"What did you think, you could shake Me in My own house? Dybbuks you cast out, Gruber—THE LORD YOU INVITE IN!"

In a last-ditch effort to take up the thread of his ordinary life, Morton went that afternoon to inspect the latest Suds-O-Mat installation. Swallowing what was left of his pride, he'd prevailed upon Jason (who tried to beg off) to take him along. While Jason was outside talking with a contractor,

Morton poked about a rainbow array of washers, testing a surface here, feeding a quarter there. He was trying to take some satisfaction in this farthest outpost of his little empire.

But nothing helped. His business, to tell the truth, had meant little enough to him these past few years. Now, in the face of recent developments, it meant even less. This preoccupation with his disembodied voice had monopolized all of the available significance. It filled him with an awful apprehension that left no room for less demanding concerns—for his native aggravation, say, or his gastric distress. But how, he asked himself, could this have come to pass? How could his brain have become so completely occupied by the fear of God—unless the space had been vacant in the first place?

He was standing in front of one of the huge tumble-dryers, contemplating his distorted reflection in the porthole glass. Is that how I look to a fish? he wondered, peering closer. Then the porthole came suddenly unlatched, opening in his face, and the voice of the Lord chastised him once again. Stumbling backward, Morton listened fatalistically and nursed his bloody nose.

"Enough hide-and-go-seek, eh Morty?" A torrid breath was expelled from the dryer. "It begins to get boring."

Hangdog, Morton sniffled a token "What do you want from me?"

"A book, boychik, only a book. Something . . . in a popular vein."

Morton was chuckling dolefully to himself.

"What's so funny?"

"Me write a book?" He shook his head. "I ain't written more than my name on a check since grammar school."

"So what? You're divinely inspired now."

Morton had to laugh over that one. So this was inspiration? Being badgered and bullied and frightened half out of your skull? Okay, all right, he would consider himself inspired. And taking the Lord at His word, Morton thereupon conceived a gem of a rejoinder.

"Look," he suggested, "why don't You just forget about this book business and spare the world." Then, drawing on some remote recollection of how things were done in the Bible, he added, "You made a believer out of a hard case like me. Ain't that enough?"

"You trying to bargain with Me, Gruber?" boomed the empty dryer drum, the door swinging emphatically on its hinges, spanking air.

"It ain't done?"

After a long moment the Lord responded, sounding profoundly fatigued. "Well . . . to be honest, the whole thing is out of my hands."

Suspicious, Morton felt compelled to ask what he thought he was probably better off not knowing. "What do You mean? Ain't You the Lord God Almighty?" Then he waited, embarrassed and uncomfortable in his role as inquisitor.

Came the voice, the big wind reduced to a balmy breeze: "The Lord, yes. Almighty not no more." Another pause, Morton folding his arms. "Y'see, I gave away all my secrets already. So now you guys are in charge."

Morton was confused. "Wait a minute. Lemme get this straight. You mean we, the humans, we're the ones running the show?"

"I cannot tell a lie."

"Then . . . " began Morton, nodding to welcome a little light. If men ran the world, then what was the problem? Sure they'd made some mistakes—who wouldn't? But it was never too late to put things back in order. Give a little here, take a little there, and everything's shipshape again. And if He could be believed, there would be no more meddling on the part of Providence.

Morton took a deep breath, the tears of gratitude welling

up, when the Lord, having apparently read his mind, threw down an inexorable wet blanket.

"Forget it, mortal. Your days are numbered."

"So You're telling me . . . what are you telling me?" stammered Morton, the clouds reappearing, mushrooming over his temporarily rosy horizon.

"Must I paint you a picture?" asked the Lord. "Anyway," He continued dreamily, "who could resist? I'd do the same if I still had the power."

Morton had heard all he wanted to hear. Irate, he was impressed by the reserves of his own audacity. His wrath restored his self-esteem.

"If You're so God-damned impotent," he shouted, accompanied by the percussion of his heart, "then what the hell am I listening to You for?"

"Because"—Morton felt himself pitched head foremost into the humid dryer—"I'm still the Lord!" The porthole slammed shut, the drum began to spin, and saith the Lord: "I AIN'T DEAD YET, YOU SHMUCK."

Braced inside the dryer, Morton ogled the topsy-turvy laundromat through the circular window. It was the way the world would look being flushed down a toilet. And cramped, nauseous, stifled as he was, Morton still hoped that he wouldn't be evicted from this vantage too soon.

Distracted now beyond reason, Morton decided to run away to some heathen country where they never heard of the Lord. But the thought of His voice speaking from shrunken heads or out of the mouths of tigers gave him pause. Instead he clung to what was familiar, driving alone about the city streets after the networks had signed off. At 3 A.M. he turned up on Louie Gold's doorstep, looking like he'd been deposited there by a storm.

"Boy howdy, you gimme a scare!" exclaimed Louie, adjusting his cockeyed spectacles, fastening his bathrobe. "What do you mean coming round here at this unholy hour?"

"Louie," greeted Morton, trying his best not to plead, "how about we take a stroll around the old neighborhood?"

As they shambled along North Main Street, Louie remarked to Morton more than once, "Don't say I never did you no favors." But in the end he forgot his annoyance, warming as always to his role as curator of their mutual past. Every gutted storefront and weed-choked lot recalled some checkered incident from their youth.

"Hey, Morty," he might say, pointing toward a tilting tenement, "remember the night we smoked muggles on Plesofsky's roof? Remember the time we rode the dumbwaiter at the Cochran Hotel? And Saturday evenings, Morty, Saturday evening. Hot rye bread, dancing pickaninnies, and tootsies . . . "

Rather than fight them, Morton tonight embraced Louie's remembrances; he silently thanked him for keeping them fresh all the years. And as they crossed the street at Auction and started back down the other side, Morton detected a few awakening memories of his own. There was Lolly, for instance, as she was when he'd met her—a plump, playful girl waving an ostrich feather at a synagogue dance. He asked her if she was there all alone and she told him yeah—smiling slyly, nodding toward a bow-tied nebbish—except for her date.

Then the whole street was busy with figments: Mr. Zimmerman hawking "irregular" trousers, Mrs. Ridblatt accusing the butcher of highway robbery, Yudl the melammed wading through traffic with his nose in a book. Though he couldn't explain it, they had all become suddenly sacred to Morton. It exhilarated him past understanding, this return by popular demand of Morton's own personal history.

It struck him that he ought to write a memoir, though what did Morton know from memoirs? And anyway, where was the sense in it, when he had it from an indisputable source that there might be no one around to read such a thing? Still, Morton's newfound notion would not let him go.

"Y'know, Louie," he opined, savoring a little the sound of his own voice, "in the beginning was the Word. So why not the same thing in the end?"

Then he had packed his bags and declared that he was going away for a while. A trip, he assured all concerned, would do him good.

"Away?" wailed Lolly, appealing to Jason and an imaginary jury—"Away where? Where away?" her powdered jaw still working in search of other combinations of the phrase.

"Papa, sit down. We'll talk," asserted Jason, clutching the back of Morton's armchair the way a matador holds a cape. Then, having made no immediate impression on his father, he took a couple of calculated steps forward, as if stepping into somebody else's shoes. "It's no use," he judged, offering his mother condolences. "He won't listen to reason, so what can you do?"

At the door Morton turned to take in the sad spectacle of his abandoned family. Even as he looked at them he missed them in his bones. Then he plodded down the porch steps cherishing his mental snapshot: his wife with her hysterical devotion, her cheeks irrigated by freshets of purple mascara; his son with his luxuriant chest hair like smoke above the volcano on his Hawaiian shirt, suppressing his unspoken affection with a "Good riddance."

"The family Gruber minus its head," he lamented aloud,

labeling the snapshot. "My family finally at a loss for words." For himself the words came so easily of late; words like *passionate*, *vulnerable*, and *clairvoyant* came tripping from his tongue, leaving an aftertaste of spices. And while he already desperately missed his place in the bosom of his family, Morton took some consolation in his newly acquired facility with language.

At midnight he boarded a train for God knows where. He could not have said whether he were fleeing his fate or running headlong to meet it. For the moment being in motion was enough; it was the be-all and end-all as far as Morton was concerned. Outside his window the darkness was interfered with periodically by lights signaling pockets of humanity. Like luminous gallstones the lights had their coefficient warmth in the depths of Morton's gut.

A riot of sensations performed themselves in his breast, while Morton identified them, like long-lost children, in the order that they appeared. "Sorrow and pity," he whispered, "chutzpah, rapture, a fine wooziness." Conspicuously absent among them, he noted, was fear.

It was as if his yearning for the past, with which he'd lately become infected, had spread to include the here and now. Whatever caught his eye he immediately longed for; all of his appetites were active. He wanted, for instance, that sandwich leaking green olives that an old man across the aisle was nibbling out of tinfoil. That flashbulb of an amethyst which the gentleman with the briefcase was sporting on his pinky. That young girl in the beret with her downcast eyes and her dimpled knees, like a pair of small faces, peeking out from under a tartan skirt. Everything he looked at had its place among his desires.

Morton wanted the words to express his current attachments, and bingo, there they were.

"That lopsided grin of a moon," he pronounced as he gazed out the window, "like Lolly's dentures in the pocket of her black negligee." It gave him goose flesh, the way he'd contracted the gift of gab. He'd come into his own exclusive voice, an all-purpose eloquence, suitable for pulpit, stump, after-dinner, or you name it.

Eventually he arrived at a station in a town on the edge of the continent. He took a taxi out beyond the swampland to a beach, then waddled with his baggage over sand strewn with the skeletons of creatures and foundered craft. He looked out across the dark water, embossed with threads of silver toward lands more traditionally associated with prophets. On the horizon there was heat lightning as if some glorious battle were in progress. There was a familiar, not-so-resonant voice, which Morton knew better than to confuse with the flashing sky.

"Morty," came the voice, sounding out of breath, as if it had struggled to catch him up. "Help me!"

"So," said Morton, folding his arms, relishing the upper hand, "You don't speak in capitals no more."

"I'm nowhere, Morty, banished from the farkokte world I created. Like something on a shelf in a hockshop, I'm waiting to be redeemed. Redeem me, why don't you! For God's sake, make me a book, give me a home!"

Morton shrugged a bit impishly, having perceived what he took to be a truth. "I guess some things ain't already written, eh, Lord?"

"Wise guy," snapped back the Lord, an impishness of his own in reserve. "You're free to guess." There was a suggestion of thunder and a couple of waves tossing phosphorescent caps.

Morton waved his hands in counterfeit fright; he whistled a spooky impersonation of the wind. "Hoo hoo," he laughed, "give a listen to Mr. Mysterious here." Then, lifting his eyes,

Morton winked at where he figured a gallery of eavesdropping angels ought to be.

Returning by the next train, Morton moved, for a man of his age and weight, with considerable stealth. He took a few prized items from the offices of Suds-O-Mat and made his way back to the old neighborhood. Dodging ghosts, he ducked down an alley, slipped behind a flap of corrugated tin, and was greeted by a timeless mildew.

In his old second-story office he rehung an out-of-date calendar, cleared the bottles left by derelicts from the relic of a rolltop desk. He arranged the photographs of Lolly and Jason, blew a mantle of dust from a yellowed ledger, and composed himself to take dictation from the Lord.

At first Morton wasn't entirely comfortable with the collaboration. God, feeling himself again, was too full of propaganda and threats. Too much "Babylon shall become heaps, a dwelling place for vermin"—that old hobbyhorse. But after a while Morton learned to temper the more sanctimonious, tub-thumping stuff with here and there an amusing anecdote of his own. As a consequence, there was soon a preponderance of narrative drawn from Morton's own very rich past. There was a danger of his eclipsing the Lord's message beyond recognition. But Morton was too intoxicated by the ease of his writing to worry. He was convinced that, if not completely faithful to the letter, he was at least being true to the spirit of the Word of God.

Under the pressure of the promised end of history, he wrote with a balanced grace. He wrote as if his book were an ark upon which he and his God and his family—and as large a circle of others as there was time enough to include—would weather oblivion. Sometimes, however, it bothered him that posterity would never read these pages. Then he thought he would tear them out of the ledger, stuff them in bottles, and fling them into the universe. Sometimes he despaired of finishing before the end.

But the ordered accumulation of words was usually satisfaction enough. And his single-minded diligence in transcribing them, Morton came to believe, was even stronger than death. If not here, then he might complete his task in heaven. There, watched over by cherubs with feather dusters, engraved upon tablets of gilded stone, the book would take its place in celestial archives. It would bear this inscription under the title, in what he prayed would not be considered false modesty:

BY THE LORD GOD ALMIGHTY AS TOLD TO MORTON GRUBER.

Shimmele Fly-by-Night

Everyone ran away from my father. My mama ran away from him into the scrawny arms of Mr. Blen the hatter, who was so frightened of my father that he fled the Pinch with my mama at his coattails. My sister Fagie ran away from him to the sanctuary of the Green Owl Café, managed by her fiancé, the bootlegger Nutty Iskowitz. The neighborhood kids ran away from him, afraid of his fiery beard, its edges ragged from the tufts he pulled out of it in his wrath. They were scared of his voice and his bloodstained apron, his colossal hands, the shredded left thumb on which he tested the sharpness of his knives, his furious eyes in the shadow of the black homburg he never took off.

The kids along North Main Street ran away from him to their mothers, who told them, "Read your lessons, eat your whitefish, don't wet the bed, or Red Dubrovner will get you."

They ran away from me too, though you couldn't exactly call it running. They turned their backs and whispered whenever they saw me, like I might be my father's spy. This I was used to since I was little. Then—running from behind my sister's skirts as we crossed through the Market Square Park—I used to chase after them. But eventually I got the idea that they weren't playing games with me, that for them the son of my father was something to beware of. So I got used to being lonely, and sometimes I thought that it wasn't the butcher but me that they feared. Then I was able to enjoy their silent treatment a little. What bothered me was when they broke their silence and dared each other to make cracks about my family. What bothered me was when some wise guy got the nerve up to ask, "Hey, Shimmie, why don't you run away?"

It was Papa's theory that our neighborhood was haunted. He believed that the gamblers and fancy women, the river rats and drunken Indians who used to live there were now dybbuks. They were taking possession of the Jewish shopkeepers and their children one by one.

"It's the truth, cholilleh!" he would declare in his borsht-thick accent, kissing his mezuzah and spitting against the evil eye. And if someone who didn't know about his rotten disposition should say otherwise, suggesting that the Pinch wasn't so bad—if they said that it wasn't Russia, after all—my father would insist it was worse.

"Some golden land!" he would groan, slapping his barrel chest. Then he would count on his fingers the ways that we were persecuted: by the infernal heat and the crooked politicians, the high water at Pesach, the diseases that followed the floods, the yokels in their white sheets that they bought wholesale at Zimmerman's Emporium.

It was the peculiar quality of my father's voice that it could grumble and bark and whine all at once. And coming as it did out of his flame-red beard, it was as good as if delivered from a burning bush. He was at his best when he was laying into his own kind.

"This North Main Street, I'm telling you, it's a regular circus parade . . . and bingo bango bongo," hopping from one foot to the other, pounding the cash-register keys, "here comes the Jews! They are shaving off their beards and peddling corsets on Shabbos, they are stuffing themselves with chazzerai. They are running away to join the vaudeville. They are forgetting their mama-loshen, which ends up where? In the mouths of the shvartzers is where. The shvartzers have stolen our tongue!"

It was true that the local colored porters and maids seemed to have an especially good ear for Yiddish. There was even a street musician who sang "Oif'n Pripechik" to his own accompaniment on washboard and jug.

"Pretty soon they pick up all the Jewishness that the Jews are throwing away. Then nu? What will the Jews have left? Cold cuts and dry goods is what."

But as bad as the Pinch was, the South outside its boundaries (according to my father) was even worse. The river was awash with dead men and snakes. Beyond our neighborhood the poor people married their own mothers and had two-headed children. For sport they wrestled pigs and cut the private parts off of Negroes, which they framed and hung up in the barber shops. The South beyond the Pinch was Gehinom, it was sitra achra, the other side; and it was seeping into Jewish homes the way the creepers poked through the tenement walls.

I had no reason not to believe my father. When had I ever been farther from home than the Market Square school? After class I went for my Hebrew lesson to Mr. Notowitz, the malammed, in his rooms across from Blockman's junkyard. An ancient mildewed gentleman with breath like a toilet, he would prod me with his walking stick through my alephbaiz; this until, convinced of my ineptitude, he sat down at the table and fell asleep. From Mr. Notowitz I went straight home to work in the shop. On Saturdays my father took me with him to shul, on Sundays to the Auction Street stockyard. During the rare unsupervised moments when I was out of his sight, I didn't know what to do with myself. Then, like my miserable mama, I tended to sit in an upstairs window and look out onto the tummel of North Main Street.

If he hadn't been the only ordained ritual slaughterer in the Pinch, my father with his temper would have chased away what business he had. But as it was, the women had to come to Dubrovner's for their kosher meats. They came to him by the dozens on Shabbos eve, carrying live chickens from the market by their trussed-up feet. As they approached the shop, the cackling would swell to an unholy pitch, reminding my father of one of his pet complaints.

"Gevalt, the noise!" he would cry, clapping his hands over his ears. He was forever at odds with the pandemonium of the streets: with the bell from the Chickasaw Ironworks, the calliopes from the excursion boats on the river, the shouts of the newsboys, the songs of the cantor at the Anshei Sphard shul—though none of them gave his own bellowing any serious competition.

In any event, when the ladies had gathered in the shop with their chickens, my father would roll his sleeves above his ham-sized forearms. He would take up his blade and, muttering a benediction that sounded more like a curse, shut the birds up for good and all. Then he would call me: "Shimmele Goylem, pipsqueak, shlemiel!"

It was my job to hang up the chickens in the stinking rear of the shop. I hung them upside down on a row of hooks so they could finish twitching and leaking blood onto the sawdusted floor. The women would look on with a kind of reverence, as if the chickens had been justly punished for daring to squawk in the face of Red Dubrovner.

Then they took their seats in a half-circle of folding chairs near the open back door. In faded kerchiefs and dowdy dresses ringed in sweat under the arms, they sat with their knees apart, waiting for me to drop a dead bird into their laps. After that they proceeded to flick the feathers, tossing them by the fistful into the air. In this way, in the sweltering rear of Dubrovner's, the wives of North Main Street became the engineers of a blizzard.

Feathers would swirl and spiral around the dangling light bulb, flurrying down from the ceiling and settling in drifts over the filthy floor. Then we were no longer in the back of the butcher shop, but in the snowy woods of Byelorussia. Or so I imagined. I imagined it not because I'd ever been in any such woods, but because my papa, resting after one of his outbursts, would sometimes recall them.

"You had the mud and the drek but what's new?" He would shrug, brushing chicken guts and toenails from his apron. "Then comes the snow—kadosh kadosh . . . " Here he closed his eyes, his fingers wriggling an imitation of falling snowflakes. "Kadosh kadosh and everything's kosher again."

It was the same snow, I once heard him suppose, that had covered the bodies of his family, murdered by Cossacks in a village pogrom. The pogrom had occurred after my father, fleeing military conscription and chasing rumors of freedom, had already run away to America. This he'd let out before he knew what he was saying. Then angry with himself for his moment of weakness, he clenched a fist to shout: "Here it only pishes dirty rain!"

That's how it was with the storms of feathers. They lulled my father into thoughtfulness just long enough to make him mad all over again. Then he would come from behind his butcher's block, swatting blowflies away from his beard, and accuse the women of everything under the sun. He blamed them for bad weather, bank panics, arson, for binding their husbands to their steam presses and lasts by the chords of their own phylacteries. And sometimes he accused them of cutting the cords. He accused them of putting ideas in my mama's head.

"Yentes!" he bawled at the wives, who had the good sense to keep their heads bent over their laps. "Where is your gossip? Y-t-t y-t-t, why don't you! Shmoose!" Then he would sway in front of them pressing his palms together and fluttering his eyelids, a housewife expressing concern. "Poor maidele, how she suffers; on a dog I wouldn't wish it . . . "

He always turned around to make sure that none of his antics were lost on Mama. Usually she was standing behind the marble counter preparing to dress the chickens. Thin as a candle, she was often caught gazing wistfully at a naked bird, like maybe she recognized it from better days.

"What do you think, that's your cousin Chaim on his deathbed?" my father would growl, making me think of the Lord goading Abraham to butcher his son. "It's a chicken, cut out his kishkes!" And later on, when he caught her hesitating, he began to say: "What do you think, that's your precious Mr. Blen?"

How Papa hit on the notion of a romance between my mama and the little hatter, I'll never know. Mr. Blen, with his nervous stammer and banjo eyes, his yarmelke riding his wavy hair like a buoy, was the least likely candidate for anyone's suitor, never mind the wife of the terrible Dubrovner. But it was like my father to expect miracles at his own expense.

"I know what you tell my Rosie," he hounded the women, always in my mama's hearing. "You tell her run away from your momzer husband. You tell her to go to the shmendrick Blen, that he's pining away in his shop for you. You tell her" —raising his voice in a rasping falsetto—" 'He needs you, which is more than we can say for the crazy butcher, not to mention your floozy of a daughter and your nebbish son . . . ' "

On her own, I don't think it would have occurred to my long-suffering mama that there was anywhere else to go. So maybe, without any faculties of resistance, she finally gave in to the power of my father's suggestion. Maybe his constant kvetching browbeat her into a glimpse of another life. Because one day, between the meat scales and the butcher paper, I saw her blush. Then the first blush must have awakened others, spreading like a rash, until the whole length and breadth of my mousy mama became inflamed.

That's how it started, the itch of her late-blooming passion. It kept her from sleep and drove her to highlight her tired eyes. She marcelled her stringy hair and swapped her drab gaberdine for a taffeta shirtwaist with lavender trim. It probably wasn't as complete a shedding of her old worn-out skin as she must have hoped for: not quite a butterfly, she was more of a caterpillar with wings. Still, it was enough to give her the nerve to throw her couple of dresses, along with her mother's candlesticks, into a carpet bag one day, and walk out of the apartment above the butcher shop forever.

Never much of a match for my ferocious father, it seemed to me that my mama and the hatter had been paired in heaven. Where neither of them had made much of an impression when they were around, now that they were gone they were legendary. Though everyone naturally fell silent when they saw my father coming, the story was in the air. Who didn't know how Mama, with baggage in hand, had entered Blen's Custom Millinery in the early morning? Who but my papa hadn't heard the women in the gallery at the synagogue, or the old kockers on their bench in front of

Petrofskys' fruitstand, repeating my mama's words: "Wolfie, mein basherter, my destined one. God help us, I belong to you."

After that it's unclear whether Mr. Blen was fleeing Mama (who pursued him) or whether they were burning their bridges together. In any case, they were last seen boarding a streetcar amid a spray of sparks.

To be honest, neither my sister nor I missed our mama very much. What was there to miss in her day-long sighs, her taking to bed with a headache, her staring dumbly at dead chickens, dumbly out the window at North Main? Papa, of course, made up for our lack of concern. He howled his shame and rifled the pages of his grease-stained *Schulchan Aruch,* looking to brand himself the male equivalent of aguneh, abandoned wife.

"Am I the only one who doesn't run away from this farkokte place?" he cried, though only Mama was gone. But that was his favorite refrain. In his tantrums he always talked like he was completely alone, betrayed by one and all. Still, I could tell that some of the heart had gone out of his hysterics. It wasn't the same complaining about Mama's leaving him, now that her desertion was fact.

Nevertheless he went through the paces he was famous for. He caterwauled and butted the doorposts with his head until he'd ruined the crown of his homburg. He bloodied his own nose, blackened his eyes, carrying on in the way that kept alive the tall tales of Red Dubrovner's mishegoss. But to me the whole thing lacked conviction. I'd seen worse when he had no reason at all to be mad.

At one point during his demonstration he tore off his lapels; he went down to the meat locker and brought up a case of his home-brewed kiddush wine. With every bottle he swilled, his roaring diminished a little, until finally he had drunk himself into silence. Then the sounds of North Main Street—the shmeikeling shopkeepers, the delivery wagons, the bells—had their turn. They took up the roaring where my father left off. And that's when I got the willies: not from the butcher's ranting, which was the familiar music of my days, but from the thunderous noise which the world made when he stopped. I was scared when all I could hear was the world and my father's small voice—when he'd pulled his tallis from under his apron to cover his head—saying a kaddish for Mama.

In the shop downstairs, however, it was business as usual. Papa continued haranguing the women, who continued flicking their chickens with heads bowed. But upstairs was another story. Abandoned by Mama, the apartment over the shop was worse off than before.

Nobody would have accused my poor footsore mama of being a housekeeper, but at least she had swept up the wreckage in the wake of my father's wrath. Now that she was gone, the place was a shameful dump. Glass dropped out of a crack in the skylight and the kitchen table listed from a broken leg. The pan under the icebox had overflowed, warping the floorboards. As I watched my father sniffing around in the debris, I saw it coming.

"Faigele!" he bawled. "Where is my shikse daughter?"

That was when he must have realized that my sister Fagie was seldom at home. Afterward, whenever she stopped by for a bite to eat or to wind her Victrola in the bedroom we shared, Papa would start in on her.

"Vildeh moid!" he wailed, with or without his audience of women. "She got to run, you know, she got to skidoo. They are missing her already in the speakeasies of Babylon

. . . " Then he would lift alternate feet in a grotesque black bottom, slapping the soles of his shoes.

But Fagie could take the hint without all of Papa's displays. Nobody needed to put ideas in her head. Hadn't she been gallivanting, chasing boys and making scandal, for a couple of years?

She was a pip, my sister—a flashy dresser, always with bracelets and beads, high-heeled pumps and seamed stockings rolled below the knee. Her short pleated skirts swished as she walked, the necklines plunging toward the bosom she didn't have. Her carroty spitcurls dangled like burlesque sidelocks, and her cheeks—feverish anyway—were heavily rouged.

"I can't do anything with her," our mama used to grieve before she went away—which was no news, as what was there that Mama could do anything with? Meanwhile Papa might call her nafkeleh on principle; he might, finding part of a barbecue sandwich she'd brought home from the Pig 'n Whistle, bellow until his blood vessels burst. But mostly, too busy with his general ravings, he took small notice of my sister's shenanigans until after Mama was gone.

Then all it took was his declaring that she would depart soon for the Unterworld, that already she smelled of sulphur and deep-fried sin, to send Fagie straight into the arms of Nutty Iskowitz.

He was the local bootlegger, owner of the notorious Green Owl Café and of the largest piece of the broken-down middleweight boxer Eddie Kid Katz. Nutty wore padded suits and two-tone shoes, and pomaded his hair until it looked like record grooves. On any day you could see him driving his Studebaker down Main Street, unaware that half the neighborhood kids were hanging onto the fenders and running boards. For all the shadiness of his reputation, nobody seemed to take him very seriously, least of all Fagie.

"The Czar of Market Square he calls himself," she would sigh to me with a ha. "He's a czar all right: He fortzes Mrs. Rosen's meatballs and it's a pogrom." She would joke about his pitted weasel features, his jaw always snapping gum. "A face he ain't got, only a pair of profiles."

But she liked him all the same. I could tell by the way that she squirmed when she spoke of him, toying with the gaudy jewelry he bought her. She bragged about his connections with ward heelers and the celebrities of Beale Street, whose gambling houses he claimed to supply with his bathtub gin. She described for me with affection the rooms above the café where Nutty held court, the green felt crap tables overhung with blue muggle smoke.

It made me nervous to hear about her life, all of it so foreign to the butcher shop. But I was glad, on the other hand, that Fagie had finally found herself a sweetheart. The others had always run away from her on account of her meshuggener father, and because, frankly, Fagie was no prize. Only it seemed like what was discouraging to everyone else was what attracted Nutty, which was maybe how he got his name.

"He thinks it makes him some kind of a macher to be seen with Red Dubrovner's daughter," Fagie told me once while buffing her nails. "It's his idea of living dangerously." And later she mentioned offhandedly that he had asked her to stand under the canopy with him.

"So I says to him, 'What do you think, it's going to rain?' " Then she left off plucking an eyebrow to squeeze my hand. "Oh, Shimmie," she said, "it looks like I found my ticket out of this bughouse."

I thought of pointing out that, as big noises went, Nutty was second only to our father in the Pinch, but it didn't seem like my place to say so.

• • •

Papa, for all his prophesying the worst, was the last to know that my sister and Nutty had become an item. This was owing partially to me. While secrets tend to make me nauseous, I had helped to keep my father in the dark. I covered for Fagie in her absences, straightening up the apartment and cooking the briskets, everything short of which my father considered trayf. So—except for Papa's appetite, which had fallen off lately—everything was going along as usual. Then Fagie had to spoil it all by waltzing into the shop with her boyfriend on her arm.

They strolled in—Fagie swinging her beads, Nutty under a fedora, a thumb in his lapel—looking like this must be how the other half lives. Behind them loomed an individual whose chest and biceps strained the seams of his pinstripe suit. I guessed that this was Eddie Kid Katz, Nutty's partial property and bodyguard, in whose puffy eyes there shone not a speck of light. With his lantern jaw working its chewing gum in time to his boss's, he took up his post by the open front doors, while Fagie and Nutty browsed the meat cases, casually approaching the butcher.

He stood in his sleeveless undershirt behind his chopping block. The sweat poured off of him, beads of it glistening in the hair on his shoulders like raindrops in a bird's nest. Busy trimming the flanks of salted beef that I was shlepping in from the locker, he didn't even bother to look up.

"Papa," said Fagie, tightening her grip on Nutty's arm, "I want you to meet my fiancé."

Still he didn't look up, though his slicing became more vigorous, and I could tell that he was biting his tongue. But though she knew better, Fagie continued to needle him: "Papa, maybe you didn't hear . . . "

I don't know what she was up to, asking for trouble that way. It was like they were sightseeing and she'd brought Nutty to show him the most celebrated temper in the Pinch.

So it must have disappointed them when Papa, who looked like he was going to explode, only fizzled.

"Lilith," he hissed, calling on the Lord to witness what a brazen thing was his daughter, that she should soak in a mikveh for ninety years. And that was it. He went back to his trimming and chopping.

Nutty looked over his shoulder at Eddie Kid Katz as if to say, "So this is the big wind?" I wanted to shout over the counter that he hadn't seen anything yet, just wait until Papa got hot . . .

Meanwhile Nutty was making motions as if he were taking control. Giving Fagie back her arm, he shoved her politely to one side. Then squaring his shoulders, checking his shirt cuffs, he planted himself directly in front of the butcher.

"Now, Papa," he began, patronizing and familiar, rocking back and forth on his heels. "We come here in good faith, didn't we, to ask for your blessing? So please, spare us the 'Vey is mir,' just say 'Mazel tov' and we're on our way." Evidently pleased with his speech, he glanced over his shoulder again.

He turned back around in time to see the vein at my father's temple pulse like blue lightning. Impaling a loin roast with his cleaver, Papa started to tremble, taking hold of the underside of his chopping block to steady himself. But the huge wooden block, despite its weight, wasn't anchor enough for his rage. As his temper rose, so did the chopping block, coming away from the floor with all four legs.

From the way that the bootlegger's jaw dropped, the gum rolling out of his mouth, you'd have thought that Papa was lifting the block by magic, and not just by dint of his awful strength. Mr. Iskowitz, I imagined myself saying, meet Red Dubrovner.

With the tendons like roots in his neck, his teeth clenched about the tip of his tongue, Papa bent his knees to hoist the chopping block over his head. Except for Eddie Kid Katz, who went on noisily chewing his gum, nobody breathed. We were spellbound watching the way that the block was suspended above my papa—like Moses about to smash the tablets of the law. In a minute, I knew, he would let loose his tongue and spit out whole plagues of abuse. He would froth into his beard.

But Nutty Iskowitz, snapping out of his stupor, wasn't hanging around for that. Taking cautious steps backwards, he grabbed my sister (whose eyes were still glued to the block) and dragged her behind him out the front doors. Not so impressed, the stone-faced palooka turned and strutted slowly after them.

No sooner had they gone than my father dropped his chopping block. He let it fall on top of his head, rattling his teeth, which bit off the tip of his tongue. It plopped like a little strawberry onto his apron bib. Then Papa folded under the weight of the block, his thick body crumpling like the crown of his homburg. The building shuddered and the floorboards splintered beneath him.

Later that evening he sat motionless in the kitchen upstairs. On the crippled table in front of him were his open *Schulchan Aruch* and three empty bottles of his kiddush wine. In his mouth was a piece of melting ice; an ice pack was perched atop his bald and swollen head, fastened there by his blue-striped tallis. Standing beside him in the coppery light, I saw a mouse crawl unnoticed over his shoulder. The Saturday night hullaballo started up outside the window, nearly drowning out the voice of my father lisping a kaddish for his daughter Fagie.

In the weeks that followed he never took his eyes off me. He must have thought, now that Mama and Fagie were gone, that I too would soon be running away. The worst of it was that he watched me without ever speaking his mind. True, he still let off steam from time to time in the shop, parading his anger in front of the women on Shabbos eve. But he would trip now over his hobbled tongue before he got very far, then fall silent. And upstairs in the apartment, which I was still taking pains to keep straight, he seldom spoke a word.

What's more, he was losing weight. Brooding at the kitchen table like he was sitting shivah, he refused to eat his bloody briskets—though he might occasionally pick at the tripes he brought home from the slaughterhouse. His shoulders had begun to droop and his beard was getting sparse and lusterless. Bags like bruises appeared beneath his eyes.

Meanwhile business, such as it was, had fallen off. The wives, no longer so shy about gossiping in his presence, still brought them their chickens, of course. But in Mama's absence they then carried the carcasses across to Makowsky, my father's nonreverend competitor, who dressed them out for a dime. Cradling the dead birds with lolling necks, they would file a little smugly past Red Dubrovner, as if there was maybe a better show over the road.

I wanted to tell him, Don't worry on my account, I'm not going anywhere; but I didn't even like to mention the possibility. I didn't like to think about leaving my father's sight. What was there, anyway, outside of our neighborhood? Swamps and vicious three-legged dogs and yokels who hitched Jewish boys up to their plows—as my papa had always assured us. And now that he wasn't shouting about it, I was more fearful than ever, now that the sounds in the distance were coming so clear: the whistles of the packet boats, the singing of the roustabouts on the levee.

• • •

But one afternoon I didn't wait, as I usually did, for my Hebrew teacher, Mr. Notowitz, to wake up and dismiss me. Instead, leaving him asleep at the table, I picked my way through his fish bones and stacks of books and slipped quietly out of his apartment.

Following my feet I found myself headed up Main Street toward the Green Owl Café. I was drawn there by my fondness for Fagie. Though she'd never hung around much, now that I knew she wasn't coming back I missed her. I missed her dirty mouth and the reek of her cheap perfume. Hadn't she always been more of a mama to me than Mama? What harm would it do, I wondered, if I paid her a visit? I would drop by briefly on the way home from cheder—it was that simple. So why did my heart hammer my chest like it wanted out?

Then I was standing on the curb at Poplar Avenue—which I'd never in my life been across—looking for any excuse to turn around. But the avenue didn't appear to be different from any other street; it was no Red Sea. The other side was still Main Street, still shops and offices, and there was the Green Owl less than a block away. So I hitched up my shorts and crossed over.

The curtained door of the dingy café was the only one on the street that was closed against the muggy sunlight. I was shuffling in front of it, having second thoughts, when the door suddenly opened and a customer came out. I expected raucous noise to tumble down on top of me, saw myself bolting away. But as I heard nothing, only the knocking of what I guessed were billiard balls, I took a deep breath and sidled in.

The men sat at tables under harsh lights, in the sluggish air stirred by ceiling fans. They were drinking from porcelain mugs which they took under the tables to refill, spitting dolefully into dented cuspidors. From my father's ravings I'd imagined that they would be brawling and sinning openly. So I was relieved, if a little disappointed, by their silence. All things considered, the Anshei Sphard shul, with its reeling and chattering daveners, was more like I'd expected the café to be.

Then I realized that the quiet was due in part to the fact that everyone was looking at me. Accustomed to being practically invisible, I was close to backing out the door when the man behind the counter, wiping a spoon in his apron, asked me, "What can we do for you, small change?"

I swallowed and told him I was looking for Fagie Dubrovner.

"Sorry, sweatpea," he replied, turning his head aside to wink. "She's already spoken for."

Everyone chuckled over the way I was blushing. "But I'm her brother," I explained.

"Ohhh," nodded the man behind the counter. "In that case . . . " and he jerked his thumb toward the stairs in back of the pool table.

Upstairs it was even harder to breathe than down. The smoke hung so thick I had to wave it aside like cobwebs in order to see. Then everything was pretty much as Fagie had described, only faded. The draperies were threadbare, the windowpanes painted an ugly red. The men in vests and gartered shirtsleeves, standing over the dice table, looked grim, like they were peering into somebody's open casket.

Fagie saw me before I saw her.

"Shimmie!" she hailed from a table in the back. At the table, which was littered with amber bottles, a group of men sat playing cards. Nutty Iskowitz was among them in striped suspenders, a cigar stuck in his mouth, and behind him in his too-tight suit stood Eddie Kid Katz. With his arms folded, the boxer made me think of a genie popped out of one of the cuspidors downstairs.

"Look, everybody," said Fagie, risen from Nutty's side, her tassels swishing as she crossed the room to hug me. "It's my long-lost baby brother." But nobody even bothered to turn around.

"Hello, brother-in-law," Nutty Iskowitz called out to me, leaning back in his chair to study his hand of cards. "I'll buy you a pair of long pants for the wedding."

"You're coming, ain't you, kiddo?" asked Fagie, breathing toilet water and whiskey in my face. "Every gonif in town will be there."

Somehow it hadn't entered my mind that Fagie would be having a wedding. On the Other Side, where Papa claimed she had gone, who had weddings? Now that I knew hers was coming, I was excited for Fagie's sake. But I was sorry for myself, knowing that the butcher would never let me attend.

"That's right," said Nutty, laying down his cards, locking his fingers behind his head in an attitude more suited to blowing his horn. "Nothing's too good for my angel drawers . . . "

Fagie beamed through her makeup as she told me how they were renting the banquet hall of the Cochran Hotel. She practically crooned the words "catered affair," waving her handkerchief lah-de-dah over the elegance of it all. But all I could think of, as she carried on, was that it was past the time when I should have been home from Mr. Notowitz's.

Meanwhile Nutty was still putting on the dog.

"Shapiro's got his whole sweatshop working on her gown," he was saying. "The train's so long we can use it for a chupeh. And wait till she gets a load of the ring." Here he crossed his legs on top of the table and shut his eyes. "We'll bring down a wonder rabbi from Chicago, and Eddie here can jump out of the cake, and to close the show, we'll set a flock of chickens free . . . "

At this Fagie's face suddenly clouded. "No chickens!" she snapped, turning hotly toward Nutty. "I want real birds—pigeons and doves."

"Awright awright," protested Nutty, "whatever my little knish . . . " Then his eyes went wide as he righted his chair, hopping abruptly to his feet. "Nail down the furniture, boys," he exclaimed, showing the empty palm of one hand, tugging at Eddie's coat sleeve with the other. "It's him again!"

At the head of the stairs stood my father in his homburg and apron. Stoop-shouldered and pale, he was resting his chin against his sinking chest, so that his beard resembled a shirt front. He was moving his lips, trying, I suppose, to tell me that he'd come to take me home. But no sounds emerged from his mouth.

The whole room, distracted from gambling, was braced for some kind of eruption. Then Fagie, having sized up our papa's condition, took the liberty of putting words on his tongue.

"I come," she said, making her voice sound Russian and gruff, "to give a blessing on my daughter's marriage." After which the gamblers relaxed into horse laughter and guffaws. Encourged by their response and Papa's continued speechlessness, Fagie went on.

"I will slaughter a bull in her honor, with my bare hands, kayne horeh."

Everyone was howling over her impersonation. Stepping from behind Eddie, Nutty sauntered over to put an arm around her shoulder. "What a gal!" He grinned, while he put his other arm around me.

I wished I could enter into the spirit of it all, but when I tried to laugh with them, my papa's downcast presence reminded me of my place. His lips were no longer moving and he appeared to be shrinking, the general hilarity affecting him like salt on a snail. So I broke away and hurried to his side.

As I began to lead him out, Fagie shook her head and gave me a look like, So long, it's been nice to know you.

When we were back across the avenue, my father's hangdog silence was even more of a spectacle. Everyone noticed how he trudged in front of their shops, his eyes fixed on his feet. Seated in a folding chair outside his dry-goods store, Mr. Bluestein was the first to say it.

"Whaddayaknow, Dubrovner's lost his temper."

That was his joke, and he liked it so much that he shouted it to his wife in her upstairs window, resting her bosom in a flower box. She passed it on to Mrs. Ridblatt in a neighboring window, who called down to Mr. Sacharin rolling a herring barrel into his market. He shared the information with a couple of firemen outside the Number 4 station, who dispatched their idiot mascot, Arthur, to Mrs. Rosen's next door. In a little while the newsboys would get wind of it. Pretty soon the whole street, when they got over the shock, would maybe turn out to give the butcher back some of his own.

It was up to me to do something.

"Papa," I said, clearing my throat to speak a little louder. "Papa, I don't think that the Green Owl is so bad."

Don't ask me how but it worked. I heard a rumbling in his belly as his chest began to swell. His beard bristled and the blue vein flashed at his temple.

"Then go back!" he cried, miraculously overcoming the handicap of his lisp. "Go to the goyim, why don't you! Gey in drerd arayn! Run away!" I was trotting to keep up with him now, staying out of the way of his flailing arms, of his fingers squeezing air.

"Or maybe you want to wait for the dark. You burn your skullcap and black your face with ashes, you hide in a shvartzer's wagon and roll away. Or sail away, that's good. You wait for the floods, you put a washtub in the bayou—you're a regular Hucklebee Dubrovner. You hop on the ice truck, you hop on the freight train that is crossing over the bridge. You tie your tallis to a stick—Shimmele Luftmensch; you sprinkle salt on the Pinch, you don't turn around . . . "

He was himself again, sounding off to spite the whole neighborhood. Mothers grabbed their children and merchants pulled down the shades inside their shops, while Papa continued his rampage, suggesting so many colorful ways of departing that you might have thought he'd considered them for himself.

But by the time we got back to the shop, he was spent. Gloomy again and short of breath, he slogged up the stairs to our stuffy apartment. In the kitchen he slumped into a chair and laid his head across the sticky tabletop. Seeing him like that, dead silent in the failing light, I thought I knew what he was feeling: that he was all alone in a deserted house.

"Papa, get up!" I pleaded, trying to shake him by his hairy shoulders. "Tell me I'm a no-good, I'm running away! Say, 'Shimmele Shnorrer, you take up with gypsies . . . ' "

Unable to move him, I was shaking myself over what might come next. In a little while, I thought, he would lift his head slowly. He would pick himself up, go down to the meat locker, and return with his ritual wine. He would drink two or three bottles, cover his head, and say the kaddish for me.

But since he was behaving anyway like I'd already left him, I left him, creeping stealthily out of the room. I went down to the locker in the rear of the shop and pulled open the thick wooden door. I hauled out a case of wine from under the hanging flanks of beef, dragging it through sawdust to the screen door in back, then down some clattering steps into the yard. Then I returned to the locker for the remaining case.

With chattering teeth I uncorked a bottle of wine. I poured it into an empty birdbath, which stood choked by rotten vines in the center of the yard. I did the same with another and another, asking my father's forgiveness for every bottle that I poured. Soon the wine was slopping over the bowl, spilling onto the broken stones, sending up steam toward the setting sun.

Down to the last bottle, I suddenly realized how thirsty my labor had made me. It was Friday evening, so I said the blessing before I drank. The first sip, which set off a pleasant tingling inside me, called for a deeper swallow. Refreshed but a little dizzy, I went over to the low brick wall that surrounded the yard, squatting there with my back against the bricks as I continued to drink. It was then that the birds began to come.

They were pigeons—some blue and gray, some mottled albino. Swooping down into the birdbath, they fluttered and splashed and preened, battling for space in the crowded bowl. Edged out, they glided to the ground and wobbled about. Some keeled over as if they were stalled; some came to rest within inches of my feet. Watching them, I worried that the wine had gone bad; they were poisoned and so was I. Then a hiccup brought home to me my own condition, and I understood the birds were drunk.

This got me tickled. The more they stumbled and capsized, making trilling sounds that might have been snores, the more amused I became. In the end I had to laugh out loud, clapping a hand over my mouth. I tried to get hold of myself. After all my father might appear at any moment—

and what would he find? Me sitting in the mud made from his own spilled wine, a flock of shikkered pigeons at my feet.

And in the midst of it, remembering my sister's request for pigeons, pigeons and doves to set loose at her wedding, I had an idea.

Wiping tears from my eyes, I fumbled back into the shop, snatched a spool of shaggy twine from a counter, and returned to the yard. I unraveled a length and bit if off, then stooped to tie the end around the leg of a snoozing pigeon. The bird only twitched a little and moaned, and I was encouraged to try another. By the time I had run out of twine, there were strings attached to nearly all of the birds in the yard.

I dried my sweaty hands on my shorts and, taking up all the loose ends, went back to the wall and sat down. Now I had only to wait for the birds to sober up and begin to stir. And when they rose into the air, I would carry them like a bunch of balloons to my sister Fagie.

I took one last swallow of wine and tied my fistful of string through a belt loop. Then I closed my eyes to imagine how they would greet me: "Hurray for Shimmele Badchen, the wedding jester!"

I was waked by a tugging that jerked me forward and up. Before my eyes were open I knew that it was my father, I could feel the wind from his wrath in my hair.

But when I looked, I saw it wasn't Papa but the birds who were carrying me aloft. Already I was as high as our kitchen window, through which I glimpsed a dark and empty room. I was dangling by the seat of my pants, swinging just above my father as he came out onto the steps behind his shop.

He might have reached up then and grabbed me, and pulled me back into his arms. He might at least have called my name.

"Shout, Papa!" I cried, still hoping he would scare the birds into letting me down. "Say, 'Cruel boychik, you give me a this, you break my that!' "

But he only stood there looking helpless and small, the feathers falling into his upturned face.

So maybe he took the grubby pigeons for angels, I don't know. By then I was over the rooftops, the neighborhood diminishing to a huddle of tenements below me. And what with all the commotion of the birds, their pitching and diving and beating their wings above my head, what with the breezes flapping in my baggy shorts, I had enough trouble just trying to stay horizontal. I had my hands full with pawing the evening air—which was smoldering red in the west, beyond the river over Arkansas. I had my own problems now with learning to dip and soar, never mind worrying about the butcher.

Aaron Makes a Match

"Aunt Esther, have you ever been penetrated by a man?" asked her nephew, Aaron Bronsky, who was concerned.

"What is this, a proposition?" replied his maiden aunt, nodding her head in a palsy. "Listen don't worry about me, worry about you. Your childhood is a mockery; your mind is a public convenience. Go climb a tree, tear your pants, get dirty. Here's another book." And with the help of her nephew, she rose from her love seat and went to the tall shelves that surrounded the room.

It had been for years Aunt Esther's habit to make Aaron the gift of a book upon each of his visits. As a consequence her library had become severely depleted. The books had originally belonged to her father's father, who had somehow managed to lug them across an ocean from Bratislava. Family tradition had it that he was mad, as the task would imply and the sepia photograph above the fireplace confirmed. His hair and whiskers were an ice storm out of which peered his terrible eyes. In the days before his spectacles, Aaron had spent hours in front of mirrors, trying to duplicate the look on his great-grandfather's face.

The books consisted mostly of arcane volumes in decaying leather, with titles such as *The Testament of Solomon* or *The Secrets of Abramelin the Mage as Delivered by Abraham the Jew unto His Son Lamech, A.D. 1458*. Interspersed amongst these were a few dubious pamphlets with naughty illustrations.

"Take," said Aunt Esther, removing from a shelf one of the heavier tomes, "read." As Aaron thanked her and made for the door with his prize, she followed him with more injunctions: "Ruin your health, go blind. Haven't you heard of recess? Haven't you heard of life?" All of which made Aaron feel that he was stealing a golden goose.

Then he had stepped into the evening and shut the ponderous front door. Looking back through its rippled diamond panes, he could see the little woman, like a harlequin in a block of ice, still standing on the other side.

Back home Aaron entered his bedroom which had come to house the bulk of Aunt Esther's library. The books were stacked about the floor in dense and tottering heaps. To negotiate a path from the door to the bed required the skill of a Theseus. Aaron himself had been known to get lost for days.

"Milton, your son has buried himself alive," his mother would complain to the newspaper behind which her husband was hidden.

Counting his books, fingering their bindings, blowing the dust from their pages, Aaron was sometimes even moved to read them. This earned him the neighborhood nickname of Aaron the Scholar, whose eyeglasses were rumored to be made from the bottoms of pop bottles, whose feces were full of undigested words.

Thus happily outcast, Aaron kept to himself. The clutter of his bedroom could not have accommodated loneliness. One thing, however, disturbed him in his otherwise comfortable solitude: that, as his own store of books was increased, his aunt's was diminished. He imagined his own house and hers at either end of a seesaw. With every book that he carried home, his house was brought closer to earth, while his aunt's—with its congeries of vacant rooms—rose higher into the air. The imbalance haunted him.

Then there was the recent confidence, imparted to him with relish by W. Cecil Blankenship, the neighborhood's evil genius.

"Unless your Aunt Esther gets penetrated by the male of the species," pronounced Cecil, "she will dry up inside and out." Then, with variations on his theme, "Her navel will fall off and her bodily orifices will . . . " But Aaron was already walking away. Although he had only an abstract grasp of what Cecil's prophecy implied, he worried that it might be even now in effect; that his aunt's wizened figure and her prunelike complexion were not necessarily due to her age.

These thoughts preoccupied him, as he sat on the floor and opened the latest addition to his library. Out of its leaves fell a yellowed pamphlet bearing the title "The Doge at His Dalliance" in formal calligraphy. Aaron inspected its contents. Through a progress of antique daguerreotypes, a man and a woman, exotically undressed, were involved in a series of impossible postures. Their activities were framed by a minimum of poignant commentary. Putting aside all other considerations, Aaron gave the pamphlet his undivided attention. When, well after midnight, he felt that he had the bulk of its details by heart, he stopped to clean his glasses. Replacing them, he caught sight of the weathered volume from which the pamphlet had fallen. Itself profusely illustrated, it was a dictionary of angels.

• • •

Though it hurt his pride to do so, Aaron went to consult Cecil Blankenship. He was usually to be found in the loft, properly known as the Asylum of St. Mary of Bethlehem, above his family's two-car garage. This was where Cecil conducted his unspeakable experiments and entertained his friends.

The Asylum was reached by passing between a Studebaker and a Dodge sedan, then climbing a rope ladder to knock at a trapdoor.

"Password," came a voice from above.

"Cecil, can I see you for a minute?" asked Aaron, impatient of protocol.

"Well, as I live and breathe," declared Cecil, "to what do I owe the pleasure . . . ?" And so on. Cecil frequently patterned his speech after the villains of melodrama. Then resuming his official tone, "Say, 'The horror, the horror.' "

Aaron complied and found himself promptly hauled into the presence of the archfiend of Alabama Street. Cecil was alone in his chambers, tastefully appointed (as he liked to say) with the furniture of bad dreams. Homemade manacles containing a human skeleton hung from the rafters; on the creaking floor were: a whip, a crown of thorns, a reinforced birdcage labeled The Iron Mask of Torquemada. On a table in the corner, amid tubes and scorched beakers, lay a rodent without a head. The austerity was a little mitigated by, here and there, a filthy magazine.

"Have you come to be solemnly mortified?" intoned Cecil with his sidewise grin, his strawberry cowlick like a wave at sunset.

Because he was anxious not to know what Cecil was talking about, Aaron, by way of an answer, produced his pamphlet. Opening it to its choicest sequence of photographs, he asked, "Cecil, is this penetration?"

After careful scrutiny, Cecil placed his hand over his heart. Lifting his pink eyes toward paradise, he became pious.

"I'm dying," he said.

Aaron took this response to be an affirmative. Seeing no reason to prolong his visit, he thanked Cecil for his expertise and turned to go. A hand at his belt held him forcibly restrained.

"Give me that," said Cecil, suggesting an alternative, "or I'll kill you."

Aaron shrugged and endeavored to open the trapdoor. Said Cecil on second thought, "Give me, and I'll make you an honorary Inmate."

Aaron thanked but no-thanked him and persisted in trying to make his escape.

"Gimme and I'll give you . . . " Cecil looked round the loft, spotted a murky aquarium. ". . . some rare and colorful tropical fish."

So that evening Aaron introduced his books to a large glass jar full of tiny incandescent fish. Through the night he watched them, like expiring matches, drift to the bottom of the jar; later on, setting out for another world, they would rise as far as the surface and float. Nothing in his books could tell him what Cecil had also neglected to: that the fish could only survive in water of a controlled equatorial temperature.

This was not the first time that Cecil had had the last laugh. Once, ransacking his own laboratory, he'd left a trail of broken glass and dead animals leading to Aaron's door. Reprisals included the desecration of Aaron's bicycle, as performed by the Inmates at Cecil's behest. After that there were notes in Aaron's mailbox to the effect that his Aunt Esther, a figure of fun, could be spied upon in her bath. The evidence consisted of graphic descriptions of the remoter parts of Aunt Esther's anatomy. The notes were signed. "Yours in regurgitation, the Inmates of the Asylum of St. Mary of Bethlehem."

Then there was the occasion of the grammar school science fair. Cecil had submitted a stillborn infant—acquired from godknowswhere—immersed in a beaker of formaldehyde. Wires were attached to it so that, when a button was pushed, it jiggled about. Despite his insistence that the child was in fact a homunculus in a *vas hermeticum,* Cecil took none of the prizes.

Perhaps it was his disappointment on this count which prompted Cecil to scapegoat Aaron. Science had never been Aaron's strong point. That year he had taken advantage of his mother's last operation to place her pair of gallstones in the fair. Floating in a small glass container, they were accompanied by a modest cardboard sign which stated simply what they were. Cecil, for it could have been none other, replaced the sign with an enormous placard:

SACRED RELIC of the TESTICLES of
JESUS CHRIST OUR LORD

announced the placard in rainbow pastels.

The prank, beyond the embarrassment which it caused his family, secured Aaron's ostracism at school. Not that Aaron was especially aware of it. The opinion of his peers concerned him no more than the oaks outside his bedroom window. The oaks lined a street in a city on a river where steamboats had once disembarked: all of which was a matter of indifference to Aaron. What concerned him were his books and, lately, the question of his aunt's virginity.

• • •

"Aunt Esther, why don't you marry?" asked Aaron upon his next visit.

"Because," replied his aunt, wistfully lifting the cover of an album on the table beside her love seat. With her crooked fingers, she fanned the pages, flashing the glossy autographed images of Valentino, Navarro, Bushman.

"Because all the best men are taken." The phrase, in this context, had a strange connotation. Then, recovering her senses, "What are you talking marriage? I got one foot already in the Bosom of Abraham."

It was true, observed Aaron, that Aunt Esther had seen better days. Her mottled scalp was visible beneath the sparseness of her iron-gray hair; the pouches beneath her eyes were marsupial in depth, and blue veins embroidered her shins. Her chest was concave. She was a comprehensive catalogue of the symptoms of desiccation for want of a man.

"Why don't I marry?" continued the aunt, ruffling under her nephew's regard. "Why don't you be a prizefighter, go to sea, you nebbish, you milksop, you bookworm . . . "

Meanwhile Aaron was discreetly making his exit. Aunt Esther had been raised to her feet by the strength of her own why-don't-you's, some of which included violence and the pursuit of sin. It occurred to Aaron, as he reached the door, that it was through no accident that the provocative pamphlet had fallen into his hands. Perhaps his aunt, to alleviate her boredom, meant to arouse his manhood prematurely through the medium of stimulating pictures. These reflections saw him through the front door and into the night, oblivious to Aunt Esther's "Wait, here's a book!"

It was the first time he'd left her house emptyhanded. She needed, he reasoned, to be left in possession of what little remained of her library. This might console her until her nephew could implement the resolution which he formulated on his walk home.

• • •

It was a resolution reinforced by an item of which W. Cecil Blankenship had once apprised him.

"Her membrane will have ossified beyond penetration by ordinary men," he'd pronounced from a shadow, as Aaron walked by.

He entered his bedroom as if there weren't a moment to lose. Without hesitation he took up the dictionary of angels and, having small patience with lesser lights, turned instantly to the chapter on archangels. Then, suddenly cautious of overmuch haste, he browsed.

The prints of the more prestigious seraphim were very imposing. There was Michael in residence in Seventh Heaven, Israfel with a scissors-hold on Jacob. Uriel was confounding Ezra with riddles, and Gabriel, seated on His left hand, was gossiping with God. Raphael, with ritual gravity, was showing Tobit the proper way to clean fish. Aaron was taken with their august countenances, both at home and interfering with humankind. But one in particular had captured his discriminating eye.

Azrael, with his mane of black curls and his magnificent wings, was taking his ease in the shade of the Tree of Life. In a drawing by Doré, he was seated next to Solomon entertaining a rajah. He was depicted elsewhere with the handful of dust that completed the assembly of Adam. He was obviously one of the more worldly and resourceful of angels. Also there was something in the penetrating glint of his eye which convinced Aaron he need look no further. Without bothering to read his pedigree, he decided aloud, "Azrael, you are it."

Then toppling a precarious stack of books, Aaron unearthed an incunabulum in a limp leather binding. The inscription on the title page professed that the following had been translated from parchments found in Jerusalem catacombs. The parchments had contained the keys to the conjuration of spirits, both celestial and infernal. Aaron shuddered to think how such a book might be used in the hands of a W. Cecil Blankenship, then shuddered to think how he intended to use it himself. He examined its pages for finger prints of necromancers who might have preceded him, and wondered about their purposes.

"Maybe I should start with something less ambitious," he considered, thinking fondly upon the relative security of white rabbits and sleight of hand. But, summoning his courage, he called upon the blood of his great-grandfather to stand him in good stead.

No doubt Cecil Blankenship would have proceeded with scientific integrity. He would have made his scroll from the vellum of a lamb that he'd butchered himself, drawn his forty-four pentacles with a quill shaped from the third feather of a gander's left wing. He would have forged his own sword and tempered it in blood drawn from his little sister, then donned a silk robe embroidered in the consecrated letters of Tetragrammaton. Or so Aaron imagined, himself a great believer in the elimination of red tape.

For an approximation of sorcerer's garb, he made do with a bathrobe, a prayer shawl, and a paper party hat. He substituted an antenna for the specified wand of virgin hazel. Clearing a space on the floor, he drew with a piece of chalk a magic circle, or rather oblong, and stepped within. Ignoring the preliminary ten-thousand-word incantation, he commenced straightaway to chant the unutterable names, guaranteed to attract the attention of the denizens of kingdom come.

Outside his room he could hear his mother, who was given

to listening at his door, complaining, "Milton, your son is doing funny business," to her husband the newspaper.

Having repeated the entire register of unutterables to no avail, Aaron took up an alternative tack.

"Azrael, come now or else . . ." he warned, reciting the list of disfigurations to which reluctant spirits are subject. Although he began zealously enough with leprosy and gangrene, by the time he arrived at hemorrhoids his exhilaration was spent. He was weary of nothing happening, losing faith. From an angel's eye he saw himself: a skinny kid in a dark room on a small planet sunk in a whirlpool of stars. What, after all, had he done to deserve the indulgence of immortals?

"Maybe I should have sacrificed something," he wondered, picturing Cecil Blankenship disembowling his younger sister. Then intercepting a tear with his finger, Aaron sat down, a little surprised to find himself so soon defeated.

"Azrael," he muttered, in broken tones, abandoning all pretense to ceremony, "my Aunt Esther needs love."

"So what does she look like, your aunt?" came a voice from nowhere in particular, which brought Aaron to his feet. Stepping out of the chalk circle, he fell over books and switched on the overhead light, then promptly switched it off. In that moment in the dark he prayed that the mistake, which he'd only just glimpsed, might be rectified, then turned the switch again, illuminating the answer to his prayers.

There in the circle, in place of himself, unaccompanied by thunder or other effects, stood a seedy old man in a threadbare black suit a couple of sizes too large. In his horny right hand he was holding an account book, in his left a rubber-tipped walking stick of standard orthopedic supply.

"I know what you're thinking already," he croaked, "but the wings I leave up there," raising his tired rust-red eyes. "On earth you take what you can get."

"You couldn't get better than that?" asked Aaron, unable to mask his disappointment.

"I'm inconspicuous," the old man protested, "and anyway what are you, the Baal Shem of Oz?" Self-consciously Aaron took off the party hat and shawl. "Now about your aunt," goaded the old man, "you were saying . . . ?"

But Aaron, having found not one hint of sublimity in the shabby phenomenon before him, was brooding. Particularly saddened by the sight of the old man's hairless pate, he was wondering if its speckled irritation could be due to the heat of a halo. Finally he asked pointblank, "Are you the archangel Azrael?"

"Yeah, that's me. Now what about . . . ?"

"Then prove it; do me a miracle."

"It's not miracle enough I'm here?" the alleged Azrael wanted to know. But Aaron's obstinate expression said not.

"So what do you want I should do? A nice card trick maybe?" And laying aside his cane, he actually produced from the pocket of his coat a deck of dog-eared tarot, at which Aaron frowned. "All right, okay," sighed the self-avowed angel, in a voice which implied that Aaron had asked for it. He restored the cards to his pocket, then withdrew what Aaron expected to be a feather duster, a scarf without end, but was in fact a small pencil.

"Your father's name in full, surname first," he inquired, opening his ledger officially.

"Bronsky, Milton G.," Aaron volunteered, forfeiting his father for the sake of curiosity.

The angel thumbed through pages, licked the lead, and made a mark. Directly a screaming was heard from the other side of the bedroom door.

"Your papa is now exhibiting the symptoms of heart failure," stated Azrael. "Falling over his newspaper, he tears convulsively at his breast." The whoops and cries for help from his mother seeming to confirm as much, Aaron was satisfied. Gloating, the angel erased his mark and blew; the screaming ceased.

"Your papa resumes his reading of the funnies," reported Azrael, "which, incidentally, are one page away from the obits."

"My Aunt Esther needs a husband," submitted Aaron.

"Ah," said the angel, interested, looking almost spry, "a coincidence. It so happens I'm in the market for a bride." Then with a wanton inflection, "Between you and me, eternity can be a very lonesome place."

Aaron could not help appearing doubtful.

"Don't worry, Mr. Wise Guy," said the angel, developing a rash, "I'm completely functional. You can start to call me Uncle, if you wish." And seeing that Aaron still had scruples, he continued with a ludicrous yellow-toothed grin, "You just introduce us, and let my charm do the rest."

"But . . . ," Aaron tried again.

"But me no but's; and to set your mind at ease, I give you another miracle." So saying, he disappeared. A plume of dust, as when one shuts a casket, ensued.

"Aunt Esther, I brought you a suitor," said Aaron, and anticipating her disapproval, "It's the best I could do."

She stood at the threshold of her pile of a house, peering past the porch light at the angel, who was bowing. The top of his head, caught in the light, served as a proxy for a crimson moon on an otherwise pitch-black night.

Then he stepped into view with his walking stick and various accessories adopted for the occasion. There was, for instance, in his moth-eaten lapel a partially decomposed boutonniere. The scent he was wearing was a heady mixture of camphor and carbolic acid. Business deferring to pleasure, he had tucked his account book away.

"Aunt Esther," announced Aaron with uncertainty, "this is Uncle Azrael from the other side . . ." ". . . Of the family," he had been about to say. But the angel cut him short, creaking forward to take the maiden aunt's hand in his own.

"I'm bewitched," he said, lifting her hand to his mouth, kissing the swollen joints. The sound complementing the gesture was that of a plaster being pulled from a sore. Aunt Esther removed her hand and examined it curiously, as if to verify it was still the original. She seemed reassured.

"Aaron," continued the angel, ogling the spinster, "you were too modest." Aaron's head felt incongruous upon his shoulders. "She ain't just a lady of culture and taste, she's a regular shaineh maidl."

Aaron was prepared for the worst. All the way over he'd imagined their reception: Aunt Esther's shock over Azrael's squalid appearance, her bristling at his impertinence. How she would slam the door, then open a window to call names: alter kocker, philanderer, toad; nor would her nephew be spared her indignation: anemic pismire who would sell his own flesh and blood.

But here she was, tittering slightly, her crow's-feet radiant as fishtails about her smiling eyes. With unprecedented impulsiveness, she had taken Uncle Azrael's arm, saying, "Aaron, where have you been keeping this delightful old heartbreaker?"

And Aaron, to his utter amazement, saw his aunt wink at his make-believe uncle, who smugly returned the confidence in kind. Then, leading him through the hallway into the library, Aunt Esther deposited the angel in her love seat and herself beside him. Aaron sheepishly followed.

Beginning to feel like an unwanted chaperon, he took a

chair opposite the heavenly host and hostess. Aunt Esther, with spasms and feverish cheeks, was cajoling Uncle Azrael, "So tell me about yourself."

"So twist my arm," said the angel, sniggering consumptively.

"You're a card, you are," persisted the aunt, placing her hand on his knee.

"That's right, I'm the thirteenth trump."

Attending these proceedings, Aaron was resentful of the ease with which Azrael had entered his aunt's good graces. Although he had always credited Aunt Esther with formidable resistance, it was difficult now to tell who was courting who.

"You're a wicked one," scolded Aunt Esther, close to a stroke. She was all aglow, eyes moist, the folds beneath her chin like curtains of northern lights. Her imaginary bosom heaved dangerously. Transported, she had squeezed Uncle Azrael's knee, causing the leg to kick involuntarily. As a result, a cherished glass decanter, standing on the coffee table in front of them, was smashed.

"Which reminds me," said Aunt Esther in the subsequent silence, "can I offer you some wine?" Then, unable to contain herself, she started to laugh. No proof against such contagion, Uncle Azrael joined in the cackling, interrupting the hilarity only to gingerly spit phlegm into a handkerchief.

Aaron was, frankly, a little disgusted. As matchmaker, he felt called upon to maintain the proprieties.

"Ahem," he said, his authority counting for nothing. The couple had become conspiratorial in their mirth.

"Uncle Azrael," offered Aaron, "is from out of town, you know." And louder, "I believe that he's traveled extensively." Then taxing his conversational skills, "Is it true that you've been as far as New Orleans?"

The angel put a finger on his lips and cupped a tufted ear.

"Did you hear something? I thought I heard something," he confessed to the aunt, who shook her head no. This was the signal for more incontinent laughter.

"Uncle Azrael is also an amateur magician," cited Aaron, who had yet to take the hint.

"There it is again," said the angel, cocking his head in the attitude of one who receives communications from beyond. "It sounds like . . . yeah, that's it; it's Aaron's mama calling him to come home." And Aunt Esther merrily threw in for good measure, "Aaron, why don't you take a book with you on your way out." Then, joining hands in a collision of fingers, they congratulated each other upon their mischief.

Trying to control his pouting lower lip, Aaron took his leave. As for Aunt Esther's books, she could keep them; he might even bring the ones she had given him back. And with this thought, he felt suddenly free, saw himself with only a kerchief on a stick, setting off for Cathay, say, or New Orleans.

But before he left, he thought he might take a souvenir. So, as his lingering presence was already forgotten, he removed from the mantelpiece the photograph of his great-grandfather and walked out the door. He carried it home to his bedroom and placed it on top of his tallest stack of books. There by flashlight he meditated upon the face, wishing that he were himself the fierce old scholar, seated in a study house in Bratislava, a volume of Mishnah open before him, "The Doge at His Dalliance" hidden inside the text.

Sometime during the small hours, Aaron, fallen asleep in his clothes, was waked by a visitation. Before him stood the down-at-heels seraph, more disheveled than usual. His shirt front was furled and his funereal suit had been pulled off of one of his shoulders. His hoary head was wreathed in lipstick traces, like erysipelas or roses.

"Your aunt and I, we don't believe in long engagements,"

he asserted, leaning jauntily against his cane, adding that the date had been set for a week from Sunday.

"Say mazel tov," he prompted, but before Aaron could respond, he vanished with nominal effects.

The family were of course scandalized over the announcement of Aunt Esther's banns. Although prepared to humor her more harmless eccentricities, they now felt obliged to protect her from herself. A December bride was one thing, but Aunt Esther was practically into her thirteenth month. And who was this luftmensch, this Azrael? What were his credentials and where did he hail from and why did he look like The Golem Takes a Bride? Where was his shadow? But after they'd met him, one by one they came under his spell. No one any longer seemed conscious of his nastiness or his pungent scarecrow's attire. They could only repeat how fortunate was Esther to have found such a doting and urbane companion for her declining years.

"But what can a man like Uncle Azrael see in a meshuggeneh like Esther?" Aaron heard his mother wonder. Already the family were calling him Uncle.

But to Aaron's mind, the angel was the unworthier party. The shame was that his aunt had so readily succumbed to the designs of a creature disreputably fallen from grace. Then, remembering how he had engineered the fall, Aaron was forced to acknowledge the shame as his own. In the days that followed her wedding announcement, Aunt Esther kept company almost exclusively with Uncle Azrael; therefore Aaron, left to his own devices, had plenty of time to indulge in regret.

Sometimes he thought he might sabotage the ceremony. When the rabbi asked if there were any reason why this man and woman should not be joined together, Aaron would step forward.

"Uncle Azrael's not a man," he would shout, "he's . . ." and the relatives would all concur; for didn't they think him an angel already?

"Where does it say that mortals are forbidden to marry with seraphim?" he could hear the more irate among them protesting.

So Aaron contemplated abduction. He would steal his Aunt Esther and smuggle her, possibly wrapped in a carpet, into countries where even angels feared to tread. They would spend their days swatting scorpions, eating grubs, and Aaron would bask once again in his aunt's abuse: you pipsqueak, you nothing. Then, recalled from his daydreams, Aaron recollected that his aunt was already happy. It was his own dejection which was making him wish that he might have left well enough alone.

Usually impatient with pathos, he asked himself, "What have I set loose on the world?"

Came the Sunday of the wedding, and Aaron was putting on his suit. It was his navy blue bar mitzvah suit, pockets full of mothballs, which his mother had laid out for him that morning. In it he remembered that he was supposed to have come of age. This thought made him as skittish as if he were the bridegroom, then led him to imagine that the wedding was his own.

"Aaron," his mother was calling from beyond the bedroom door, "come on already, we're late."

"I'm not going through with it," said Aaron to himself, practicing second thoughts, picturing a synagogue full of outraged relations.

"Huh?" said his mother, who thought she heard something. "Come on. Don't forget you gotta give the bride away."

At this Aaron tried on the resolution which practice had made perfect.

"I'm not going through with it." And blaming his books for finally crowding him out of his room, he opened his window and stepped into a tree, then leaped out of earshot as his mother paged him again.

In lieu of faraway places, Aaron was in search of the childhood which his aunt had accused him of losing. Without an authentic chum to give him asylum, he made his way toward the Blankenship garage.

"The horror!" cried Aaron, rapping upon the trapdoor until it opened.

Straight away he was hoisted by a couple of Cecil's lieutenants into the groaning loft. Flanked by half a dozen kids in surgical masks, in rain slickers doubling as laboratory coats, Cecil sat cross-legged in similar attire, saying, "To what do we owe this unexpected . . ." etcetera.

"I ran away from Aunt Esther's wedding," admitted Aaron, thus explaining his suit; though he wondered why, given the circumstances, he should feel self-conscious.

"Your visit is very opportune," said Cecil, his mask puffing in and out of his mouth as he spoke, muffling his voice. He explained that this afternoon he had gathered his colleagues to witness a mysterious biological phenomenon.

His colleagues fidgeted and poked one another impatiently, ill becoming the solemnity of the occasion. The truth was that they were Cecil's faithful disciples only as long as he kept them entertained. And as they had lately grown bored with the customary atrocities upon animals, their host (or warden, as he preferred to be called) was forced to greater lengths to amuse them. Already, embezzling the St. Mary of Bethlehem treasury, Cecil had managed to engage the services of Desdemona Malone. For half an hour she had tick-lishly submitted to the anatomical researches of the Inmates; after which, weeping disconsolately, she asked for a priest. Today Cecil promised something altogether different.

"So if someone would provide Aaron with a mask . . ." he suggested, as preliminary to their getting under way. A comical kid took from among the instruments of torture the bottomless birdcage which served for the Iron Mask of Torquemada. This he placed over Aaron's head, who sat down from the weight of it. Unwieldy as it was, he thought better of trying to remove it, at least until the comical kid had taken his foot from its crown.

When the laughter subsided, Cecil went on, "Today we have with us Mr. Genghis Padauer, come all the way from Leath Street in the interest of science." Not to mention the five dollars out of Cecil's mother's sinking fund.

A gangling, flatheaded older boy in mufti sat to one side, gravely scratching his acned chin.

"Under our strict clinical supervision," said Cecil, "Genghis has agreed to show us sperm."

At a signal from Cecil, Genghis took a checkered handkerchief from the pocket of his dungarees, spreading it over his lap. He might have been about to eat his lunch. Then, searching for something, he slipped his right hand underneath the kerchief. Directly the handkerchief, coming to life, stood up and jerked about. Genghis appeared fascinated by the activity in his own lap, as if waiting for an imp he had captured to be still. The floorboards accelerated their bouncing, and Genghis, rolling his eyes toward the rafters, grunted once. Then, tugging at a furtive zipper, he held forth for inspection the kerchief containing the residue of his passion.

The Inmates climbed over each other for the privilege of being the first to see. While a couple pretended that they were going to be sick, the rest were unusually reverent.

Crawling forward, Cecil dipped a finger into the nacreous substance, proving its ropy consistency.

"Gentlemen," he declared, removing his mask as if to punctuate a successful operation, "I give you the elixir of life."

From inside his birdcage, Aaron was impressed. Although he essentially hated and feared Cecil Blankenship, he couldn't help feeling at that moment a glimmer of brotherhood.

"And now," said Cecil, while he had their attention, "for our next experiment, let us turn to Aaron the Scholar. Take down his pants!"

The Inmates, in their inflammable mood, needed little encouragement. Howling diabolically, they pinned his arms and pulled his blue serge trousers to his ankles. Thus overwhelmed by boys in masks, Aaron was robbed of his composure.

"For your express delectation," Cecil shouted over the din, coruscating in his plastic rain slicker, "we present to you this album of photographs, entitled *Aunt Esther's Honeymoon*" —holding open before Aaron's eyes the pamphlet called "The Doge at His Dalliance."

Gazing disinterestedly at the pictures through the bars of his cage, Aaron was elsewhere. He was standing beside the chupeh, proudly consigning his aunt to her marriage. He was applauding as Uncle Azrael crushed the glass. Then, despite his distance, he was recalled to the immediate proceedings by the awareness of his risen member.

Sitting up, Aaron took stock of the details of his humiliation: his bitterness, his certainty that he would never forgive, the sudden high-pitched ratcheting sound which superseded the fiendish laughter, Cecil Blankenship's ecstatic broken-toothed grin; which was the last thing that Aaron saw before the lights went out and he found himself temporarily in midair.

The beams which supported the loft had snapped, the floorboards given way. The collapse of the Asylum of St. Mary of Bethlehem, from an excess of pandemonium, was as complete as that of the House of Usher. The boys dropped through darkness onto the roofs of the Blankenship family vehicles, from which they tumbled off into adolescence; all except Aaron who merely fell out of his cage.

Pulling up his trousers, Aaron ran several blocks without a backward glance. Crossing Poplar Avenue, he did not stop until he reached the doors of a ponderous copper-domed building, its stained glass windows garish with the setting sun. Stepping in out of the afterglow, he passed through a vestibule and entered the sanctuary, vacant of its congregation. Prompted, however, by distant music in a nonliturgical mode, he left the shul and ascended a flight of stairs. In the assembly hall, beneath a succession of lambent chandeliers, the wedding reception was already winding down.

Kitchen porters were removing plates of chicken bones, marzipan crumbs, and gold fillings, decanting wine. A few elderly guests were still seated at the long banquet tables; some dozing, some resurrecting old quarrels and complaining of pain. Meanwhile an orchestra, looking as if it had emerged from the face of a clock, was playing a waltz. Pregnant cousins and their apprehensive husbands, uncles and infant nieces, the bachelor rabbi and his sister were shuffling about the polished floor. In their midst, executing a kind of geriatric apache, the newlyweds amorously doddered.

Looking a bit like a superannuated ringmaster in his tails, Uncle Azrael lurched with his bride through a series of hyperbolical postures. Aunt Esther for her part, breathless in white satin, clung to the groom for dear life. The other dancers, a little frightened, tried with varying success to make way for them.

Standing unnoticed at the edge of the dance floor, catching his breath, Aaron seemed to have, at least momentarily, outrun his shame and indignation. Not many Uncle Azraels, he whimsically considered, could dance on the head of a pin. And watching the married couple turn like a broken dreidl, he exulted.

"Tonight my aunt will get laid," he sighed, dropping a tear into his spectacles. A corollary to this thought occurred to him: If matrimony could make of his dilapidated aunt a woman, perhaps it could make of an angel a man. Hence the old spellbinder's preposterous animation: he was celebrating his return to mortality.

"Mazel tov," whispered Aaron, imagining a cozy future. He saw himself and his aunt and uncle, seated before shelves to which he intended restoring their borrowed books. His aunt would be knitting an endless scarf for his uncle, who would sit reminiscing about the life to come; while Aaron luxuriated in their contentment, safe from his enemies, growing wise.

Just then, stepping forward in his waistcoat, the violinist had become a fiddler, striking up a lively tune from a recent Broadway show. Aaron saw Uncle Azrael's wrinkles rearrange themselves like paper catching fire. He was smiling at Aunt Esther, as if this were their song, taking her agued hand. Aunt Esther in turn took the hand of a cousin, who took the hand of a husband, and so on, until the entire unseated wedding party were concatenated. Then, led by Uncle Azrael, lifting his spindle shanks unnaturally high, they hokey-pokeyed.

They moved around the floor in a serpentine romp, eventually passing Aaron, whom his uncle incited the relations to encircle. Without interrupting the dance, Uncle Azrael greeted him, tweaking his cheek in transit.

"Wouldya look at what the cat drug in!" he exclaimed. "We thought you'd been stolen by gypsies."

Next came his aunt, who was finding it difficult to simultaneously hop and speak.

"Aaron, you fragment," she managed to scold him, "you made me give myself away." And her lips, particularly bloodless that evening, shaped a coquettish kiss.

Aaron blushed, while the rest of the dancers filed past, beckoning him to join the chain. Thanking them, protesting his weak linkdom, he modestly declined. Nevertheless, orbited by so many faces, he was feeling slightly indispensable.

The dancers wove a circle round him thrice, then moved away, following their leader, whose kicking legs revealed his gartered socks. Aaron might have applauded had they not left him richer by a goblet of wine in either of his hands. Thirsty, he drained the first glass to the health of the newlyweds: long life. Then, to assuage his worries that their health might be impaired through behavior unbefitting their years (be they three score and ten or, in the case of the groom, ten thousand), he drank the second. Through the upturned crystal, emptied of wine, he viewed the galloping procession; trailing out of an exit behind Azrael and Esther, they appeared to be dissolving into the bottom of Aaron's glass.

The fiddler stopped playing and Aaron's heart sank. Turning to place the goblets on a table, he happened to see Uncle Azrael's metal cane among the bread crusts and ashes. Obviously the sprightly bridegroom had no real use for it.

"But on the other hand," reasoned Aaron, looking for a loophole, "there might be a sentimental attachment." The cane did, after all, convey a sense of authority, not to mention its many practical uses. Surely his new uncle would be grateful for its return.

"Bless you, boychik," Uncle Azrael would say, "and so

long as you are here, why don't you accompany your aunt and myself on our honeymoon?"

Speculating on the places where retired angels might go (the constellation of the Great Bear, maybe, or New Orleans), Aaron picked up the cane and fled the hall. On his way out he caught sight of his mother, seated on a bench, informing an open edition of the *Hebrew Watchman*, "Milton, your son's run amok."

Aaron bolted down the steps and shoved through the wedding guests, who stood on the sidewalk throwing rice at a departing black taxicab.

"Wait for me!" he called, sprinting after it, swallowing exhaust for the length of a block. As the taxi accelerated, undaunted, Aaron vaulted fences and streaked down alleys. Never before so fleet, he felt lighter by at least an entire roomful of books.

After running for some minutes, he reached his aunt's house, in front of which a shadowy driver was loading trunks into the back of a taxi. Hurtling up the steps, Aaron made straight for the library, whence issued the screams.

On the carpet in front of the love seat, Aunt Esther in her bridal gown lay shrieking. Desperately she held onto the ankle of another, an upright Aunt Esther, distinguished from the prostrate by her sensible, if wintry, traveling attire; and by her transparency. The standing Aunt Esther, while attempting to retain her balance, shook the foot to which her corporeal counterpart was fastened. She might have been trying to kick off an ill-fitting shoe.

Meanwhile Uncle Azrael, restored to his somber worm-perforated suit, was holding his open ledger in one hand while tugging at the ankle of the fallen Aunt Esther with his other.

"This is highly irregular," he groaned in exasperation.

With a grace becoming her newly acquired matrimonial status, the upright Aunt Esther welcomed her nephew. The room swam through her pellucid countenance, as she beseeched the boy above the noise of her double, "Aaron, you doormat, be a sweetheart and make her let me go."

Despite his trembling, Aaron managed to hang on to his wits. Anxious to be of service, wanting to redeem his absence from the wedding, he quickly weighed his allegiances. Hadn't his sympathies always lain more with the spirit of Aunt Esther rather than with the flesh? Reasoning thus, Aaron dropped the cane and knelt on the emerald carpet. He grasped the hands of the dying woman and prized her crooked fingers, one by one, from about the scrawny ankle of her soul. There followed a medley of all the rigors that the former old maid had been heir to over the years. Then, with the surcease of her rattling, Aunt Esther said, Gott in Himmel, and gave up the ghost.

"Good riddance," sighed Uncle Azrael, sneezing, wiping his nose with a sleeve, offering his arm. "Come, my neshomaleh, my queen, let us fly."

And so the ageless couple departed the house, exchanging its vestigial library for an evening in April. Left behind, Aaron considered closing the mouth and the terrified eyes of the corpse, lighting candles, sitting vigil beside its putrefaction for the remainder of his days.

"I will be the friendless custodian of this solitary house," he told himself, just to hear how it sounded. Satisfied that it sounded absurd, he shouted, "Wait, I'm coming with you!" then staggered after the angel and his mate out the door, bearing the cane.

Azrael was committing the soul of Esther to the back seat of the taxicab. He turned around at Aaron's approach, discarding the ledger in favor of the cane. This he tore out of Aaron's hand and lifted above his head. It was a gesture of such furious and mighty dimensions (rending the seams of his suit) that his bareboned frame could scarcely contain it. To assume it, he had first to rise in stature, to fling back his head, had nearly to spread his wings. Aaron, protecting his face, fell backward onto the grass. Through the lattice of his fingers, he observed how a crescent moon sat athwart the tip of the upraised cane like a scythe. Then the angel had ducked into the taxi and roared, "Take us home!" to the driver who screeched away.

Aaron sat on the curb and felt sorry for himself. He would have liked to be left with a little something more in exchange for the sacrifice of his aunt. A garter, perhaps, or a bridal bouquet. But all he had to console himself with was the gift of the ledger, quarto-sized and with a pencil stuck in its spiral spine. Inspecting its columns of debits and credits, he frowned, as if an account book were all that remained of his childhood.

"Thank you for nothing!" he inveighed against heaven, and as it seemed so far away, "Kiss my you-know-what." Which, lifting his flank, he indicated, so that there might be no mistake.

Then, by the light of the streetlamp and with the help of the wind, he thumbed idly through the pages of the ledger, looking for familiar names. Among those he recognized, there was of course his own and that of one Blankenship, Wolfgang Cecil; beside which, removing the pencil, he made a mark.

Leonard Shapiro
Banished from Dreams

"He was revolted by the thought of known places and dreamed strange migrations"

—from *Sweeney Astray,*
translated from the Gaelic by
Seamus Heaney

I. 194? Infection

Leonard Shapiro was ambushed on the way home from school one day. Mook Weiss and Speedy Plesofsky grabbed him by either arm as he turned the corner into North Main Street, causing his books to scatter over the sidewalk. They gave him the bum's rush down an alley, between the slats of a wooden fence, and into a storage shed behind the ironworks. It was there, among spider webs and tools encrusted with age, that Bernard Rosen, the grand inquisitor of Market Square, held court.

Frightened as he was, Leonard heard himself saying in some remote corner of his head, "Rosen, call off your dogs!" But the words never found their way to his stammering lips.

"So all right," sighed Bernard, a dark-eyed, world-weary kid sitting cross-legged on a keg of nails. "Let the nebbish go."

Bernard's lieutenants reluctantly unhanded Leonard, muttering their disappointment that he had yet to put up a fight. Shaking his head in sympathy with Weiss and Plesofsky, uncrossing his legs so that they dangled from the keg, Bernard said to Leonard,

"Shapiro, you know what you are?"

Leonard considered, by process of elimination, some of the things that he wasn't: Daniel among the lions, Sidney Carton on the scaffold . . .

But Bernard wasn't waiting for him to find the temerity to speak. "You're nobody," he told him, taking the occasion to spit. "You ain't even here."

Then, in case Leonard had missed the point, Bernard aimed a forefinger and stated ex cathedra:

"It's for the crime of being a nobody that you been brought before this tribunal."

"Guilty!" chorused Weiss and Plesofsky, over which Bernard had to hang his head.

"Shmucks!" he groaned. "You were supposed to wait till I prosecuted him."

Plesofsky mumbled something about having to get back to his old man's store, and Weiss seconded the need for haste. Anyway it was not as if this were the first time that Leonard had been thus arraigned. It was a thick-as-thieves neighborhood around North Main Street, and a kid as willfully solitary as he was bound to be fair game.

So far, however, all their hazing had proven a pointless exercise. Unpantsing him in public, pelting him with garbage, dunking him in the ritual bath beneath the shul—such efforts as these gave diminishing returns. Leonard's passivity to their abuse was even more aggravating than the remoteness which had provoked it in the first place. And worse—as his books captured more of his attention than the world at large—Leonard tended to forget whatever happened almost immediately after the fact.

It was this kind of incorrigibility that had prompted Bernard Rosen to take matters into his own hands. Evidently he intended to scare Leonard out of his stupor. But cowardice notwithstanding, Leonard still retained a certain confidence: There was no fear that Bernard could employ to drive Leonard out of his seclusion that would be a match for the fears that kept him in.

He hadn't counted on Bernard's craftiness.

"You're a spook, Shapiro, a dybbuk," Bernard was saying, emphasizing his accusations with the drumming of his heels against the keg. Then he allowed himself half a smile over the alarm he must have seen registered in Leonard's face.

"A dybbuk, Shapiro," he repeated, satisfied that he'd struck a nerve—because figments made more urgent claims upon Leonard than the population of broad daylight ever had. Further encouraged by the smirking of Weiss and Plesofsky, Bernard pursued his advantage:

"You know what we do with dybbuks, don't you Shapiro?" He paused until Leonard had shaken his head in the negative. "We ex-or-cise them, and that don't mean no constitutional. We flush 'em out like drek—which is what you are, ain't it, Shapiro?" He paused again until Leonard, forced into a nod by Plesofsky's hand on his scalp, had concurred. Then he arched an eyebrow and adopted a cooler tone.

"We're flushin' you, Lenny . . . but scientifically, by the rites prescribed in holy kabbalah."

Hopping down off the keg, Bernard went to a shelf below the cloudy windowpanes. With the formality of a rabbi taking scrolls from an ark, he took down what looked like a phone book but for its moldy leather binding. This he brandished in Leonard's pasty face.

Closing his eyes, Leonard squirmed against the injustice. Weren't books his own personal fetish? So how was it that he should be threatened by one of his own? Feeling betrayed, he let go a couple of tears and submitted bitterly in his own defense.

"What'd I do? Aren't we s'posed to be the people of the book?"

Bernard was in a corner setting fire to a trio of cattails. Over his shoulder he reminded Leonard of his place. "You ain't people, Shapiro. You're a spook."

Then keeping one for himself, he handed the ignited cattails to each of his confederates. With his free hand he took up the book and read aloud a hybrid of arcane Hebrew and pig Latin. As he read he marched around Leonard with Weiss and Plesofsky in his train, the two of them repeating a rough approximation of his chant.

The interior of the shed was darker for the light of the torches, their blazes eclipsing the faces of the boys. The revolving flames gave Leonard the sensation of standing at the axis of a spinning room—a room, say, caught up in a whirlwind. Dizzy, he shut his eyes once again and tried to imagine where he might be set down. But without some printed page to navigate by, he lost his bearings. He grew confused, his efforts distracted by a hissing sound like a slow breaking of wind. It was a noise that had its disgraceful echo at the seat of Leonard's pants.

When he looked, he saw Bernard extinguishing the torches in a bucket of water, Weiss and Plesofsky making a show of holding their noses and pretending to retch.

"Show some dignity!" barked Bernard, then himself made a face over the smell. Regaining his composure, he thrust the cattails solemnly toward his lieutenants. They in turn—once they were prompted—grasped the stems with alternate hands, leaving Bernard to crush the scorched ends in a crowning palm. Then, with his blackened hand foremost, he stepped up to Leonard and smeared the ashes across his sweating forehead.

"Consider yourself cursed, Shapiro," he said. "A homeless dybbuk, doomed for a certain term to walk the night."

Behind him the other boys snickered into their sleeves.

Leonard shambled back to his family's apartment above

the millinery shop. He wiped off the ashes, changed his pants, then locked himself in his room. Warm as it was, he closed his window on the come-on's of the shopkeepers, the newsboys crying the current progress of the horsemen of the apocalypse.

"Home free," he sighed, reaching for the nearest book and sticking his head in it. In a while he emerged, surprised at how little he had to show for the events of the afternoon. There was no fat lip, no molasses or eggshells to wash out of his woolly hair, nothing, in short, to indicate what he'd been through.

"So what happened?" Leonard had to ask himself, because the memory had already grown dim; it had practically vanished in the face of the story he'd started to read. And as for the curse: "Maybe I left it in my other pants," he giggled, wise guy in the privacy of his own room. For if it was about his person at all, the curse was lodged so deep that it would be decades before it ever surfaced again.

II. 197? Remission and Reappearance

"You were born scared, Lenny."

That was the accusation that his wife, Cathleen, had leveled at him throughout the long years of their marriage. It was what she said whenever he complained that he was frightened about money or history or losing sleep; frightened of making love in strange places, of talking to salesmen and waiters, of being married, meeting neighbors, flying, the dark. And lest, in some reckless moment, he should forget that fear was the source of his reluctance in all things, there was Cathleen to remind him.

"At least you give me credit for having been born," Leonard would sometimes reply, with reference to a condition that he seldom gave himself credit for.

The issue of Leonard's elemental fear, however, had arisen less and less as the years wore on. As a consequence, he was grateful whenever his wife bothered to take him to task, because it implied that he had never changed.

They'd met during his student years when Leonard, spooked by an axiom concerning all work and no play, was on a brief holiday from his studies. He was taking the grand tour, so to speak, of real life before settling down to his terminal make-believe. He'd ventured on his excursion as far as a barroom some quarter-mile from his dormitory, where he saw her dancing.

With her enormous eyes flashing mischief, her swirling skirts and furious auburn hair, she danced with a series of partners. Each one complemented her fluid movements until he could no longer sustain the pretense that she was dancing with him. Then they deferred to the next partner. Asking someone her name, Leonard couldn't help thinking: Cathleen ni Houlihan, the arch-shikse who inspires men to a courage beyond their means.

Which was how Leonard found himself cutting in on one of her partners, presenting himself like a cop assigned to retrieving legendary heroines escaped from the pages of books. She probably wouldn't have noticed him any more than the others, had he not been standing still. When she also stopped dancing and asked what was his problem, Leonard began to excuse himself; he'd made a mistake.

"Wait a minute," she said, as if she'd noticed something, like maybe his soul was a sliver in his paw that needed drawing out.

And as Leonard continued retiring, Cathleen, her curiosity piqued, followed. Such deadwood as he would make excellent kindling, she thought, offering to provide the sparks. Leonard asked her please not to do him any favors. But a sucker for a contest of wills, Cathleen had persisted; she went so far as to attempt using his books as leverage to pry him into the world.

"What is it that Zorba says?" she might ask him, her eyes great with expectation. "You've got to take off your belt and look for trouble?"

To which Leonard would more than likely reply, "I take off my belt and my pants fall down."

In bed she might tease him, "Let's do it like the lovers in *For Whom the Bell Tolls*—y'know, so the earth moves under us."

And Leonard: "Get off my stomach before my bowels move under us."

If she then became moody, he was quick to second her exasperation, repeating his motto: "Disgrace under pressure—to coin a phrase." It was his way of making jokes that were not jokes.

Sometimes in her frustration Cathleen had thrown food and drink in Leonard's face. She had, being the stronger, knocked him down on occasion, unpantsed him and spanked his bony behind. And Leonard endured it all with the long-suffering passivity that outraged his persecutor even more. But what angered her most was that, minutes after her every outburst, he pretended that nothing had happened.

Their wedding had been like that: Leonard standing beneath the canopy as at his own auto-da-fé, while his bride (having blithely professed her conversion) circled him with a candle several times. And afterward, should he be called upon to perform any husbandly duties, he had first to be reacquainted with the fact that he had a wife.

In the end, realizing that her efforts made Leonard cling all the more desperately to himself, Cathleen conceded defeat. "Temporarily," she qualified, still refusing to give up the hope that Leonard's dormant vitality might one day erupt. Having gambled all of her own resources on his rehabilitation, she was prepared to play a waiting game.

Leonard commiserated, "Our lady of lost causes."

Leaving him to his own devices, Cathleen occupied herself with the details that Leonard neglected, thereby allowing him an even more self-absorbed grace. She saw that the food was purchased, the plumber summoned, the taxes paid. She tended to all the leftover reality with a devotion that compelled her to keep her own two feet (so previously accustomed to dancing) firmly on the ground. Thus confined to a limited terrestrial movement, she put on weight. She became dowdy, having forfeited her own grace for the sake of her husband's.

More disgusted with herself than with him, she suspended her attacks and cajolery. She stopped daring him to let his hair down, eat a peach, get her pregnant. Her most venomous barbs she reserved for herself. Finally she was forced to admit the infectious nature of Leonard's faintheartedness.

Careful not to gloat, Leonard was nevertheless relieved about Cathleen's broken spirit. That she had become matronly and no longer so desirable—this was an advantage, as Leonard saw it, since it made her less likely to distract him from his so-called studies. He was free to inhabit a solitary country of which he fancied himself the sole owner and proprietor. And if his only wife was excluded from therein, then it was a kind of tragedy. But the tragic sense, he told himself, was useful, even essential to his particular style of dreaming.

In an unprecedentedly relaxed mood after dinner one night, he revealed to Cathleen the ambience of his mind. "It's like Yoknapatawpha County, it's like Oz." They were the kind of remarks that, for all her reserves of patience, Cathleen could not let pass by.

"More like a Warsaw Ghetto, if you ask me," she replied, wearily extending the metaphor: that Leonard would have to be bombed out of his complacency. Then he'd sulked and accused her of anti-Semitism, working himself into a state.

"What more do you want from me?" he cried, with more fervor than the situation demanded. (Cathleen applauded the display.) But it was one thing to show disrespect to himself and quite another to blaspheme Leonard's invisible kingdom.

Cathleen pressed her hands prayerfully in front of her face and confessed that there was indeed nothing more she could ask. "Each day I count my blessings," she said, without a trace of sarcasm, touching forefinger to forefinger as she began to itemize. Number one was that, having lost faith in her own life, she had another's to be wholly responsible for. And two, she had a house which Leonard, despite his lack of substance, had graciously provided her with.

"This is surely the best of all possible worlds," she asserted, secure in her feeling that such a statement did not violate the sanctity of Leonard's impossible world.

Bought with the money his father had killed himself making, the house—trellised walls, casement windows, slate roof—was a testament to coziness. Like a cottage where beauty or royalty is secretly domiciled, it sat on a shady street a stone's throw from the college where Leonard taught. In a sense the house was a chip off the hallowed prettiness of the campus, itself an ivy-trimmed Gothic affair surrounded by arcades of elms.

It was the college where Leonard had taken his various degrees. Afterward, having made a steadfast fixture of himself, he managed to stay on in the capacity of instructor, then associate professor. Ultimately he was made a full pro fessor and resident eccentric, with tenure. He had no special love for the place or for his vocation, which he associated with a shamelessness tantamount to daydreaming out loud. But he did enjoy the unassailable aura of safety with which the campus was suffused.

"Come the end of days," he was fond of saying, "the college will be spared." In fact it was already a precious anomaly in a city that looked otherwise prematurely visited by the end of days.

Since the War, Leonard's hometown had been in a serious state of decline. Truthfully, it had never advanced very far into the twentieth century, but having burned all its bridges in the name of urban renewal, neither was there anywhere for the city to retreat. So there it stood crumbling in a perpetual present. And nowhere was the decay so evident as in Leonard's old neighborhood, to which, if he could help it, he seldom returned.

Instead Leonard dwelt in a timeless space in his room insulated by books at the top of the cottage. In that room passions were embroiled, destinies lost and found, men transformed by sorcery, peril, or love. It was a portable spectacle which, at his convenience, Leonard could fold and tuck discreetly under an arm or away in his head. He could smuggle it through dappled streets loud with calling birds, carry it up to an office insulated by books, and set the passions loose again. In this way, with only the odd interruption of classes and the occasional nod to married life, Leonard had crossed over the border into middle age—without, as he liked to think, showing a passport or paying a toll.

In fact, whenever he bothered to look, he observed that, unlike his wife, he was aging gracefully. Sparseness became his unkempt hair, salt-and-pepper lent dignity to his beard, and his frame, despite sedentary habits, had remained slim.

Where heretofore it had never much concerned him, he realized that for a mature man he was not unattractive. But just as he was congratulating himself on having eluded the crises that so often beset men at his age, he experienced a certain unsolicited restlessness.

He, Leonard Shapiro, for once in his life began to feel a little claustrophobic. The atmosphere in the cottage was beginning to cloy, its familiarity a touch contemptible. It was a passing sensation, of course, though after some weeks he was still unable to shake it. It agitated and bewildered him, drove him out of his room, and moved him one evening, as he stood at the foot of the stairs, to speak out of character: "Why don't we sell the house and go prospecting for gold?"

Cathleen looked up stunned and blinking from her knitting. Grown listless with the years, she was by now resigned to a terminal hibernation in their snug little house. But her husband's remark seemed to have stirred some long-lost something, awakened an old conviction—that any change, for instance, was a change for the better.

So while Leonard braced himself to deny his own words, Cathleen gave him a glance that threatened to make him eat them.

"Be careful I don't take you seriously," she said. After which she returned to her knitting and Leonard slunk away up the stairs.

Still his restlessness persisted, and he began to think that maybe he wasn't such proof against the pangs of middle age. Meanwhile a new symptom had developed, one for which he was thoroughly unprepared. He'd begun to leer at his female students, and was likewise convinced that they were wantonly observing him. This was unnerving; scarcely ever had Leonard attached sexual significance to objects in the physical world. Only his wife had ever similarly disturbed him, though not since her figure had acquired its zaftig dimensions. That was a blessing which had freed him to heed more attentively the sirens that called from his books, but lately the sirens had faces, and the faces were those of the girls that he lectured to.

There was one in particular, a mousy blonde, with dewy eyes that seemed to alternate between innocence and dizzy depths. She came to his office wearing half-buttoned blouses, asked to show him her poems, talked about books like forbidden fruit that she'd gorged herself on while her hunger remained unsatisfied.

Leonard wasn't used to such attentions from students. Although a curiosity as a teacher, he had never been popular—nor had he desired that status. Always a miser concerning the details of his life among books, he tended in his lectures to tantalize rather than inform. It was as if, having kissed, he would not tell; not that his classes had necessarily been all ears. How was it that his image had altered so that the girl might want to trespass where students had never been welcome before?

She was doubly unwelcome on this afternoon in early spring, when Leonard was busy discarding his latest essay. This was the product of another recent phenomenon. Of course he'd done modest critical pieces throughout his academic career, but during the past few months he'd been seized at odd moments by what he hesitated to call inspiration. He wrote for hours in a driven frenzy, filled pages with oracular interpretations of the philosophies of the creatures of dreams. Then, in the calm after composition, he would realize how he'd given himself away and would reject the essays as unfit for popular consumption.

The girl sat feverishly inhaling her cigarette, flicking ashes into the wastebasket containing his wadded scribblings. She made Leonard nervous with her questions, her slenderness, her crossed legs and kicking sandal-shod foot. Chafed with desire, he lost patience and told her that he had to prepare for his class. He told her that he had indulged her all he could, that he was weary of her persecution, that her kind—while they might visit—could never survive the rarefied atmosphere of literature.

"What more do you want from me?" he exclaimed, aware of an echo, looking at the girl as if to inquire: Did I say that?

Having gotten a bit more than she'd come for, the girl controlled a trembling lip. She apologized for the intrusion, dropped her cigarette butt in the basket, and hurried from the room.

To compose himself Leonard took up a book and began to read. A hero had descended into a place of belching chimneys and titanic ugliness. So vivid was the passage, so intense his concentration, that Leonard could smell the smoke and hear the crackling of flames. He coughed and rubbed his watering eyes, delighted at the sympathy of his response, when he observed that the metal wastebasket was on fire.

Bolting from his chair, Leonard fumbled through the smoke that filled his office. He covered his face with a sleeve and began to stomp the burning paper. Wedging his foot in the bottom of the basket, he kicked wildly to keep from setting his pants leg aflame. He snatched up the still-smoldering basket, rushed it out onto the landing, then down to a broom closet at the foot of the stairs. Dumping the whole conflagration into a basin, he turned on the tap, waving frantically at the smoke that billowed up beneath the running water. With stinging eyes he managed to pour the soggy ashes into a garbage can. Then, a bit shaken from his brush with danger, Leonard wiped the sweat from his forehead with a dirty hand.

His entrance into the classroom provoked some mild hilarity; but this was nothing new. Leonard's circumspect lectures and mania for privacy had long since made him renowned as a figure of fun. And having made his own bed, he was willing to accept a certain quota of disrespect as his due. But enough was enough. His nerves were already on edge, and the continued snickering seemed especially out of order today.

"What's so funny?" he protested, fooling no one with his appeal to authority.

The girl in the front row, the same one he'd expelled from his office, tapped on her forehead. Leonard thought at first she was implying his brain was cracked, but as she persisted, he touched his own brow with a finger that came away smudged. Excusing himself, he went out to the lavatory.

In the mirror he saw the troubled face of Leonard Shapiro, old born-scared Lenny with his squinting eyes and bulbous shnoz, his forehead smeared with ash. But while the reflection, except for the coal-black daub, was perfectly recognizable, he had the sudden thrilling wisdom not to claim it for his own. This Leonard in the mirror was not real. He was nobody, a golem, a ploy like a wooden horse used to gain entrance to the habitations of human beings. Inside of himself, frightened, he'd hung on for dear life; he'd kept coiled up and quiet lest anyone find him out. But it came to him now that the danger was past, that caution and his dour face had outworn their usefulness, and he found it astonishingly easy to let go.

Back in the classroom he remembered that he had yet to wash off the ashes, but no one was laughing now. The students seemed to be collectively holding their breath, waiting—as Leonard perceived it—for him to unriddle his presence there. He bit his lip as if trying to crack a nut, tugged at his hair until it stood up like horns. When he felt that he had it, he chuckled out loud.

"Instead of my lecture on . . ." he began, shrugging when

he couldn't recollect the topic for the day, "I want to speak to you about the character of the curse."

The class stirred uncomfortably and exchanged doubtful glances. Then Leonard, so evasive throughout his career, began to confide what had only just been revealed to him.

Sitting atop his desk, keeping cadence with his drumming heels, he established that there was often a fine distinction between a blessing and a curse. He explained that it was in the nature of some curses not to take immediate effect. They might, for example, tick away like a bomb, like a fetus that takes years to ripen. You sometimes think they're defunct when they're only dormant, like henpecked husbands and comatose kings slumbering away the millennia in enchanted places. You think they're lost when they're temporarily displaced, like a prophet who makes a detour through a whale. You think they're ashes until they gather themselves up and spread their wings.

"They're in remission, you think, when in fact they're lurking like the famous syphilis of Monsieur de Maupassant, who thought it was rapture that bled him of a thousand stories, struck him blind, left him crawling on all fours in a madhouse where he ate his own shit . . ."

To illustrate his point Leonard had mounted his desk on his hands and knees, and was making chomping motions with his jaws. That was how the class, climbing over one another to get out of the room, left their professor that afternoon.

Back in his office, Leonard locked the door and made an effort to get hold of himself. He felt light-headed after his lecture, as if his brain had spilled its ballast, as if his head were an ark that had let down its gangplank, debouching legendary passengers with crazy baggage. "Wait for me!" he called out, laughing himself to tears. Any moment now he supposed his old reliable prudence would return to put him in his place. It would remind him of consequences and prompt him to read a book. But looking around him at the overcrowded shelves, Leonard saw a city of closed doors behind which no one was home. And as he seemed to have shaken his common sense, a/k/a his fear, he could not think of a single reason to hang around.

He was possessed of more energy than could be confined to a pigeon rib cage or a size-five head. Estranged from his own anatomy, however, he recognized its peculiar advantages, possibilities he'd never had the inclination or the nerve to explore. But now, if he wished, he might poke his head out through the latticed window; he might grab hold of the ivy tendrils and begin to clamber down the wall.

His office was in a bell tower built by the family of a local adventurer, who, having traveled everywhere, booked passage on a junk and vanished without a trace. That the memorial to a man who never knew the meaning of fear should contain the cells of so many busy with its definition—this had always been amusing to Leonard. But now he was happy to be escaping such ironies. Lowering himself by awkward degrees on the vines, he celebrated the ache of his awakening bones. He tore his jacket and grazed his hip, scraped his shins on the jagged stones, rejoicing with every bruise.

Having dropped in a sprawling heap onto the grass, Leonard looked left and right, a little disappointed that no one was yet in pursuit. Propped on an elbow, he took a moment to appreciate the architecture, how the Gothic facades seemed to have acquired a somber authenticity and age. Today was the day, he decided, when everything became what it pretended to be. So what was Leonard Shapiro pretending? That the patches on the sleeves of his chestnut tweed sport coat concealed mouse holes, that the stray twigs and leaves caught in his hair were the remains of a wreath.

His body, so long inactive, uncoiled like a jack-in-the-box. He bounded and capered, hotfooting it away, acquainting himself with his muscles as they emerged from their suspended animation. Staying low in the shadows out of sight of the students, he vaulted fences and scarpered through a dozen backyards. He got tangled in garden plots, fought to extricate himself from shrubs and wisteria vines. He hugged the trunks of blossoming dogwoods, got sticky with their sap, got dusted with the pollen of tiger lilies. By the time he arrived home he was as tattered as a castaway.

The cottage seemed alien for all its tranquillity, suspiciously serene, like a place under a spell. To approach it demanded extremes of stealth; this much Leonard understood—which was why, instead of using the door, he climbed an oak at the side of the house and waited amid the leafy camouflage until dark.

He was squatting on a limb just outside an open window, peering into a room more cluttered with books than the one he'd so recently flown. "My study," he had to remind himself, as if it were decades since he'd seen it. He wondered how, in all the years of his hermitage, it had never once occurred to him to step out onto this limb. Could it have been the same reluctance that inhibited his stepping onto the window ledge now?

At dusk the lights had come on in the lower part of the house, while the study remained in gloom. Then it was also lit up to reveal a woman standing in the doorway. She was wearing an outsize terry cloth bathrobe and a towel wrapped turban-wise about her head.

"My wife?" Leonard asked himself, staring with such intensity that his gaze dissolved her several chins. He was fascinated by her scrubbed complexion, by the ruddy blush of her cheeks. From his perch he sniffed the floral scent of her, and imagined a leap in full armor into the depths of her enormous, doleful eyes. Then, having conceived an answer, he informed himself under his breath: "My bride."

Hands shoved into voluminous pockets, she was browsing the shelves with a knowing fondness, as if whoever she were looking for might be hidden between the pages of some book. Then, with a shrug that was half a sigh, she switched off the light.

Leonard lowered himself from his branch to the casement window. Slipping inside, he tiptoed through the study, careful not to disturb the settled dust. He padded downstairs into Cathleen's domain, stealing into a parlor appointed with old things that her patience had made new again. He hesitated, then furtively approached where she reclined on a sofa munching popcorn, her attention divided between an open novel and a television set.

Standing over her, Leonard was breathless, compelled by the warmth of the scene. He was drawn to it as if he'd come out of a storm, stretching fingers that seemed to need thawing within inches of his unsuspecting wife. He understood that he was in the presence of a primal domesticity; here was a woman worth sinning bravely for, worth returning to through untold escapades.

Her robe was disarrayed to the waist, exhibiting a single, lolling, rosy-tipped breast. Studying it scrupulously, Leonard was at first transfixed, then enflamed. With what began as a whimper and ended as a savage cry, he flung himself over the back of the sofa, desperately seeking her nipple with his lips.

The book fell, the popcorn spilled, the voices from the television were subdued by her terrified scream. Straddling her, Leonard threw back the lapels of her robe, all the better to nuzzle her breasts and burrow into her leavening abdomen. Beneath him Cathleen jackknifed and thrashed, grabbing fistfuls of his hair, her terror transformed by degrees into a joyous delirium.

"Thank God!" she cried, welcoming him home with passionate nibbles, with fingernails and tears. "My incubus, my love, you're out of your skull!" She tore off her turban, releasing a small cascade of silver-streaked auburn hair.

As they tumbled from the sofa and rolled through the popcorn, the noise like a crush of dead leaves, Cathleen opened herself to accommodate her husband. Hastily shoving his pants down to his shoes, Leonard clutched his swollen manhood like an angler. He rolled his eyes and relished the pain of anticipation, feeling it seep from the core of him toward his extremities. In the same way the moment seemed to overflow its place in time, spreading out toward immeasurable horizons. It was a moment in perpetuity which defied any actions that Leonard might take to conclude it; and, impotent, he raised himself droopingly to his feet.

"Not here," was all he could find to say.

Cathleen lowered her outstretched arms, while her body, still receptive and abandoned, contradicted her stricken disbelief.

"Then where?" she panted. "In the bedroom? The shower? Where?" Starting up, she barked at him, "Damn you, this is your home!"

But Leonard only shook his head—a slight tremor, as if he'd developed a tic. Cathleen gathered her robe tightly about her throat and slid away from him across the rug.

"You know what, you're out of your skull," she told him, with no trace of her former delight.

Leonard tried to rekindle himself. "You could come with me," he submitted, but Cathleen extinguished him with an angry glare.

"Come with you!" she gasped. "So who are you, Peter Pan?" Sniffling a little, she bundled up, hugging herself in her robe. Then she let go and began to pick up the scattered popcorn, dropping the pieces back into the bowl.

Backing toward the door, Leonard stumbled over his pants, stooping to draw them up from around his ankles. He paused a few seconds before leaving, long enough for the pain to fill him completely, occupying the space left vacant by fear.

III. Autopsy

Bernard Rosen, the celebrated attorney, was showing his third wife around the old neighborhood. They were en route to Miami Beach for a honeymoon when Bernard suggested that, for a lark, they make a detour through the city of his birth. They would stop only long enough, he promised his bride, for him to show her where he grew up.

"I don't believe it, I just don't believe it," Bernard kept repeating, lamenting the derelict storefronts, the gutted buildings and overgrown lots along North Main Street. "That was Mr. Goldstein's delicatessen, and over there, that was Saccharin's fish market . . . I just don't believe it."

Despite her attempts to dig in with her stiletto heels, Bernard's wife was helplessly dragged along behind him. "Bernie, it's getting late," she reminded him at regular intervals, fussing with her stole. Then, almost grateful at the opportunity to vary her complaint, she added, "It's starting to rain."

"Where'd everybody go?" Bernard was asking a row of boarded-up facades. "Hey, Mook Weiss! Plesofsky! Come out and talk some trayf . . ."

He got for an answer a clap of thunder, the broken windows illumined like dragon's teeth. Taking shelter from the sudden downpour, Bernard and his wife ducked into a doorway. They huddled on tiles whose mosaic, spelling out Dlugach's Sundry, sent Bernard into further elegies about his old haunts. He invoked the Idle Hour Cinema, and what they poured on Rosie Dubrovner from the balcony; the Kol Nidre night when they outfitted the Torah in lady's lingerie. There was the kidnapping of Mrs. Teitelbaum, the exorcism of Leonard Shapiro, the sabotaging of Izzy Lipman's still . . .

"Oh, we were bad kids, Selma," boasted Bernard, "and I ruled the roost. Such a pisher I was, but smart? A regular wizard."

Meanwhile Selma, practically groaning, was looking this way and that as if for help. She double-took at the sight of a curious figure lowering himself out an upstairs window of the empty shop across the street. As he dropped into the alley and trotted toward the curb, oblivious to the storm, she could see the rain unfasten the knots in his matted hair and beard. She was stunned by his outlandish apparel, his coat composed more of patches than original material, resembling a mantle of autumn leaves.

He paused beside a dustbin and, interested, drew forth a floppy fedora and a book. After brief consideration he put the hat on his head and tossed the book back into the bin. Then he shook himself and looked their way.

In her misery Selma was afraid that he was about to cross the street toward them. He was going to take advantage of her husband's preoccupation to carry her away. It was a ghastly thought (all the worse for being not entirely unattractive) which left her tugging urgently at her husband's sleeve.

"Bernard," she pleaded, "there's some nut over there!"

Irritated at being jerked back so abruptly from a distance of more than thirty years, Bernard snapped, "What's the matter with you?"

She repeated her cause for alarm, indicated its source. But behind the heavy curtain of rain that swept across North

Main Street, the pavement was bare.

"You're seeing things," chided Bernard. "There's nobody but ghosts around here." Then, never one to dwell in the past, he relaxed; he brightened and gave his new wife a pinch.

"Sweetie," he reassured her, "let your mink stole be your umbrella. Miami, here we come!"

The Book of Mordecai

My Uncle Mordecai, at seventy-nine, was what you might call contented. Not really my uncle, he was my father's stepfather, whom my father had always called Uncle, as did I. He had a mild and sunny disposition, simplified by the excision of numerous obsolete organs. Nevertheless, he retained his portly good health.

"Go ahead, give it a potch," he would urge me, proffering his venerable belly to be thumped. And after I had obliged, "You see, I am hollow," laughing the way owls might laugh, if they could laugh.

He had white hair like spindrift over most of his head, white tussocks in his ears, cheeks ruddy and varicose, moist eyes. He smelled pleasantly of mildew and cigars. In the far corner of our living room he sat, smiling perpetually, removing his dentures before bed so that his teeth might carry on smiling as he slept.

My uncle's famous complacency had been ruffled only once to anyone's knowledge. This was during the demise of his wife Naomi years before. A competent, maternal, and generously bosomed woman (affectionately called the Gezunteh Mama by the family), Grandma Naomi had lost her dignity toward the end. She seemed to be suffering under the illusion, or rather misconception, that she was in labor. For months she lay in her bed of travail, lamenting between convulsions the fate of women, losing weight. As her considerable dimensions shriveled, so did her lamentations increase in their volume and pitch. Finally she was nothing but a mouth in an outsized nightgown. The ample woman, size twenty-two, had given birth to a caterwauling seventy-two-year-old infant, size four.

Nor, according to my Uncle Mordecai (who seldom complained), did her shrieks necessarily diminish with her passing. They continued to resonate throughout the rooms of his little house in its shady bee-loud street. Not even the racket of his radio would drown them out.

"For a swan song, it ain't too sweet," my uncle confessed, adding that he might look for an apartment somewhere. But my father would never hear of such a thing.

"I could hear of such a thing," said my mother under her breath, protesting aloud that Uncle Mordecai must not live alone. "Please don't thank us; after all, what's a family for?"

So it was that Uncle Mordecai came to our house. Not wishing to become a burden, he brought with him only the barest essentials: some photographs and old newspapers, mildew and cigars, his antediluvian radio and an encyclopedia. The latter—the *Book of Knowledge,* edition of 1908—was the bar mitzvah gift of his father, who peddled tinware.

"Mazel tov," his father had said, dropping the crate of books, which rattled the building. "I paid for these with my youth." And though Uncle Mordecai could not remember ever having opened them, he'd shlepped them along with him all the way from Henry Street to Tennessee. They weighed as much as had his father when a young man.

Although Uncle Mordecai was given a room of his own at the back of the house, he went to it only to sleep. He preferred to sit unobtrusively in his corner of the living room, the benign proprietor of his little store of mementos.

"There's a corner of the living room which is forever Uncle Mordecai," said my mother, who was sometimes waspish.

He kept his radio turned up just loud enough to neutralize the quarrels among my family. Shaped like a tabernacle, the radio crackled with static; the voices inside it sounded as if they were broadcast from a burning bush. But to my uncle they were of no more concern than the squalling of my little sister, who might also have been on fire.

Through it all Uncle Mordecai would sometimes doze, sometimes look through the window at an oak tree hung with children. But mostly he would sit, imperturbable in his waistcoat and watch fob, an out-of-date newspaper in his lap, an unlit cigar depending from his smile.

In those days my uncle was my hobby. I watched him the way people watch crocodiles in a zoo, wanting to be there if he should move.

On Saturdays my father drove him downtown to the business which Uncle Mordecai had come into fifty years ago. Before his retirement at sixty-five, the store was known simply as M. Pinsky Dry Goods; but since my father had taken over the management, the premises were expanded by a couple of adjoining buildings, becoming Lipman's Department Store. While my father saw to his ledgers, the old man would wander the carpeted aisles. Under fluorescent lights that whirred like cicadas, he looked for the warped wooden floors, the ceiling fans in need of oil. Invariably my father would find him confounded by some cul-de-sac, stranded amongst notions or between bolts of cloth.

"You're a good boy, Isador," he would say to my father, who led him out of the building and around the corner to the barbershop.

He would nap in the chair, while the barber gingerly trimmed round his tonsure, keeping the scissors at a respectable distance from his dreams. Hair would fall onto his shoulders like rime. Then the barber would slap him awake with a stinging lime-scented liniment. Following this exhilaration, my uncle would rest, taking his seat under the awning outside the shop. He would gaze down the street toward the levee and the sluggish river, listening to the old yokels seated next to him. They were trying to remember sin.

"Ida Upjohn," recollected one, his arthritic fingers tracing impossible contours. Uncle Mordecai, anchoring his smile with a cigar, might take out his pocket watch and scrutinize the clock face until my father came back to get him.

At meals my uncle seldom spoke, eating his soup as if in prayer, farting delicately. The chicken gristle or the noodle pudding, which his stomach sent back up, he discreetly received in his napkin. And always he retired to his corner, which the maid regularly cleared of cobwebs. Because our house was larger than the needs of my family, it was easy to take Uncle Mordecai's presence for granted.

When I was eight or nine—and Uncle Mordecai had been with us for about two years—my canary passed away. A pale yellow bird that had never demonstrated any particular love of life, it toppled one day beak first from its perch. Lying on its side beneath the cuttlebone, it maintained the precise pose which was its custom when erect. There was little distinction, I had concluded, between life and death.

Then the shvartze maid picked it up by the tail feathers and flushed it without ceremony down the toilet. As I watched King Solomon—for that was what I had named him—spiraling into oblivion, I was curiously unmoved. Later on I passed by his empty cage where, in place of a jaundiced canary, there was fear.

For several nights after, I could not sleep for falling off perches and spinning in toilet bowls. I would call in my mother to verify that my room was still inhabited by myself. In the bathroom my turds were canaries; I avoided the maid, whom I associated with the headsman of Lille. In a few days the fear, like a bout of the measles, finally left me alone. But not before it had infected my Uncle Mordecai, who lacked the resistance of youth.

The first of his symptoms to declare itself was cantankerousness. He turned up the volume of his radio, which overwhelmed the sounds of my family embroiled. He pinched the maid. Then came his unprecedented heartiness of appetite at supper. He began to approach meals as if each were his last and he meant to take as much as possible with him. What wouldn't fit in his mouth might serve to dapple his cheeks and decorate his waistcoat. And once, retiring to his corner armchair, he kindled a cigar. With the butt of the first he lit another, and so on, transferring the same light from smoke to smoke. Henceforth he never slept beyond the occasional catnap, always awakening before the cigar could go out.

His smile went all askew, then disappeared. The corners of his mouth fell without the promise of a curtain call. His moist eyes grew narrow and bloodshot, a little resembling the tip of his cigar.

"Maybe the visions of sugarplums danced out of his head," submitted my mother, becoming nervous. But who could imagine fugitive sugarplums, when we'd always assumed my uncle's head was empty? Like a cage without a canary.

On the second Saturday after the bird's quietus, my father had taken Uncle Mordecai downtown as usual. He'd dealt for a while with his ledgers, then left them to see what the old man was up to. There was an aisle between racks of furs that terminated in a triptych of mirrors—into which Uncle Mordecai was pissing. The crowd of Uncle Mordecais in the glass were returning his salute. The effect was like the reverse of a fountain of youth. As my father endeavored to lead him away, my uncle recovered his arm.

"Meshuggener," he snarled, "what do you take me, to the lost and found?"

At the barbershop, when the barber slapped on the lotion, Uncle Mordecai returned the gesture in kind. He left the shop with the sheet still tied round his neck, announcing to the yokels outside, "I go to lie with a totsie with tsitskehs this big," holding out his liver-spotted hands to embrace a world.

Following rumors of a wandering curmudgeon wrapped in a pinstriped flag, my father finally located him on the cobbles along the levee. He was gazing upstream as if he thought that the Mississippi flowed out of the River Dvina.

At home, his orneriness temporarily spent, Uncle Mordecai was backed once again into his corner—from which he never re-emerged. He had reached another stage in his affliction, characterized by despair. With no other recourse, he called for a pen and paper; he pushed back the radio full of ancestral voices and made room for a spiral notepad.

"I, Mordecai Pinsky," he wrote, then tore out the page and tossed it away.

"Dear Naomi," he started again. "Tonight I can feel your big toches."

This is how Uncle Mordecai, albeit deliberately, toppled beak first into the past. He fell for the space of about thirty-five years and landed in bed with his wife. He had fallen past hundreds of other nights in bed with his wife to arrive at this one, which was nothing special. Except that her hair—

dense and black, streaked with silver—had come free of its rollers and net. It lapped about them like the waters of a ritual bath. And he, a poor swimmer, floated on her oily abdomen, whose large pores exuded a scent of garlic; he peeled from her hips a kimono that shimmered like scales.

"My wife is some mermaid I rescued from a mikveh," recorded my uncle in wonder. For it seemed that this woman, so traditionally unresponsive, was someone of whom he had never had the pleasure.

He might have tarried for many more pages with Naomi, exploring the mysteries he had somehow missed the first time through. But such transports, alarming in a man of his conservative temperament, warned him that the fear which drove him to write was even now at his heels.

His corner had become unhygienic. In an otherwise tastefully appointed house, it was a slum. Peach pits, zwieback crumbs, fishbones, half-empty cups of Ovaltine, and blowflies littered the floor. The maid would not venture near. In fact, the first time she saw what the old man, in collaboration with nature, had done in a chafing dish, she withdrew her services from my family. My mother erected a screen which was covered with roses. It did nothing, however, to conceal the smell of a midden and the sulphurous odor of the fear itself. So my mother was moved to deliver an ultimatum.

"Isador, it's either him or me."

While my father was considering, my mother slipped behind the screen. I believe that she may have been armed. She emerged momentarily, screaming, her dress torn open, brassiere and girdle in evidence, coiffured hair in disarray.

"It's a phase," said my father, patiently responsible.

My mother: "Eighty-year-old men have infirmities, not phases."

Father: "He's only seventy-nine; it will pass."

Although Uncle Mordecai was composing his memoirs back to front, subtracting year after year, he was not getting any younger. On the contrary, though his appetite remained unappeasable, my uncle was losing weight. His filthy waistcoat was emptied of its paunch; his several chins collapsed into a wattle. Stubble frosted the hollows beneath his cheekbones, and his hair boiled over. Except to consort with his meager possessions—to corroborate dates in his pile of newspapers, rifle his photographs, tune his radio (with its voices of persons selling laxatives in hell)—Uncle Mordecai never left off writing. At night you could see him through the screen as in a tableau. His silhouette appeared like a scribe in a cloud of roses.

Once, during the early weeks of his labor, my uncle broke his silence to call for strong drink.

"Schnapps I want schnapps I want schnapps!" An unusual request from a man who seldom took anything headier than seltzer.

"Go ahead," said my mother, renowned for her ultimata, "give him schnapps, then say goodbye to me."

My father, seeking a loophole, took a bottle of pink muscatel from a cabinet and passed it behind the screen. He passed it down the years to my uncle, who was celebrating his honeymoon. It was Miami Beach before its heyday, circa 1921; so that, by the time that Uncle Mordecai received it, the wine was vintage. He raised his bottle to the ambered photograph propped in front of him and proposed a toast to everything that he'd originally taken for granted.

"L'chayim my bride who won't be touched because she is still in mourning," he wrote, taking a drink. "L'chayim her son who only eats to spit up. L'chayim the flea-bitten hotel where the guests are as old as the population of paradise.

L'chayim papayas, l'chayim the bellhop, l'chayim the game of canasta. L'chayim the cockamamie moon. L'chayim the sea which is suddenly full of monsters with fancy tails." And he'd slung the empty bottle through his window, which admitted the first breeze of autumn.

My mother packed a bag, took my sister, and left the house. "Him you can keep," she had said, meaning me. For, to tell the truth, I was a singularly unattractive child. And moreover, the time I spent watching my uncle increased my guilt through association.

"Schnapps I want schnapps, etc.," the old man cried, having retreated as far as his wedding.

He'd assembled about him a party of photos, most of them featuring the cast of the above-mentioned honeymoon, which was yet to happen. In addition there were pictures of sodden relations, stepped forth from a receiving line. Thus, in depicting the occasion, did Uncle Mordecai draw from life but once removed. Except for the case of Mendel Lipman, or rather his ghost, which my uncle drew from death.

" 'Mendel, where were you the first time I did this?' I ask," he wrote.

It should here be mentioned that Mendel Lipman—my grandmother's first husband, my father's father—had been a neighborhood friend of my uncle's youth, who had vanished one day from his sewing machine. When next heard from, he was in the South, proprietor of a dry-goods store, head of a family, victim of cancer of the heart. Unable to get rid of the latter, he thought he might get someone to take care of the rest. He appealed to my Uncle Mordecai, who'd arrived from New York just in time to step into his vacant shoes.

"He stands before me," wrote my uncle, "across the table sagging with kugel and sesame cakes. He is wearing black serge, what you might call the opposite of a birthday suit.

His face is dripping off of his bald head, so that he looks like a dressed-up yahrzeit candle.

" 'Turn around and show me your wings,' I say," he wrote, "but he only stares like I'm the dybbuk, with the whites of his eyes turning green.

" 'Mendel,' I say, 'we were never that close; yet you call me from my pushcart full of nothing to this city of the Old Man River. You make me, who had not the spare change to put over your eyes, the heir to your life. Why, forgive my asking, such mazel for Mordecai?' But he's looking at me like the business is a headache, the wife don't like to shtup, and in this city they never heard of a bagel. When he speaks, the words rattle like the top of a teapot.

" 'Who else do I know is meshuggeh enough to come?'

" 'Mendel,' I say, 'you'll pardon my frankness, but I love you.' And I upset the table in my haste to embrace him. Meanwhile the fiddler has struck up a tune, so we're dancing, the ghost and I. The guests are wondering why, with my brand-new bride, I must dance with myself; and who is it steps on my toes? Who makes me shudder like I'm already old, so that I have to turn the page?"

When he'd filled one thick notepad, he called for another. My father, disconsolate for several days, packed a bag.

"I'm going in search of your mother," he said, and judging from his resignation, my mother might already have been in heaven. "Be kind to your uncle."

Honoring my father's departing wish, I lurched behind the screen, tendering a receptacle in which to catch my uncle's overflowing memories. By the time that I reached him, he had spilled all the years subsequent to his thirteenth birthday, when he was given the *Book of Knowledge*.

"Thank you, Papa," he wrote, grateful for everything in retrospect.

His corner had become his alcove on Henry Street, the armchair his Murphy bed. At his feet was the crate from which he selected a book, breaking its spine. From the dust which arose and the ratcheting, he might have been opening the door to an oubliette. In this way my uncle entered volume L.

"Laboratory, labyrinth, lady's thumb," he inscribed, hooting his owl laugh. "Lamentations, lamp—any of various manmade devices producing light—subjectively the experience aroused by . . . locomotive, Loki, lymph . . . "

With great industry he took items from the copious encyclopedia and transferred them to the virgin pages of his notepad. Once he interrupted this operation in order to remove his fetid false teeth and soak them in wine. It was then that he appeared to notice me.

"I am a fmuggler," he confided, his scarlet eyes wet with pride; "a fief." For his lexical contraband, of relative value in its own original context, became priceless once it was spirited into his life. Or so his celebration would imply.

He continued to expropriate words, transcribing each letter with clerical devotion, marveling at how they itemized themselves. When he'd sufficiently plundered one book, he took up another, beginning to gloat.

"Sabbath, Saladin, salt (NaCl)," he wrote, his corner converted from alcove to counting house, "scaffold, shamrock, ship—the vehicle by means of which . . . dream, Dürer, dwarf, Gabriel, Galicia—region on north slope of Carpathian mountains where Pinskys are coming from, gentian, glass, god—see theism, religion; guillotine . . . "

In his acquisitive fever, he was unable to discriminate between the cheap words and the dear. He devalued his catalogue, hoarding phrases from whatever caught his ears and eyes.

"I *crackle* her *crackle* this is your *crack* so she sold it. . . . Valentino Dead . . . Isador's first tuxedo . . . a kosher full-bodied specially sweetened muscat grape wine . . . " And so forth ad delirium, at which point my uncle dropped his pen. He began to fan the pages and press them to his lips, hug them to his breast. Then, looking furtively over each shoulder, he put down the notepad and slammed its cover shut.

"Take this and bury it," he beseeched me, "and bring me more paper."

And so I came into the knowledge which Uncle Mordecai's father had given his son.

As my uncle's accomplice, I stayed home from school. I left the house only to purchase more provisions—bologna and herring and notepads, cigars and schnapps (which I purchased with forged orders stamped with my father's notary seal; I was growing resourceful). I took down my mother's rose-covered screen; thus was the living room made to share some responsibility for the foul rag-and-bone shop of my uncle's corner. I emptied the chafing dish.

Not that he noticed my least ministration. He was writing now with a cumulative fury, seldom eating, frequently drinking, stalking his own biography toward its source, pausing only to raise his eyes to the chandelier and beyond, asking, "Where were You the first time I did this?"

His once stout frame had diminished to Mahatma Gandhi. Indeed, in divesting himself of his former anatomy, he had shed as well his revolting apparel. All that remained were his boxer shorts, brindled with stains, which he'd gathered about his loins like a breechcloth.

His hair and whiskers had assumed the texture of smoke,

so that his gaunt face appeared to have been conjured out of his own cigar. His right hand made an insoluble knot around the ballpoint pen as the pen stumbled precipitously across pages like Hans Brinker with a limp.

He had retrogressed as far as the chapter of his life entitled "Ellis Island."

"Or is it Mount Ararat? And are we not privileged creatures that traveled steerage on the Ark? With the inside-out eyelids, the smarting prostates, the trousers around the ankles, we peer across receding floodwaters to where the future favors a jawbone full of broken teeth."

Then he had bid the future farewell. He was six years old and fallen into grace (which resembled the intestines of the S.S. *Siglinde* out of Bremen). He was passing between wooden bunks down a narrow aisle deluged in upchuck, mostly unkosher. He was climbing a sticky companionway onto a deck strewn with sleepwalkers, hailing the ghost ships that attempted to navigate between the sea and the starry sky.

Swiftly he reeled in the remaining years. He was up to his ankles in the mud of Zhmerinka, leaning against a rust-colored butcher's block, lightly dusted in yellow pollen. He was a little while in the tumbledown synagogue and a little while on top of the stove. He spent some time among the vinegary folds of his mother's somber skirts and some time in the crib that his father had crudely painted with roosters and dogs. From a rafter above the crib hung a dreidl on a string; it spun in the slightest draft, chuckling musically. Lying beneath it, looking up, my uncle had come under its spell. For some eighty years his head would be filled with the spinning and chuckling which rendered him tranquil.

Until: "The string breaks, the dreidl falls and k–nocks me on the kop," he wrote, illustrating the event by banging an empty bottle against his forehead. A plum-colored swelling (which I half expected to sprout a horn or an eye) ensued.

My uncle continued, "And for the rest of my days I see stars."

Consequently there was no rest for him even in the cradle. By now the fear which infected and compelled him had spread as far as his remotest recollection. Ailing internally, he had fled through a dozen notepads hemorrhaging memories through as many ballpoint pens.

"I am bleeding ink," I heard him whisper, and begin to cry. Because the emptying of Uncle Mordecai had been so much more important than his filling up.

To cheer him I produced a cream-filled cupcake on a platter. For want of another, I'd stuck a memorial candle in its midst. It was, incidentally, the candle which my father lit annually in homage to old Naomi.

"Happy Birthday," I said, having happened to notice a calendar.

He was describing a room with a low sloping roof that is leaking into buckets. There is a samovar and a window steamed up from the breath of a man looking in from outside. There are women moving about and one on a mattress with a small bloody parcel between her legs. The women are unraveling the parcel. There is: a flash of scissors, a syringe seeking nostrils, a hand potching toches, a filthy gesture against the evil eye. Then there is Uncle Mordecai, wailing hysterically.

"I am born," he wrote, soaking with his tears the parched page. Then, on second thought, he dried his eyes, inserting with a flourish the prefix "un-" before the last word in the final sentence of his story.

That was how my uncle escaped into eternity, where the fear was unable to follow him. He fell out of his armchair and lay in the garbage and books, his knees tucked up under his chin. I took the cigar from his mouth and stubbed it out, lest it set us all on fire. I turned off his radio. His eyes were already closed.

When my family returned, some days later with color in their cheeks, they set about purging the house of my uncle's remains. They put the rubbish in containers and his body underground. They restored his infamous corner to its original serenity. On the whole the fumigation was successful but for the odors (sulphurous and cigar) which clung to my person.

"What did you bathe in, the River Stynx?" said my mother, holding her nose, forbidding my father and sister to love me.

I took some consolation in the gift of my uncle's estate, for so I regarded the memoirs which I had salvaged. They make a dubious sort of book that begins at the end and vice versa. Sometimes I read it backwards like a holy book; sometimes I start at the front, which is dusk, and read continuously until dawn.

Though it's been in my possession for a long time now, I can't say that the book of Mordecai has been any particular blessing. My own life has been for the most part beneath contempt. Nor do I think that, at my death, the scholars will want the book. I don't think that the scholars, into whose hands it will not pass, will be looted by pirates who are converted by saints who bury the book in a mountain protected by a curse. Nevertheless, the book is my gift, and I live in constant fear of losing it.

The Ghost and Saul Bozoff

"When you awake you will remember everything"
—The Band

"I wouldn't mind coming to a place like this when I'm dead," said Saul Bozoff, gazing out the row of dining-room windows onto a meadow of virgin snow.

"Rumor has it," replied Iris Gronauer from across the breakfast table, without bothering to lower her newspaper, "that you already are."

Saul aimed a mock smile at the paper from behind which Iris, an essayist and reviewer of formidable reputation, continued to release the black clouds of her muttered outrage.

"Can't resist the cheap ones, can you, Iris?"

The paper descended enough to reveal a snub-nosed, round-spectacled face, highlighted in varying shades of smugness. Her foggy eyes, narrowed to slits, implied that, sarcasm notwithstanding, she never joked. Then, as if this were overmuch truth for such an early hour, she raised the paper again.

Turning away from headlines back toward the windows, Saul allowed his fake smile to broaden into the genuine article. For all of her crankiness, he had taken to Iris in their two or three days' acquaintance. Detached as he felt lately from the current events against which she constantly railed, he was nevertheless entertained. She managed to remain an incorrigible malcontent even here in paradise, and Saul aspired to her example.

But where Iris viewed the Colony as nothing more than a glorified haven for debtors, Saul was there on an honest retreat. ("Further into yourself?" Iris had suggested at their very first encounter, upon which Saul hung his head over having been seen through. He enjoyed being seen through.) A novelist of modest renown, hailed at his debut by one reviewer as "a brave new chronicler of failure," he had failed to fulfill his initial promise. He had, in the twenty or so years of his so-called career, written himself into ever diminishing circles of confinement.

As the great real world had seemed to be increasing in peril, so had the world of Saul's fiction—which he was dug into as if into a storm cellar—shrunk in inverse proportion. It had become so small in its self-conscious sphere of concern that it excluded the majority of his original audience. It had excluded his wife, who took the hint and left him a little over three years ago. And lately, despite the gauntness of his long, stoop-shouldered physique, it had excluded Saul himself—which was why he'd decided he could do with a change of scene.

Taking advantage of an invitation to spend a month at the Colony—a hallowed old sanctuary for artists tucked into a wrinkle of Vermont hills—he'd come out of a self-imposed exile in the South. In fact, the Mississippi River town of his current hermitage was also Saul's place of birth. It was where, but for an obligatory footloose period in his youth, he'd spent a relatively uneventful forty-five years. Which had never deterred him from regarding the South as a place of exile. Dwelling as he did among cakewalkers, tobacco chewers, speakers in tongues, devourers of the entrails of pigs, he maintained a kind of diaspora sensibility. He rejected most opportunities to travel, preferring to stay at home, where he might better cultivate a lifelong yearning after some faraway golden land. But now, past the age when he thought it could matter, he'd arrived at the Colony, and was disturbed by its resemblance to the landscape of his yearning.

It was midwinter, and Saul, for whom snow had been mostly hearsay, felt that he'd come to an inland sea of the stuff. There were broad troughs and rolling swells of it, drifts like tidal waves, coves with snow-laden trees like masts of furled sails. There were vistas, an armada of white mountains in the distance. There were groves of snowy woods camouflaging a couple of dozen artists' studios—designed, Saul surmised, by the architectural firm of Currier & Ives. There were snow-banked winding lanes along which the colonists, in knitted caps and flying scarves, trudged or glided on skis.

Solitary and purposeful, they traveled the lanes with their heads inclined against the wind. Hunched over a canvas or a satchel of books, they looked as if they might be concealing something else—some spark which, once they'd reached their destination, they would try to fan into flame. Or so they appeared to Saul, who wasn't ordinarily given to such whimsical notions.

That was the fundamental problem with the place: Its postcard pastorale distracted Saul from more pressing concerns. It turned his thoughts to matters incompatible with the project at hand, the project slated to set in motion again the wheels of his stalled career. For Saul had hoped that in this alien setting, revitalized by the new and strange, he might plant the seeds of his masterwork. He would commence a book that was both a bold departure from his previous work and a coming to terms with an apocalypse which he expected daily. Once and for all he would purge his pet fear of the end of days; readers sharing the catharsis would declare themselves saved. A prophetic task, it made sense that he'd left a place where he was without any honor to begin in more sympathetic surroundings.

But so far, not much had been translated onto paper. This wasn't, however, for want of a vehicle; to Saul's mind the book had an irresistible premise. Its protagonist, Felix by name, amnesiac after a universal cataclysm, sits in a cellar under the rubble trying to remember the world. As a metaphor, this was a natural: a (for all intents and purposes) dead man trying to remember the life he'd lost. Every glimmer of recollection would appear to him sacred, suitable for framing, resplendent with purpose. What would transpire during the telling would be nothing less than the reinvention of human experience. But in the absence of humanity such labors unhappily would have no application, and Felix, survivor and demiurge, would fall victim to this cruel paradox.

Artistically speaking, it smacked of high tragedy; it was worthy to the point of redemptive. It was a project which would not only vindicate his decade or more of self-indulgence; it would enable Saul to make his peace with the worst that could happen. So what—he was forced to consider—if the worst came to pass and his cautionary tale were atomized along with everything else? Then life would have blindly imitated the cosmic irony of his book, and Saul would have had the pleasure of saying I told you so. It was an inspired concept, altruistic, a godsend, in fact; in the face of its execution, however, Saul couldn't help but feel inadequate.

The hangup was that, once he had made the necessary identification with Felix, Saul, like his character, drew a blank. He was unable to decide what on earth was finally worth salvaging; baby and bathwater seemed to him indistinguishable. Then Saul worried that, given the ritual monotony of his days, he might not have experienced a sufficient depth of feeling to realize such a book. He might not have suffered enough. To write it one would have to go to hell and back in his mind; he would have to beat a hell-bent planet at its own game. But Saul wasn't certain that it was possible to get to hell from here.

He blamed his failure of nerve on the environment. Constitutionally accustomed to standing water, to rusted chassis on cinderblocks and flyblown neon signs, Saul was at odds with all this idyllic beauty. Beauty was never a medium he was comfortable with. Naturally the situation called for more patience; he ought to give himself a few days to acclimate. Then a few days had passed, and, but for some haphazard notes, Saul had yet to write an earnest word.

He spent his time poking at the fire in his studio's huge stone hearth, seeing in the flames the incineration of his best intentions: easy come, easy go. He sat at the broad oak desk and looked out the leaded windows into the pines, their boughs folded under a burden of snow like half-opened umbrellas. Freed for once of material pressures, he tried to focus the whole of his anxiety exclusively on the forthcoming end of the world. But, lulled into a sense of tranquillity foreign to his apprehensive nature, Saul had lost faith in that inevitable end.

He watched for the frosty-faced owl that sometimes lit on a branch outside his window, blinking at Saul in an indecipherable code. Sometimes, languidly, he read the catalogues of names on the "tombstones." These were the wooden plaques that decorated the wainscoted walls, engraved with the lists of former occupants dating back to the Colony's founding. Some of the names were auspicious, even immortal. In their presence Saul would alternate between wanting to apologize and resenting them for having absorbed his studio's potential for creating in. But the other less than household names—the forgotten artists, writers, composers—they were the ones that began to get a little under his skin.

He thought of them, even the most recent, as already deceased and rattling their chains, lamenting eternally some great work they had left unfinished, and with his native fatalism Saul anticipated joining their company in that vertical graveyard.

As homage or penance he recited aloud, in descending order, the roll of the unknown: "Birdie Weed/composer/1981, Finbar Truckle/poet/1975, Arthur Brief/artist/1969, Harriet Ringold/writer/1957 . . . " Occasionally, from the peculiarities of their signatures, Saul got a phantom taste of the flavor of their lives. Ethel Alabaster/limner/1948, for instance, must have been a chaste and ethereal soul, a painter no doubt of happy martyrs. Maxwell Daly/author/1939 was a portly and methodical writer, regular as his name, who wore a suit to his desk; his neighbors set their clocks by his habits. Cisco Malachi/dreamer/19?? was a poet of unwashed eccentricity, who kept a pet scorpion and took pride in having been marked for an early grave. Leah Rosenthal/writer/1917 . . . but hadn't Saul heard of her somewhere before? The name seemed to ring a bell. Still, it was unlikely that he would know a writer from what he'd come to think of as the antediluvian period of the Colony—the time before the hurricane in the late 1930s which had wrecked so many of the studios. Their tombstones still bore the watermarks, though Leah Rosenthal's inscription, while among the earliest, was strangely well preserved.

To kill some more time Saul visited the Colony library, where the works of former fellows were kept. A wide stone keep of a building, lashed to its base by leafless ivy, it was the traditional setting for Colony functions. Concerts and recitals were held here, each followed by an incumbent cocktail party. Saul had heard apocryphal tales to the effect that these parties had on occasion led to scandalous goings-on. If so, the hermetic atmosphere (funereally appointed in Gothic tapestries and glass-framed bookcases crowned with tintypes of the founders) was giving nothing away.

Entering in the middle of the afternoon, Saul realized he was walking on tiptoe. Spooking about in the hours when the others were hard at work gave him the distinct feeling that he was trespassing, a feeling he found not at all disagreeable.

Browsing among the mementos of the notable, he came upon some of the books of his studio's obscurer tenants. These he examined at first with only a mild curiosity; then, with the growing sense that he was searching for something, his interest took hold. He was amazed at the accuracy of his uneducated guesses, how they bordered on clairvoyance—a faculty he hadn't known he possessed. There were few surprises. In almost every case Saul had determined something of the style and content from the name. And all of them—under- and overstated, outspoken and tongue-in-cheek—had in common the unquestionable stamp of mediocrity. They had, Saul concluded—his verdict redounding a little too close to home—earned their place among the obscure.

He'd been working his way more or less chronologically back down the years, his breath coming quicker the further he got from the present. Having arrived, refugee from the future, at the second decade of this century, Saul understood how he'd been teasing himself all along. He'd been aggravating his suspense by sampling the works of others preliminary to Leah Rosenthal, about whom he maintained a murky presentiment.

Her name had not evoked any special manner of writing—maybe some precious variation on a biblical theme, maybe some long-winded account of one family's pathetic decline. But all he could find on the shelves to her credit was a single slim volume of stories, extravagantly entitled *Courts of Miracles and Last Resorts*. Saul opened the book and was satisfied that he'd never encountered her work before. Nor for that matter had he ever read anything like it:

in their communion of archaic and slapstick sensibilities, their illicit marriages of Old Testament and pagan themes, the stories were hard to pin down. They seemed, despite their situation in an undeniably authentic turn-of-the-century Lower East Side, anchored to no particular place or time.

Saul, whose jaded palate was a hallmark of his disposition, was nevertheless captivated. For one thing he was biased toward the habitat of her stories. Outlander that he was, Saul had a weakness for the immigrant scene, which he sometimes regarded as a birthright he'd been denied. But beyond that, it appeared he was in the presence of a natural-born storyteller, and how long had it been since he'd remembered the name of their mutual calling?

He was especially taken with the way that, amid the ghetto cacophony of Henry and Hester streets, the supernatural mingled so casually with the mundane. Peddlers, spinsters, and piecework tailors had frequent commerce with fallen angels; bakers and seamstresses braided and embroidered their handiwork with arcane spells. In one story an illiterate greenhorn, having once inhaled smoke from a tzaddik's library burned in a pogrom, discovers himself in America suddenly possessed of a golden tongue. In another a rabbi's daughter, at her dying father's behest, smuggles the Golem of Prague across the ocean rolled up in a carpet, installing him in the loft of a shul on Rivington Street. In yet another a terminally ill old man is locked out of his tenement flat. Wandering, he meets an old woman whose time has been previously filled with the daily observances of holidays and anniversaries. Having waked to a day on which she finds nothing whatsoever to commemorate, she has also taken to wandering. Together they gate-crash a wedding at the home of a wealthy man.

Saul turned the pages as if he were being pursued through the book. Something about its incantatory cadences had the feel of the forbidden; the library, for all its hushed furnishings, was too public a place to read it in. Difficult as it was to interrupt his forward momentum, Saul stashed the book in his overcoat pocket and made with his contraband out the door. But even as he crunched along through the pines, he had to take the book out again, reassuring himself that, like a jewel smuggled out of a dream, it hadn't turned to dust.

With his nose stuck in its pages, Saul missed the greetings of other colonists slogging past him. Nor did he bother to look up at the eminence of Mount Manifold as it shouldered its way into view. On previous walks Saul had made a point of picturing to himself a mushroom cloud billowing above the mountain's bald dome. This was his standard reflex in the face of any spectacle that threatened to overwhelm him with its grandeur. But today it was easy to ignore the scenery in favor of the printed word.

Arriving at his studio (called Prospero's Cell for its remoteness from the other Colony buildings), Saul restoked the fire and settled into a ladder-back rocker to continue reading. From time to time he turned over to the jacket flap, memorizing the tantalizingly terse biographical note:

> Miss [Saul was for some reason thankful for the Miss] Rosenthal was born in 1893 in the Russian Ukraine. At the age of three she accompanied her family to New York City. She was educated at City College and later taught grammar school until her death in 1920.

He remarked that the publication date of the book was also 1920. So she had been one of those ephemeral Brontë-like women, born to conceive a single passionate volume, then expire after the effort. Repeatedly Saul turned back to the bio, as if maybe there were something he'd missed, but it refused to give up any further information. Moreover, the starkly unadorned, age-yellowed dust jacket was barren of any photograph.

When he'd read the book cover to cover, Saul automatically started over again—like a man caught in a revolving door, he told himself dubiously, though it was more like riding a carousel. Once or twice he attempted to bring to bear the critical faculties by which he set some store. He tried to place the neglected writer and her posthumous opus in their rightful niche in the history of Western literature. But her work eluded categories; it defied his capacity to command the cold distance needed for such considerations. So why bother? As he rocked before the hearth in time to the ticking of a snowfall against the ice-glazed windowpanes, Saul was contentment personified.

"So you never heard of her?" Saul offhandedly inquired of Iris Grounauer over dinner that night. He was sounding her out, nourishing the selfish hope that he was the only living soul with a knowledge of his newfound authoress.

Iris was typically grousing about the evening's fare. In her penchant for behaving as if the artists' refuge were a workhouse or an orphanage, she was a woman after Saul's own heart. But tonight his heart had come loose of its usual moorings. When she'd finished berating the American-style goulash as the cook's contribution to the Cold War, Iris came around in her own good time to Saul's question: "Leah who? These Jewish lady writers proliferate like termites; the woodwork is lousy with them. You should see how they've reduced my library to pulp." She narrowed her eyes to strike a more serious note. "Y'know, their bite is infectious. You might, God forbid, wake up some morning to find yourself one of them . . . "

Saul allowed, without being heeded, that he was deeply sorry he had ever asked. ". . . They're under every rock . . . " she was ranting, when Saul, having assumed that he was beyond her regard, ventured to wonder which one she herself had crawled out from under.

"The cornerstone of Western thought," she snapped, pushing up her glasses for emphasis, "and don't you forget it."

Saul bowed his head in deference to Iris's intractability. "Listen, Iris"—trying to redirect the conversation to its source—"this Leah Rosenthal, she's—you'll forgive the expression—the real thing."

Iris arched an intolerant brow as if waiting for present company to be included, but Saul was too single-minded to take the hint.

"She writes like an angel on a high wire," he rhapsodized, fluttering his fingers like wings. "Her people hop off the page and get into your hair, under your skin; they romp in your underwear."

"You talk pretty good for a man with his foot in his mouth," remarked Iris with both brows rampant, upon which Saul checked himself. The secret, he realized, was devalued in the sharing. Now that he'd rashly broadcasted his new obsession, he wished he could take it all back again.

"Did you know," he tried falling back to an attitude of dismissive small talk, "that she was only twenty-seven when she died?" Iris confirmed that he'd already told her, while Saul clucked his tongue over the terrible waste. And that, he hoped, was that. But Iris was not about to let him off so easily. Since there was no fun in defaming Leah Rosenthal, who had dropped out of the competition decades ago, she leveled her caustic attentions at Saul himself.

"Necrophile," she accused. "You spend your piddling allowance of passions on a dead woman when the place is so full of the quick and still kicking?" At this Iris batted her eyes in the dense bubbles of her lenses, and actually gave his shin an untender kick beneath the table. She tossed her head coltishly despite the petrifaction of her silver-streaked coiffure.

Saul's jaw came momentarily unhinged over the spectacle of Iris's attempt at flirtation. Reassembling his sagging features to approximate a smile, he let her down as gently as he knew how.

"Frustrated and abrasive though you may be, Iris, you're still not quite my type. But know that I am flattered nonetheless."

Iris assured him that she had no idea what he was talking about; though even if she had, she certainly wouldn't have lost any sleep over it.

Meanwhile Saul had grown pensive, trying to remember the last time that anyone had bothered to flirt with him. When had he last been receptive enough to notice? Where some took early retirements, Saul had taken an early menopause. Since the anticlimax of his wife's walking out on him he'd been celibate these past three years. His appetite for women was among those he had relinquished in the process of what he'd come to think of as weaning himself from the world.

But tonight, in an environment tailor-made for the continuance of his hibernation, Saul had to admit to pangs of gregariousness.

"Iris," he learned forward to confess, apropos nothing at all, "God help me, I feel good."

He looked around the oak-beamed, snowbound room at his fellow colonists gathered at their candlelit tables. Having kept aloof for the better part of a week, he felt for once other than oppressed by the air of general convivality. On the contrary he was experiencing what might have passed for goodwill.

He observed that among the fewer than twenty current residents the women greatly outnumbered the men, which suddenly seemed to him a happy state of affairs. What was more, the handful of men that were present were a largely self-absorbed lot—too incurious or aged, too uncertain of their sexual orientation. Around these parts the healthy male animal was practically extinct; or so it seemed to Saul in his humble snap judgment, including himself in that red-blooded number for the first time in his life.

The women, on the other hand, were in the main a vibrant and communicative group. In age they varied from a salty old hack to the kittenish conceptual artist who scattered trompe l'oeil monkeys among the fir trees. There were the novelist and the biographer, flushed and inseparable, for whom the Colony functioned as both diet farm and ski resort. There was Helene, an artist in a shapeless greatcoat who kept much to the shadows, cautious of the effects of her own dark beauty. There was Iris, of course, and Katya, a zaftig emigré composer given to near-epileptic fits of backslapping camaraderie. There was Bonny, who wrote for the slicks and came swaddled head to toe in furs; and Consuela, a Spanish filmmaker who mascara'd her eyes like a bandit and punctuated her curses with a flamenco tattoo of her heels.

In their knotted scarves and bulky sweaters, boots laced to the knee, they might have just returned from a hunt. When they pulled off their knitted caps and shook loose their hair, it was as if they'd removed a lid to release a flame. They sang songs after dinner and swapped secrets, reclined on the hearthstones in seraglio poses and sipped mulled wine from pewter mugs. Watching them, Saul felt an admiration that called for greater intimacy. Dormant sensations stirred from their long winter's nap, and he thought he might yet live to see another spring.

Try as he might to curb his impure thoughts, in the end Saul gave himself up to daydreams. Throughout the next morning, without leaving his studio, he prowled furtively about the estate in his mind. He spied on the lady artists, so carelessly attired at their labors, dropped down their chimneys and sullied their necks with sooty kisses. They spun in his arms, screamed, "What the hell are you doing?" and bum's-rushed him out the door. Later on a tribunal of Colony fellows expelled him into the outer dark.

Foundering in his fantasies, Saul hung on for dear life to the buoy of Leah's book. (On such intimate terms with it now, he took liberties with the author's given name.) *Court of Miracles*, etc., had apparently shaken something loose in his congested head. The stories, striking eldritch chords, had tapped his sleeping energies, which ought by all rights to have been channeled back into his own work. But it was a delinquent kind of energy, a volatile stuff, which Saul didn't have the heart to waste on his miserable Felix, who wouldn't have known what to do with feeling good.

He thought about Leah, and how it might be a lark to write something to do with her. Why not, since he was already so preoccupied with wondering exactly who she was? But whereas he was enchanted with the setting of her life, the few fragments of Leah that he had to put in it weren't enough from which to assemble a palpable woman. Besides, his governing impulse had graduated from the merely mimetic, and in place of the ardor of writing, Saul thought he would prefer to have a good time.

Narrator by profession, occasional lecturer and veteran of numerous teaching appointments, Saul was often at a loss in situations where amateurs shone. But tonight, under the influence of Iris's sherry, sparkling in its goblet with asterisks of light, he was holding forth to a captive audience. The table, composed mostly of women, goaded him on when he paused to drink; they begged him to for God's sake finish his tale of the resurrection of his Aunt Bessie Fried.

"Like I told you," he reveled in his sudden knack for finding miracles in his own family history, "she was declared clinically dead on the operating table. After a team of surgeons managed somehow to revive her, she insisted that she'd stood in the presence of the Lord. One of the doctors, teasing, wants to know what He looked like, and she scolds him this is no joking matter. She winks solemnly and says, 'He's a good-looking man.' "

The table laughed their appreciation and assured Saul that he wasn't the antisocial creep they'd taken him for on first impression. Then, expressing regrets that it was time to attend a reading over at the library, the company commended him to Iris. Aware of a dangerously inflated sense of self-esteem, Saul also looked to his prickly friend to take him down a peg.

Her eyeglass lenses, infernally reflecting the cavernous dining-room hearth, offered him a glimpse of himself in hell. But for the moment there was no second-guessing Iris's thoughts.

"I was never much of a drinking man," Saul apologized, playing it safe. "Now you say," he prompted, inaccurately aping her voice, " 'Drop the *drinking* and that statement rings even truer.' "

When she turned her head, however, emptying her lenses of glare, Iris appeared to have no interest in casting stones. In fact, her tongue, behind a curl of chapped lips, had been in unbarbed abeyance all evening. Unused to so much approval, Saul was giddy to the point of nausea from a surfeit of limelight. Understanding that it was finally up to him to puncture himself, he searched for some old scab to pick, and remembered his marriage.

"I deceived my wife," he told Iris without fanfare. Iris congratulated him on being human, an uncustomarily generous concession for her. She primed his glass again experimentally, curious to see where his excessive lubrication might lead.

"I deceived my wife into thinking I was somebody else," Saul qualified, sloshing his wine and begging pardon for a resonant belch.

"Maybe you are somebody else," suggested Iris, but Saul asked her please not to muddy the issue. He went on to explain how he'd courted his former wife, Lucy, a pretty, provincial shikse whose Emma Bovary-like longings he had shamelessly promised to gratify.

"I came on like some kind of buccaneer maudit," he confessed, grimacing over the fraud. "Then after the wedding I dropped the masquerade, and she was a good enough sport to admit that the joke was on her." In a few years, without children to moor her in place, she drifted away, while, submerged in a book about the failure of a marriage, Saul scarcely noticed her leaving.

"To Lucy, wherever she is," Saul proposed, despite the impediment of his tongue, raising an empty glass which Iris perfunctorily refilled. She clinked his glass with her own and said hear hear, while Saul appended, "May I meet her wandering spirit in a better world."

Iris assured him on principle that he wouldn't know a better world if it bit him, nor, for that matter, a wandering spirit from a lamppost, given the shape he was in. But Saul never heard her, so transported was he by his latest revelation.

"I see it all clearly, how writing retarded my character at

an early age. I've been an emotional defective, a troll, since I wrote my first story. But strange as it seems, here in my middle years, now that I've got all that silly scribbling out of my system, I'm suddenly getting . . . " he put down his glass to caliper his temples with a forefinger and thumb ". . . growing pains."

"I don't think I'm prepared to know this much about you," complained Iris, her upraised hands pleading uncle. "What you need is ballast," she judged thoughtfully, "and I know just where we can find it." Draping his overcoat over his shoulders, she coaxed Saul out of his chair and shoved him in the direction of the library.

The reading-in-progress came to a temporary halt at their entrance, when Saul, despite Iris's guidance, stumbled over feet and apologized too loudly. Then disengaging himself from his attendant, he flopped onto an already crowded sofa. He turned left and right with a finger pressed showily to his lips, then tilted his head in an attitude of rapt concentration. But, as if the cumulative cramps of a sedentary lifetime had chosen this moment to catch up with him, Saul found it hard to sit still. He was uncomfortable with the subdued library lighting, more suited—he decided—to lying in state than sitting erect. Feeling prankish, he borrowed Consuela's sorrel braid, dangling over the chair in front of him, and used it for an impromptu moustache. He considered raising his hand to be excused.

Meanwhile, without the humor to turn the interruption to some advantage, the reader, one Murray Vincente, had cleared his throat several times and proceeded. Apparently in revolt against a colorful family that figured largely in his poems (his father a gangster, his mother a dancer, his sister born with a beard), Murray, as Saul perceived it, was dull with a vengeance. Whenever some germ of a gritty experience threatened to contaminate his work, Aquinas or Carlyle or Freud put in appearances in their surgical masks.

Saul squirmed and recrossed his legs, hooking a foot around his calf until he'd practically made a caduceus of himself. He muffled a hiccup as Murray, a bashful man in spite of his burly physique, introduced a poem he'd written at the Colony. It was about the Colony, in fact, depicting an atmosphere where the living artists fraternized with the dead. Conventional enough in theme, antiseptic with erudition, it nevertheless touched a nerve in Saul. It was a concept made all the more feasible by his sodden condition: how, in this place, the line between the here and the hereafter could sometimes get a little blurred. Sometimes it seemed not to exist at all.

After the reading came the ritual gathering about the reader to console him, as Saul saw it, for what he'd done. Grown drowsy, Saul was ready to make an exit, but given the commotion he'd caused, he felt obliged to pause and pay his respects. He insinuated himself into the knot of colonists surrounding Murray and patted him on the shoulder.

"Your poems," he began, trusting the momentum of his mouth to see him through, "are just like you."

There was an awkward silence during which Murray's features alternated between gratitude and indignation. Then the lights came up and the muted room was raucously profaned by the sound of tinny rock and roll. The women, having rolled back the carpet, began to make their token attempt at enticing the men into dancing, while the men, in turn, pleaded the usual frailties, clutching hearts and spines, parodying nonetheless legitimate complaints. This, as Iris at Saul's elbow was heard to observe, constituted its own song and dance.

Giving up a little too quickly on the others, a few of the women had dragged Murray into their midst. As engineer of the evening he was obligated to pay some lip service to mirth. For a minute he pranced about ticklishly, like a man being scrubbed by handmaidens while standing in his bath. Then, obedient to some internal clock that told him his time was up, he samba'd discreetly out of their circle. He was not missed by the women, who seemed content to dance with themselves.

Nodding to the beat of their respective drummers, they warmed to movement by degrees. They surrendered to tics and spasms, followed the lead of their senses, shucking formality as if they were wriggling out of stays. Some performed interpretations of native (if only to themselves) dances. Katya broke into a lumbering mazurka; Consuela executed an aggressive tango with an invisible matador. Bonny did the seven veils with her furs, while Helene appeared to be walking in her sleep. Only the novelist and the biographer were paired off, bunny-hugging in tandem.

As he watched, though he'd already said goodnight, Saul felt an unaccountable tugging in his blood. With his reason already put to bed by the wine, a maverick fancy came into play. Now that the other men had retired to corners or left the library altogether, Saul saw himself more than ever as an interloper. He was an uninvited witness to the way that women shed the lendings of civilization whenever the backs of men are turned. If they caught him spying, they might tear out his eyes and worse. Then the other, less paranoid side of his fancy was this: that the solitary dancers were not alone; their partners were the phantom residents of the Colony's past. With a little more to drink, Saul might even be able to see them.

He took up a random bottle from the makeshift bar on top of the piano and, seeing that it was rum, felt slightly piratical as he swigged it straight. He shivered as the alcohol baited his nerves into cantankerousness. Then, before he had caught his breath, he was grabbed by an anonymous hand

and hauled into the general undulation.

Saul's instinct was to beg off with the standard excuses. But while considering whether to blame his reluctance on his heart, head, or lily liver, he remarked how his feet had independently begun to shuffle about. Shod in his very first pair of hiking boots, with indestructible hobnailed heels that gave him an extra inch, Saul graduated from shuffling to stomping. In moments he was high-stepping about the room in boots that took seven leagues at a stride.

Ebullient, he allowed himself to be passed back and forth between the novelist and the biographer, who spun him like a game of blind man's bluff. Thus wound up, he gyrated dizzily away on his own. He moved from one woman to another, attempting a complement to the peculiar styles of each. In this way Saul cut in on Consuela's invisible partner, while she made little yipping sounds and flashed him an ivory grin. He held a bottle on his head and danced Cossack-style with Katya, shouting peace to the bones of pogrom-murdered ancestors. Unbuttoning his shirt, he circled Bonny predatorily; he orbited Helene, waving his fingertips at hers, playing a duet on her imaginary harp. Then, convinced that he'd been all things to all women, he began to dance alone.

So long out of touch with his gangling anatomy, Saul renewed his acquaintance with his knock-kneed legs in their baggy corduroys. He rolled up his flailing sleeves and welcomed himself to the nativity of his second childhood. Bumping and jogging in place, he shook out the dust mop of his wintry curls. The women who'd stopped dancing to clap their accompaniment could have been figures on a distant shore, now that Saul was so far embarked into frenzy. Somewhere he was conscious of making a thorough fool of himself; but since he was never going to live such an exhibition down, he might as well live it up.

Outdistanced however by his headlong spirit, sabotaged

by a shortness of wind, Saul eventually stumbled and fell over in a panting heap.

Iris, who'd been standing by as if for this very moment, was the first to take hold of his arm. She glowered at Consuela, who, tugging at his opposite arm, told Iris that Saul was no longer her personal property. In her guttural English she declared that, after such a performance, "che belong to the world." Raised to his feet, Saul accepted some water offered him by the novelist and the biographer. "Give him air!" he heard someone say, before he recognized the voice as his own.

Now that he was still, the room took its turn to start spinning. Faces revolved around him, and, like a dial on a wheel of fortune, Saul wondered which one he would come to rest upon. But the spinning accelerated until the ring of women were indistinguishable one from another. To keep his eyes from trying to match their revolution, Saul (muttering "I never felt better") snatched his overcoat up off the sofa and threw it over his head. Like a man abducting himself, he lurched out of the library into the snow, where he leaned against a tree and was sick.

In his clearing head there was not a trace of mortification over the spectacle he'd made of himself. On the contrary, having danced all of the kinks out of his system, Saul felt refreshed. To his right were the saffron lights of the sprawling reconstituted barn that served as a dormitory. There was the gable containing the suite of rooms he'd been issued for the length of his stay. Designed on a miniature scale, it was snug as a matchbox, though tonight the thought of his suite made Saul claustrophobic. What was cozy before was now only confining. And rather than head toward the lights, Saul turned his back on the habitations of men, directing his steps into the woods.

The sky above the pines was so dense with stars that it

looked threadbare; you could see through its fabric to the other side. The lane was luminous, a river of mercury in whose current Saul was helplessly swept along. At the turning where the silvery pate of Mount Manifold loomed into view, he looked behind him for the lights from the hall. But they were no longer visible. Crunching and sliding down the hill toward Prospero's Cell, Saul had the feeling that he'd passed a point of no return. Somewhere women would be waiting for news of his progress; they would, when he failed to return, perhaps mount an expedition by dogsled to find him.

Entering his studio, he nudged the hot coals with more kindling, then offered his backside to the ensuing blaze. The warmth relieved him of his excitation the way a valet takes a coat. With a yawning stretch he peeled off down to his long johns, wrapped himself in a down-stuffed comforter, and folded his length onto the unmade daybed. Letting go an extended sigh as he watched the fire, Saul reviewed the events of the evening, and tried out of habit to accuse himself of disgrace. But it was useless; he was too much at peace with himself to feel anything akin to shame. He closed his eyes and saw himself again at the hub of a wheel whose spokes were composed of women. As he drifted toward sleep, he saw the wheel, unfastened from its place in time, blindly careening into the unknown. Apprehensive about its ultimate destination, Saul abruptly snapped open his eyes.

She was standing at the foot of the daybed, the white of her antique gown upstaging the darker flesh of her face and bare arms. Beyond the quickening of his heart, more the aftereffect of his nightmare than from the presence of his visitor, Saul felt no particular surprise. He accepted that this was the kind of thing that happened to the kind of man he'd become tonight. Propping himself on an elbow, he squinted through his grogginess in an effort to puzzle out her identity. She was too slender by half for Iris, say, never mind Katya. So maybe it was Consuela—the gown, like an old-fashioned bride's shift, was something that Consuela might wear. It wasn't chic enough for Bonny or frumpy enough for Helene, though who but Helene could have entered his studio so stealthily? Pursuing what seemed like a logical process of elimination, he didn't rule out the possibility that this might even be his prodigal wife. But there his logic broke down.

Not that it mattered. Tingling as he was with such unlocalized lust, Saul was ready to give himself to any generic Lilith. Her identity was surely her least important attribute. Crooking a forefinger, he called her with an assurance in keeping with his newly posited devil-may-care.

"Come over here and get warm." He lifted the edge of the comforter to make room.

There was a high-pitched titter as if he'd said something naughty, but the figure didn't move. With the pert intonation of a maiden aunt, the lilt of a girl, she replied, "I've been cold for over sixty years, sweetheart. Do you think you can change that in a night?"

Sucker for the power of suggestion, Saul broke out in gooseflesh himself, and lowered the edge of the comforter.

"Anyhow," she continued, compounding her mystery with a riddle, "what kind of girl do you think I am?"

Saul was no longer entirely certain that he wanted to play this game. Was she making fun of him? And what was that business about sixty years? It was like a guessing game out of some tale in which, if you answered correctly, the woman would disappear.

Meanwhile she had glided away from the bed toward the fireplace. The flames, rather than silhouetting her, seemed to light her up from inside. They showed her stranger's face, framed by dense black hair working its way out of a bun, to be a little on the haggard side. Her cheeks were hollow, exaggerating the length of her drooping aquiline nose, while her eyes shone with a drollery that contradicted the bitter set of her lips. It was a face which, though not graced with a single prepossessing feature, was somehow beautiful.

Saul was fascinated by the way her eyes contained, like candles in saucers, the flames that hopped behind her. The hearth itself seemed visible (a kind of Joan of Arc light) through the filter of her insubstantial form. It was an illusion, of course, brought on by the collision of his fuddled perception with the filmy muslin of her gown. But the evidence of his senses persisted, overruling his doubts. It was not an illusion; the lady was transparent. And with a tremor that wrenched him sober and left him sitting bolt upright in bed, Saul began to understand.

"You're a ghost!" he cried, drawing a bead with his forefinger, withdrawing the gesture lest it give offense.

She lifted her brows in a delighted expression that awarded him full marks, whereupon she promptly disappeared. There was a fragrance the mixture of boiled chicken, dry rot, and gardenias, and her disembodied voice, emptied now of its tartness, saying, "I prefer to think an angel."

Without an immediate awareness that he'd done so, Saul had leaped out of bed. Frantic and irrational, he sniffed about the place from which she'd vanished, looking for what? A trapdoor maybe? A rent in the fabric of reality? He stuck his head up the chimney, then bolted for the windows, where he did not see her floating across the face of the moon. Searching for some proof of her visitation, some souvenir, he was at the same time looking for anything resembling a normal response in himself. Alone in a haunted house at night in the frozen woods, he ought at least to have the sense to be frightened out of his skull. But all he could think of was, now that he'd guessed who she was, she might not come back again.

"Iris, you'll never believe this . . . " Saul assured her over breakfast the next morning. He had hoped for a sign that he should try her anyway, but she wouldn't make it that easy for him. Studying the dregs of her fourth cup of coffee, pretending to see ill fortune, she replied with indifference, "So why tell me?"

Why indeed, wondered Saul, except that the storytelling itch was upon him. After his last night's visitor he'd hunkered on the daybed, waiting for some seismic shock to take its course. But as it was slow in arriving, he finally gave it up and (insomniac on much slighter excuses) fell dreamlessly asleep. He woke early, fully revived and apparently passed over by the morning-after effects of his debauch. He rose thankful for daybreak, made for the toilet, and resolved a chronic constipation with a bold eruption of the bowels. Rumpled and unshaven, lightheaded, he threw on his overcoat and, with an aerodynamic flapping of his coattails, sprinted back to the Colony hall.

He burst into the dining room with the look, Saul fancied, of a long-lost traveler returned from a realm of miracles. Several of the early risers glanced up from their tables, smiling indulgently or shaking their heads at his impetuousness; it seemed that he'd become popular overnight. But while he had it in mind to bend the ear of the first colonist he saw, Saul found himself reconsidering. He waived the attentions of the others in favor of Iris, his designated confidante, who was sitting alone over an eviscerated grapefruit with her familiar black cloud above her head.

A little daunted, however, by his first attempt at penetrating her mood, Saul thought better of trying again. He knew what ordinarily came of going public with one's visions, especially in company as cynical as this. Only today, what the hell, he was a glutton for Iris's abuse—in the same way that he was gluttonous for whatever consequences his present state of mind might hold in store.

"Leah Rosenthal came to my studio last night," he blurted, waiting for his stupefaction to prove contagious. And when it didn't: "Leah Rosenthal, the writer I told you about," he persisted, then louder, in case she might be hard of hearing, "y'know, the one that died in 1920."

Iris continued her preoccupation with her coffee cup, the tension in her jaw indicating that her patience had limits.

"A ghost, forgodsakes!" Saul insisted with an emphasis that caused heads to turn. "I saw a ghost!" He wriggled his fingers spookily, tousled his hair into a fright wig. Then, no match for Iris's impassivity, Saul admitted defeat, and began to sag slowly into his chair.

"If you're trying to deflate me," he sighed, practically sinking under the table, "you're doing a very good job."

His period of grace having formally ended, he was an easy prey to the deferred symptoms of his hangover. His head throbbed, his capillaries smarted; not to mention his muscles which, awakened last night from their flaccid slumber, now complained bitterly of the outrage. He felt his age, the weight of nearly half a century bowing his head. And worse, the earthshaking events of the night before were diminishing in Saul's mind into pot-valiant side effects.

Lifting her head, Iris might have been opening a door against which someone had been hurling himself, only to find him slumped in the hall. Satisfied that Saul was sufficiently broken, she administered the coup de grace.

"I've seen your type here before, Bozoff," she asserted with the cool authority of the veteran. "You come here to stage what you probably consider a well-earned nervous breakdown. Why not, since who could get hurt here in the lap of such scenic repose? Like a mural in a padded cell, am I right? So for once in your tight-assed life you cut loose; you play the fool and expect everybody to love you for it. Well it won't wash, dearie. So if I were you, I'd drop the Saul o'Bedlam routine and go back to writing my lugubrious books. Because this ain't a sanatorium and I am not your nurse."

Here, to say the least, was a marked departure from her old line of acerbic cajolery. Saul tried to write it off to sulking; she was getting even for his failure to reciprocate the attentions she had paid him. But as her severe demeanor seemed to say don't flatter yourself, Saul threw up a defenseless hand. He hoisted himself by unsteady stages from the table and made an unvaliant stab at saving face.

"What'd I say?"

He went back to Prospero's Cell and cooled his muddy brain in the ice-etched windows. From time to time he let go a sound, the unhappy marriage of a chuckle and a sigh. To Leah Rosenthal he now assigned the status of hallucination, evoked by the imprudent mixture of novelty and too much wine. To novelty he also ascribed his excessive zeal for Miss Rosenthal's stories. An orthodox realist, he was too advanced in years to be turning mystical. Iris knew best: it was time he remembered what he'd come here for. He should stop indulging himself at the expense of his work, stop wasting these precious, if not final, days.

But when he tried to think about his freshly hatched Felix, hunkered in his cellar beneath the detritus of history, Saul's already queasy stomach became more upset. In order to write the thing convincingly, it was essential to identify with one's protagonist; if ever there was a cardinal rule, it was that. But his protagonist, a voice from a premature burial, was already as good as dead. It had seemed such a natural, not to say imperative, projection for Saul to make. Only now, when he asked himself what he honestly wanted to do, he had to admit that fomenting Felix was not it. Moreover, whatever *it* was, he considered glumly, it ought to be a little fun. And there ought to be women involved.

"Felix, you putz," Saul practically spat, "what you need is a good lay."

Then it was as if he'd uttered a secret word; and down into Felix's cellar, which Saul suddenly perceived with a cobwebless clarity, descended an angel. In his preliminary grave beneath a wasted world, Felix was being visited by an angel. While his stunned senses began slowly to awake to her brilliant beauty, she vouchsafed him this confidence: that she was a young woman cut off in her prime without even the opportunity of having had a child. The child—she blushed to say it, suffusing the cellar in a rosy radiance—would have completed her life.

But Felix, whom you will recall had just emerged from a sluggish state of shock, was slow on the uptake. The angel asked if she had to spell it out for him. The earth, divested of humanity, was no longer a fit place for bringing up children; so the Lord, always anxious to increase the population of heaven, had given her a dispensation. She and Felix, the survivor, would conceive together, and she would return to paradise to have his child.

Helpless to prevent the story from unfolding in his otherwise deserted mind, Saul protested aloud, "What shlock!" It was a hackneyed fable, barren of the earmarks characteristic of a Bozoff story: his famous self-pity, his exhausted verisimilitude. It was an unconscionable perversion of his original theme, the product of a kind of careless breathtaking inspiration that Saul hadn't known for how long he couldn't say.

But material such as this belonged in the hands of your professional woolgatherers, like what's-her-face. Then he actually had to consult her book in order to remember her name, the sight of which recalled the ring of her voice saying, "Nu?"

Saul's head swiveled round like a marionette before the rest of him got the message. There stood the dead lady, arms folded demurely over the smocking of her gown, her back to a sunlit window on the adjacent wall. Despite her grainy appearance in broad daylight, as if the dust motes had assembled in female formation, she appeared to have more substance than the night before. In fact, her translucency was essentially limited to the fabric of her thin white gown, through which the sun revealed her naked limbs.

As before, Saul waited patiently to be dumbstruck. With every bat of his eyelids he registered some classical response to ghosts: Topper demanding decorum, Mrs. Muir clutching her bosom, Charlie Chan's no. 3 son aghast beneath upstanding hair. But Saul remained stationary throughout, trying to decide whether at this unlikely hour he ought to believe what he saw.

Meanwhile she'd proceeded to speak in her saucy East Side dialect. Waving a hand like she was wiping a window—Saul thought it made her face come even clearer—she'd assumed that a conversation which had yet to begin was already in progress.

"So what I'm saying here is this, Mister Bozoff isn't it, why don't we collaborate?"

With the illusion of chumminess thus thrust upon him, Saul had missed the moment when he might have screamed. Then it was too late, and he'd become as fascinated with her presumption as with her spectral presence.

"I mean," she went on, leaning toward him at a vertiginous angle, "I had this cruelly aborted life, as you know," putting a hand to her porcelain forehead like a burlesque Camille, "so I never got to finish what I started to say. Whereas you"—she made a face whose implication Saul was vaguely aware of resenting—"you're still breathing, so to speak; but the little you had to tell, you already told." Here Saul would have begged her pardon. "So what I'm going to do for you, my impoverished friend, I'm gonna make you a proposition . . . "

He wanted to tell her slow down. Without giving him a chance to exercise his obligatory fear and trembling, she had already weaned him from astonishment. What's more, she'd insulted him, then had the audacity to offer some kind of a deal. It was more than too much.

"You'll serve me in a sort of secretarial capacity," she was saying, winsome for all of her huckster's locution. She explained how he would transcribe her stories just as she related them: "You'll be my ghostwriter, as it were. And you can take all the credit when the stories are published. To see them nestled cozy as cats in the bookstore windows"—pressing her face against an imaginary pane which nevertheless flattened her nose— "that's all I ask. So, boychikl, what do you say?"

Saul could only stare. So far only on the receiving end of a dialogue with the supernatural, he didn't know how to participate. It was as if, after a long paralysis of the tongue, he'd been called upon to utter his first words. He swallowed and hemmed until satisfied that his vocal chords were still in working order, then managed, "Let me get this straight." And on the strength of this much lucidity, he rose falteringly to his feet and continued. "You want *me* to take dictation from . . . " Having tapped his breastbone in confirmation of his own finite entity, he pointed a finger at her.

The shade of Leah Rosenthal responded with a hopeful

nod that left her head cocked expectantly. Then, with the sound of an unstoppered cork, she allowed it to capsize, rolling chin over crown down her arm like a painted egg. She caught it in the cup of her hand and restored it with a thunk to her scrawny neck. Then smiling sweetly, she tucked a wayward strand of her hair behind an ear.

Where her stagy decapitation only revolted him, it was the gesture with the hair that somehow released in Saul the dread that until now had been delayed. Mushrooming in his chest, it was a sensation that threatened to displace his heart. Feeling crowded to the point of panic, he heard his own desperate voice still refusing to surrender his will.

"No, sorry, it's impossible. I only work solo."

He was shaking his head in a stubborn fervor, resolving not to take any more of this seriously. Apparition aside, he was anyway old enough to be her father. While, on the other hand, as her affectionate diminutives kept reminding, she was better than twice his age. Saul understood that, in the light of these circumstances, such considerations might be accounted depraved—which made him all the more furious to speak out in his own self-defense.

"Besides," he demanded, trying not to choke on the words, "who says I'm dried up? The truth of it is, I'm a regular fountain of invention. Why only this morning I concocted this crazy tale . . . " But something in Leah's altered expression—her unsolicited sympathy, that was it—brought him up short. Taking a quick mental inventory of his stock of ideas, he discovered that the cupboard was bare; he realized who'd been responsible for its brief replenishment. "You," he mouthed a silent indictment, and silently, raising her eyebrows and biting her thumb, Leah let it be known that she could not tell a lie.

Under his breath Saul muttered that it was a lousy story anyway. Then there was a terrible moment when he recognized himself as the victim of an authentic possession. "I get it!" he maintained, wagging his head to affirm he was nobody's fool. It had come to him in a flash: how out here beyond the clamor of a mechanized age, demons could ply their trades undisturbed; they could snatch your soul.

He rubbed his eyes in a feeble attempt to flush her out of existence. Amateur exorcist, he submitted a subvocal "Succubus, fuck off," and when that didn't work, clapped his hands over his face. But it was scarier in the dark where nothing made any humanly sense, save the voice of a dead woman calling softly, "What's the matter, kepeleh, don't you want me to be your muse?"

Saul peeked through the screen of his fingers, half expecting to find her juggling her own plum-sized breasts or sawing herself in two. He was a little relieved to see her standing there with the look of a lonely girl in need of a partner for the dance. Nor was he entirely proof against the charm of her ebony eyes, spying avidly from behind the oval mask of her face. He told himself, Don't be deceived; for this one the party was over definitively. Though where were the signs, beyond her native transparency about the edges, to suggest it?

He recalled his own liveliness of the past few days, his celebration of her extravagant stories. Was it so awful that what he'd taken for solitary cavorting turned out to be a pas de deux? An owl hooted ruefully outside the windows, and Saul had the sudden chivalrous urge to say. They're playing our song.

But ever distrustful of spontaneous impulses, he stipulated cautiously, "Let's say I agreed. Then no more of your parlor tricks, your special effects? My nerves won't take your special effects."

Leah crossed her heart, which flared up like a scarlet beacon in the cage of her ribs, until, in deference to Saul's request, she solemnly extinguished it.

He looked at her skeptically but swallowed hard. "Okay," he said, "what have I got to lose?" hoping that his better judgment wouldn't answer that.

Then he waited to be staggered by the stupendous knowledge that he was now among the elect of the muse. But since the ghost still appeared to be waiting herself—as if, the tables turned, she was trying to believe in Saul—he thought that some further gesture might be in order. Tentatively, somewhere between offering his and reaching into a separate dimension for hers, Saul held out his hand. She gazed at it with a palm reader's studied interest, then smiled impishly, her lips sealed over what she saw. Her sigh, in the second before she vanished into vapor, was the essence of heliotrope and sour cream.

That evening at dinner Saul sat alone at a table beneath a hanging lamp as under a halo. Such were the depths of his complacency that even the most comradely of his fellow colonists kept their distance. Only Iris, probably assuming that his withdrawal was the result of her last tirade, wanting perhaps to make her peace, tried to engage him in conversation. But her small fund of patience was no match for his vacant responses, his awful serenity, and after an exasperated few moments she removed herself to another table.

"Mr. Quiet-After-the-Storm," she remarked within his earshot to anyone interested. "I suppose he sowed his wild oat. From a Cossack to a cabbage in just one night—a nine days' wonder, minus eight." But as he only continued to smile beatifically, she shrugged and directed her abuse toward the food.

For his part Saul had nothing but fond regard for his fellows. He was pleased to be among such an exalted company, who for all he knew were conducting their own assignations with spirits. At some point it might be illuminating to compare notes. But for the time being he was content to dwell in his own speculations, the current involving the place to which specters retire when they disappear. Could the humming in his head, like a wind from beating wings, possibly be taken as a clue?

After his meal a couple of others attempted gingerly to draw him out. There was a concert of trio sonatas in the library, an expedition down to an inn in the village for drinks—all invitations that Saul graciously declined. He even resisted Consuela's inducement to a game of table tennis, despite her having asked in such breathlessly wanton tones.

"I've got to get back to work," he told her, suddenly aware of a state of emergency.

Under a low ceiling of stars he scuttled back down to Prospero's Cell, shades of a rabbit late for an appointment underground. Composing as he walked, Saul entered the studio writing, sat down at his desk and typed three pages before bothering to take off his coat. But this was not what he'd been led to expect, not dictation; it was inspiration pure and simple. It was bliss of the kind that he hadn't enjoyed since the forgotten days of his apprenticeship, back when he wrote with an explorer's passion for following his sentences to their elusive ends. Only then, his thoughts had frequently pulled up shy at precipices or collapsed into tautological bogs. But this evening he was writing with an intrepid conviction, each word succeeding the previous with an assurance that amounted to something like manifest destiny.

Always a morning writer whose intensity was spent by early afternoon, Saul wrote nonstop through the night. He worked with a perfect concentration, oblivious to daybreak and the chuckle of falling icicles, to the man who left his lunch basket on the doorstep. By three o'clock he had a complete draft of his tale about Felix's liaison with the angel. True, he didn't have a very clear idea of what he'd written; it had all been accomplished in such a white heat. But overcome by a pleasant exhaustion, he decided it was time for a nap. Later, while waiting for the next flood tide of his powers, he could coldly survey the aftermath of the first.

He slept until dusk and woke up hungry, teasing himself that his review of the manuscript could wait till after dinner. At the Colony hall he moved like a poacher, lurking at a corner table just long enough to swill his soup and gnaw a bone. What he didn't eat he stuffed into a market basket along with the leftovers from one or two other abandoned plates. Without taking the time to shave his beard or change his dirty clothes, he tucked his spoils under his overcoat and beat it back into the night.

If behind him tongues flapped over his sack of the dining room, Saul never heard them, his thoughts having already turned back to the work at hand. In Prospero's Cell, having satisfied his bodily cravings, he pounced on his manuscript, anticipating food for his soul. But where he'd looked for nourishment, Saul found instead a tasteless, insipid pap.

It couldn't be; but regardless of how he tried to readjust his focus, squinting and looking askance, the pages would not come alive. The language was lame, clodhopping syntax without rhythm; the images were random and rarely appropriate. The plot was a mawkish and juvenile contrivance. Desolate, Saul sank into his chair and wondered how he could ever have been so deluded.

Then the canny voice that heralded her abrupt materialization said, "So, pupik, is it really that bad?"

She was standing at his shoulder in an inquisitive pose, head craned, hands tucked behind her back. In the soft light of the desk lamp, none of her diaphanous effects were apparent anymore. Where before it was hard to tell if she were coming or going, she now had a density about her that suggested an aggressive commitment to being there. The incarnated midnight of her hair seemed to have acquired gravity, its thick bun—Saul worried—about to cascade. Contrarily he fanned the typescript pages on his desk.

"In short it's drek," he explained.

Leah shook her head sympathetically, tsk-tsk'd her tongue. "Look again, why don't you?" she advised him. "It's maybe not such a mishmash as you think."

It was pointless, of course, but how much more pointless to argue with a ghost. When he looked, however, Saul observed that the lights were back on in his story. The lumbering sentences, healed of their limping, jigged across the page, outfitted in tropes of many colors, performing nimble turns of phrase. The wooden characters, Pinocchio-wise, had disengaged themselves from the strings of language, the better to relate to one another without compromising entanglements. First draft? Why, this was as finished as anything Saul had ever done. It was the product, moreover, of a sorcery beyond his control, in the face of which he could only feel superfluous.

"What did you do?" he demanded, frowning over a pronounced lower lip.

Leah made a blithe little shrug, coquettishly protesting her innocence, but Saul thought he understood what was going on. He'd been seeing life and literature through her eyes. And his lapse in faith with regard to the latter, that was her doing; it was just to remind him where all of this lovely afflatus was coming from. Albeit such moonstruck logic still did not sit so well with Saul.

"You told me you didn't want any credit," he complained.

"So I'm fickle," said Leah, having dropped her born-yesterday routine. "Listen, once the stories are delivered, they're your business. But a gezuntheit or two while they're coming to term wouldn't do me any harm."

"But wasn't *I* the one who wrote the story?" Saul appealed, his irascibility compounded by the knowledge of his own thanklessness. "Didn't I beat it out on my little typewriter?"—pounding a fist on the keys, which bunched against the carriage like an audience crowding an exit. "Doesn't the story rightfully belong to me?"

Shielding her face, Leah made a pretense of having been frightened by his display. She wrung her hands like a heroine threatened with eviction. Then she relaxed and told him, "Don't you know we spooks are the ones who are supposed to inspire fear?" And when that failed to appease him: "Come, neshomaleh, leave us not quibble over technicalities."

But Saul was busily entertaining doubts which, on another day, might have been called common sense. How had he gotten into this unholy alliance in the first place? Was it all for the sake of a story whose beauty resided nowhere but in the eye of the beholder? Making blinders of his hands, he directed his gaze back to the typewritten pages, which winked at him and shimmered, words like electric minnows, like a veil of northern lights. A trick of Leah's it might be, but Saul was nonetheless dazzled, his heart in glorious arrest.

He looked to the slip of a ghost, her hands on her angular hips, her bare foot tapping out the time it took the writer to return to his wits. Then he could have sworn that, for all of her bruited insensitivity to the climate of this world, they were goose pimples that textured her shoulders and arms. It was a notion reinforced by her rigid nipples, conspicuous beneath the bodice of her gown. Also, if he was not mistaken, there was a moistness about her eyes, caused (Saul conjectured) by a fragment of his reflection lodged therein. And wasn't she even blushing a bit under his unrelenting leer?

"Leah," he began what was intended for a grudging acknowledgment: He meant to concede for the record her authorship of his exaltation. But other still nameless sentiments were pulling rank.

As if to distract him from what she knew was coming, the ghost spun her head pinwheel-fashion, then around like a weather vane. It was the act of an unruly child who refuses to sit still for the photograph. Then sorry for this breach of their contract, she apologized. "But Saulie," she felt obliged to add, "you should stop already with trying to imagine me back to life."

Saul hung his head in a perfunctory admission of guilt, but felt no shame. He was glad that Leah had changed the subject, even if to one more sore. The origin of Felix and his celestial mistress no longer seemed to be an issue; the fact of the story took precedence over anyone's responsibility for it. It was a fact with respect to which Saul's stinginess of spirit had dissolved into a giddy gratitude.

"Leah," he tried again, this time with a fib which his saying made retroactively true, "I missed you."

"Then why," she chided, "do you persist in looking this gift horse in the mouth?"

As it happened, it was anywhere but at her mouth that Saul was looking. The lamp, in cahoots with the lambent firelight (improving an act performed earlier by the sun), gave away the wraithlike contours beneath the folds of her shift. Whereas, Saul reflected, her mortal coil might have long since moldered to dust in some Brooklyn graveyard, her spirit was still a fine, if boyish, figure of a girl. In fact, relatively speaking, she appeared quite young for her age.

Suffering his rapt appraisal, Leah, to Saul's utter delight, began to fidget self-consciously. For once in their brief relationship Saul was able to feel more than gratuitous; he may even have had the upper hand. Where did this sudden talent come from, this ability to make nervous the dead? It was almost as if he were haunting her. But as befitted their collaboration, Saul assumed his share of the embarrassment. Alarmed by a twitch at the lap of his corduroys, he shifted in his chair and crossed his legs.

"Haven't you got something a little less . . ." he asked, moving his fingers as if through fabric, ". . . skimpy?"

Leah lifted and let fall her shoulders regretfully.

"It's what I was buried in."

Left to his own devices, Saul reassessed "Felix and the Angel," and was satisfied that he had never executed anything so graceful before.

"The first draft went straight to my head," he quipped aloud in case Leah might be listening.

So what next? he wondered, rubbing his hands together, looking out the window as if for a clue. Somewhere beyond the pines the old moribund world was still rallying, he supposed, for its pyrotechnical swan song. So what else was new under that smudge of a sun? For his own material, thank you, Saul would prefer to look closer to home, where there were no end of tales to relate. Here, as beneficiary of Leah Rosenthal's invisible estate, he was heir to a prodigious fertility. Stories grew on trees! And all that Saul had to do to harvest them was to be there when they ripened and fell to earth.

Making a profusion of feverish notes, he was a man frantically gathering up manna. Previously a creature of regular habits, he was indifferent now to the passage of time. He was unmindful of the meals he missed, his lack of sleep, the pungency of his unwashed person, the gossip he provoked. All that concerned him was the apprehension of new ideas, which, once captured, he confined to his spiral notebooks while they matured.

There was a story he couldn't wait to write about the son of a ferocious butcher who is carried away by birds; another just as compelling about a seedy old peddler who is literally too stubborn to die. There were secret heroines, Jewish were-wolves, holy fools—all of whose driven antics Saul, the unbeliever, subscribed to wholeheartedly. Displaced throughout his life, he felt that in the markets and on the tenement roofs, in the galleries of theaters and synagogues, he'd found his natural milieu. But no sooner had he settled in than Saul began to wonder what would happen if he imported the whole cockamamie circus back to his Mississippi River town. How would Second Avenue look resurrected atop bluffs named for Indian tribes? How would the old world visionaries get along with dirt farmers, swamp rats, the high-rolling Negroes around Fourth and Beale? How would they adapt to sitting on liars' benches or pushing their carts across the plank-paved bridge with its creosote aflame in summer?

Such bracing speculations, however, were at odds with Saul's fundamental attitude toward his work. In former endeavors, an abject fear, in place of an active conscience, had been his guide. His perennial anxiety over the failure of his powers, his conviction that every piece would be his last, that the world was about to end—these were the considerations that had goaded him through his working day. But he no longer embraced any such fears. Now that he'd accumulated enough projects to see him into his declining years, he felt a loss of urgency. Time was not of the essence. It was nice just to sit by the fire taking tally of his future tables of contents.

Granted, here was another instance of Saul's lingering

stinginess. He was Scrooge in the countinghouse, just begging to be visited by recriminating ghosts. But this time he would not be so hesitant to give credit where it was due. For it was Leah and Leah alone to whom he owed his current richness in spiritual goods. And since their initial encounter, having made the grand tour of his emotions, Saul had come back to contemplating love.

Resting his arms on the typewriter, cradling his teeming head in his arms, he realized that, in a sense, he was playing possum. If his industry kept Leah discreetly away, then his idleness might summon her return. He longed for some password by which he might beckon her at will—something with verve, like, say, "Gevalt!"

In a while, when the bittersweet voice inquired, "Saul, darling, what are you doing?" Saul was very proud of himself.

In fact, he was so happy to see her disapproving presence there on the hearthstone that he had to laugh. The very idea of it, that his witness to the comings and goings of this sprightly phantom girl was second nature to him now, suddenly struck Saul as wildly funny; it left him in stitches.

Obviously uncomfortable with his laughter, Leah adjusted her shift, brushed some empyreal hoarfrost from a shoulder. But her least movement served to add fuel to the writer's hilarity. In the end, with a sigh of boredom, she was forced to ask him, "Vos is?" And as that had no effect, "Did I miss something?"

Saul tried to inhale his laughter, choked on "Excuse me," and coughed out more of the same. Such rowdy behavior was liberating; it gave him a sensation of outright recklessness. Feeling candid as a drunk, he had it in mind to spill everything: how the most intense carnal desire of his life was affixed to a thing of ether and kitchen smells. Oh, it was rich! But all he could manage to get out through his wheezing was, "I guess you had to be there."

Leah gave him a knowing look which implied that she was.

His hooting dropped into a lower register, then subsided while he wiped his nose and dried his eyes. There was a contrite moment when Saul wondered if all of his levity were somehow at her expense. She did appear genuinely put out and unlike her usually pawky self. In any case, this time his "Don't know what came over me" was relatively articulate.

"So fine, so mazel tov," Leah conceded, waving a hand that might have been cleaning a blackboard. "So now you know there are more things in heaven and earth than were dreamt of in your mishegoss. Now can we please get back to transacting the unfinished business of my interrupted life?"

Saul nodded by all means, then saw an image of Leah, a tin angel, on a shelf in a hockshop waiting to be redeemed. He tried to keep a sober face, but it was useless; he couldn't stop enjoying himself.

"But," he teased her, gleeful at the temerity it took to tease her, "I'm fresh out of stories."

Leah folded her arms like she'd heard that one before, turning her head only to nail him with a sidewise glance.

"How can *you* be fresh out? *I'm* not fresh out, so how can you be?"

Saul made a search-me sort of shrug and replied, "I'm not you."

"That's a moot point," snapped Leah, practically squaring off.

But Saul wasn't ready to be reasonable, as what did any of this have to do with reason? It was as if they'd traded places, he and Leah. Now he was the impossible one, and it was up to the ghost to bring Saul Bozoff back down to earth.

"I need a subject," he equivocated, then caused his eyebrows to hop lasciviously up and down. "Maybe you would like to sit for one of my stories?"

Leah rolled her eyes heavenward. "Give me strength," she intoned, her voice eerily reverberative. If there were chains, thought Saul, this was the moment to rattle them. Then she'd composed herself, she who after all had all the time in eternity. So he was going to be difficult; difficulty she could accommodate. "Okey-dokey, nudnik." She smiled in smug defiance. "Write a story about me."

Saul made a show of diligently rolling his sleeves up, brandishing his pen. "Of course," he said slyly, pushing his inch toward a mile, "I'll have to research it first."

"Tahkeh," nodded Leah, fussing a bit with her untidy hair. "Sure, sure." Saul was amazed by her compliance.

She was leaning against the mantelpiece with an air of dramatic languor, as if actually posing for her portrait. "Pity you can't draw me from life," she sighed, then delicately stifled a yawn. She was playing with him now, or rather they were playing with each other, Leah having gotten into the spirit of things.

With his license to presumption, Saul asked her to begin at the beginning, and was as pleased with himself as with her when she obliged him. As she spoke, he kept up his pantomime professional front, conscientiously taking notes. But when he realized that she was telling her story in earnest, he dropped the charade and allowed himself to be captivated.

Occasionally, while reciting her alleged biography, Leah would interrupt herself to complain that this was all a digression. "From the grave I came back to get nostalgic over Yiddishkeit?" She would hesitate, putting Saul a little in mind of his misbegotten Felix—the one who, after the formal annihilation of his world, was damned if he could recollect anything at all. Only in Leah's case the intermittent amnesia was maybe a blessing, which freed her to embroider at will.

Her rambling narrative included a first glimpse of Manhattan, ringed in masts and boilers like a fogbound forest of thorns; the gauntlet of Hester Street run by marauding children spilled from an open hydrant at the corner of Orchard. There was a perpetual blizzard of feathers in the pillow-making sweatshop, eternal spring in the paper-flower factory, clothes hung in the airshafts like flags at a naval regatta. There were flaming bodies that plummeted from the Triangle Shirtwaist Company like a flight of phoenixes. There were the gentile streets from which cheder boys never returned. There was the holiday of a gangster funeral, the sanctuary of the Seward Park library, of the Cooper Union on Shakespeare night. There was Yom Kippur, when the Jews threw their sins off the Brooklyn Bridge.

There was the gallery of dreamers at the City College evening school: the good-natured Carpathian hokey-pokey man who asked her if she would like to do dirty, the stone-faced kosher prostitute who had the first book of *Paradise Lost* by heart, the fat rabbi who claimed that Karl Marx was descended from the house of David, the young poet who hanged himself for love of the lady firebrand who attended class festooned in paper chains . . .

Of course none of this was any news to Saul, not a single character introduced of whom he hadn't already had the pleasure. Everything she told him he heard stereophonically, saw in 3-D, since he and Leah shared the same depository for their mutual pasts, i.e., Saul Bozoff's brain. So he had the sense of listening to a story he'd already heard—albeit his favorite story, which he still couldn't get enough of.

But rather than as heroine of her own narrative, Leah had cast herself in an incidental role. In fact, the more the details accumulated, the less Leah figured into them at all. What was more, with the unburdening of each memory, she faded another degree. She was scarcely visible now, the scant silver thread of an arabesque; and Saul worried that, having thus turned her insides out, she might vanish with no reason to return. Nothing would remain but her cameo appearance in one of Leah Rosenthal's stories, or Saul Bozoff's, depending on how you viewed their joint venture.

So, in a desperate effort to salvage something of the authentic young woman in his midst, Saul broke in abruptly to ask her, "What about your love life?"

A hint of color came back to her, milk poured into a glass. There was the familiar playfulness about her eyes as she assured him that, oh, there were boys.

"There was the Talmud scholar who recited the Song of Songs on my fire escape, accompanying himself on a borrowed barrel organ. There was the blacksmith who knocked his donkey cold as a demonstration of the strength of his love, the garter-maker who sent a message by carrier pigeon that he'd taken his broken heart to sea. But those were funny times, and I had my priorities. I had my own stupid ideas about romance."

Saul seized upon the note of regret in her voice, thoughtlessly blurting, "You mean you never . . . that is, you haven't . . . what I mean is, ummm."

"Alas, I died undefiled," Leah declaimed, peering mischievously from under the hand she held to her brow. "Is that what you wanted to hear?"

Saul wondered how it was possible he could believe that there might still be hope for him.

He marveled at the way his mooning after a dead lady had thrust him further into life than he'd ever been. He was beyond turning back to his old preoccupations. For the clinical reduction of experience, Saul had lost his stomach; that kind of stuff was for clammier and more detached souls than he. Lately Saul saw himself not so much as a writer than as someone to be written about.

He was tickled by the stir he made whenever he put in his unscheduled appearances at the Colony hall. There were titters running the gamut from cagey appreciation to disgust; proposals of confinement to attics, references to the Phantom of the Opera and King Lear. Even in this safe harbor for eccentrics, it seemed that Saul was cause for alarm. His eyes were wild, his features sere from loss of weight, his clothes in unlaundered disarray. Bursting through the doors from the terrace, he sometimes looked sinister, even predatory, like an uninvited guest at the wedding bent on revenge.

But when he spoke, which he now did compulsively, he was sociable to a fault. His own past had lately become for Saul an album whose contents had to be shared, whether or not his audience was so inclined. Memories he'd long since discarded now seemed, give or take a little embroidery, to be sources of absorbing anecdote. Ignoring whatever discussions might be in progress, Saul would descend on some random table and begin to reminisce about his childhood in the South.

Tonight was the story, based on unverifiable fact, of how he used to run with the black kids on Beale Street—"like their mascot or something, and there was one kid who everyone thought was mute. So I go with them to see the barge come in with the Cotton Carnival royalty, and the dumb kid—as soon as he sees this lily-white carnival queen, he starts to jabber. He's speaking in tongues; only it's a kind of glorious folk poetry, lyric and fluent, all about how his queen is a gospel dove, how she was carved from a cypress knee by Jesus himself, that sort of thing. Well, sir, he never shuts up and pretty soon he's famous. He's written up in the newspapers, the preachers shout Hallelujah, the professors take sedulous notes. And all the time he's languishing, doesn't eat or sleep, just jabbers about his white lady and languishes away. Then after a while he dies. Can you believe it? The sonofabitch died for love."

After which Saul promised his few remaining listeners that there were plenty more where that came from.

Used by now to being regarded as a figure of fun, he was not above exploiting the role. With relative impunity he extolled the ladies for their desirability. He twitted them to gather pinecones while they may, threatened self-inflicted wounds if his overtures weren't returned. He yanked tufts of hair to show how his satyriasis was making him molt. For their part the women, judging him harmless enough, suggested moderate remedies, such as growing up. But where they chose not to entirely ignore him, they encouraged him—all except Iris, who didn't have to try hard to look bored.

For her Saul reserved his most heartfelt expressions of delirium, though she held her ears whenever he came near.

"Iris," he told her in all sincerity, "I feel pretty. Even my aches are exquisite. I thought you might like to know."

While she never dignified his remarks with a comment, Saul suspected that in her way she was looking after him. The extra sandwiches he found whenever he bothered to look inside his lunch basket he attributed to her, not to mention the multiple vitamins. Despite heaven-sent competition, Iris was playing at being his anonymous guardian angel.

Meanwhile, in sympathy with his ruttish behavior, a premature thaw had set in. The snow was melting and the damp brown earth beneath it was exhaling its sweetness and rot. The pines presided over a chorus of assorted fragrances, and here and there a crocus bloomed.

Saul had been feeling cramped in Prospero's Cell, doing

nothing other than looking forward to Leah's next reappearance. The manuscript pages of "Felix and the Angel" were limp from his constant perusal. How many times did he need to convince himself that the story was first-rate; it was good enough to belong to the canon of *Courts of Miracles and Last Resorts*. He was restless, the muddy lanes beckoned. Turning vagabond, Saul discovered that his dialogues with Leah no longer required her presence.

Slipping down pathless slopes, mounting boulders and dodging trees, he spoke to his muse. He wanted her to come look at how at home he was in the out-of-doors. The birds might perch on his shoulders, the rabbits feed out of his hands. But he never saw her, not in the moss-carpeted amphitheater or beside the freshly unfrozen waterfall. Then her absence seemed a kind of judgment, as if she wouldn't have been caught dead in these woods. And Saul had the guilty feeling he was playing hooky. It frustrated him that, for all his having pictured her in front of fish stalls or in the slanted sunlight under the Division Street El, he could not now imagine her anywhere but in his studio.

He went back to Prospero's Cell and waited for Leah. "Gevalt!" he called out at intervals, pronouncing the word like the name of a pet, but still she didn't come. In the meantime all his rapturous agony was losing its edge. What he'd done, he realized, was to abandon their collective endeavor, leaving the ghost in the lurch. He'd left her without a translator into the language of the living. It was a crime in atonement for which he now revived his old habit of worry, trying on this one for starters: that as it required a living being to finish her labors, it would likewise take flesh and blood to complete his excruciating love for Leah.

Then, without ceremony, she quietly appeared.

"Saul," she said, and right away he missed her patronizing terms of endearment, "wasn't there something you had to do?"

She seemed to need reminding herself. He wondered what had become of her brass, her pushiness, her Fanny Brice routine. This was no way for such a phenomenon to behave. Since their last encounter, she had yet to recover her full materiality. Her presence had no more consistency than smoke, and her features, where they were discernible, had about them a profound weariness.

Saul waited to receive his comeuppance, longed for it in fact. Bring on the fireworks: brimstone clouds and multiple self-amputations would be a welcome relief from this dismal silence. But as there was no hint of anything seething beneath her sullen frown, Saul took the initiative.

"I know I've let you down," he confessed to her vestigial feet, "and I'm sorry." Then, as that had not been a fervid enough demonstration of his remorse: "I'm sorry I betrayed you, Leah."

The ghost made some minimal movement, a sniff. "Ach," she sighed as if to dismiss the whole affair, "it was a farkokte idea anyway."

They sat and stood respectively in their dumb admission of defeat, Saul Bozoff and his beloved silent partner. Then Saul felt that the dead weight of their mutual speechlessness would crush him if he didn't fight back. So their collaboration was a little less fruitful than it might have been; was it too late to pick up the thread? And bargains aside (their own having remained officially unsealed), didn't she feel for him some semblance of what he felt for her?

"Leah," he began, intending to put the question. But losing his nerve in mid-resolution, he opted for something more rhetorical: "What's it like to be dead?"

At this she came into slightly sharper focus. "You would

know better than I," she bristled, and Saul applauded him self at having struck a nerve. "I'm what you might call undead," she continued with injured pride. "As who would know better than you, I never, at least not in the bona fide sense, let go of my life. I was hanging around for the right somebody to take the trouble to pry me loose."

Here Saul made some noise expressive of his bottomless mortification, which Leah ignored.

"This place was particularly hard to let go of," she went on, further agitating Saul with her air of resignation, her use of the past tense. "And by the same token, it was particularly easy to haunt. Let's face it, what on earth is closer to heaven than the Colony? Very convenient to commute. Anyway"—almost inaudibly—"this is the only place I ever had a good time in."

Saul was bewildered. "What about the night they turned on the electric lights in the Flatiron Building?" he ventured to ask. "What about Thomashefsky's impromptu Yiddish Hamlet in Schreiber's Café?"

"What about, what about?" she scoffed at him. "What about mock cabbage soup and boarders with nasty ideas and forced labor in the sweatshop of dreams? Where've you been, you never heard of the distinction between art and life?"

Saul blinked as from a shock of cold water, falling back on his most basic assumption: "But you have to admit they were innocent times."

Leah gave him a look like she was sorry there was no Santa Claus. "From the fruit of the tree of the knowledge of good and evil," she stated flatly, "we had our lifelong stomachaches."

Much as he would have liked to drop this hopeless exchange, Saul couldn't let it go. He felt compelled to draw her attention to certain insidious differences between her age and his. There was, for instance, the Bomb, which fruit had not yet ripened in those callow days. But the end of mankind and its invalidation of all human efforts to date seemed not nearly so pressing as the utter dissolution of this single pallid girl. Not wanting to argue, Saul submitted what was almost a question:

"You at least had the future."

"What future?" she replied as he might have predicted. "I died in my twenties."

Then she was fading, blending into the hearth, her contours confused with the hollows of the stones. Saul anticipated the aftermath of their unresolved affair, how he would burrow back into his solitude and sit a perpetual shivah for a woman more than sixty years in her grave. But why must that be, when it needed only a step across a threshold to join her forever? Didn't all his lonely years, spent virtually rehearsing to be a ghost, stand him in good stead?

Just this side of visibility now, the girl looked bedraggled and sad, her hair in lank disarray, a shoulder of her shift slipped halfway down her arm.

"Leah," cried Saul, rising from his desk with arms outstretched, "take me with you!"

While her vanishing act was momentarily arrested, her voice was curt: "What are you, nuts? You're still alive."

"That's a problem which is easily solved," he assured her, casting about for some implement of self-destruction. Then further provoked by the hand that Leah had raised to calm him down, he shouted, "You think *I'm* afraid to let go? Ha!" snapping his fingers. "That's how afraid I am to let go." Because nothing was worth hanging on to if it meant letting go of Leah.

But when he reached out to hold her, his heart already plumping itself to pillow her head, he embraced only air. Having lurched clean through her, he wheeled around crazily, and thanked God that she was still there.

She had taken a seat in the ladder-back rocking chair facing the fire.

"Now are you satisfied?" she said to him, quietly brooding. Gazing into the embers, she avoided Saul's stare, as if she were deeply embarrassed by her own untouchability. From the corner of her eye swelled a tear like an inflating balloon. Enormous, it mirrored the room: a crystal ball. Peering into it from where he stood, Saul could see himself, and beside him Leah—like a rustic husband and wife in their cottage in the pines, like a pair of ghosts. Then the tear dropped from her eye and burst into nothing.

That was when it struck Saul how their failed undertaking was only a symptom of a common malaise. It wasn't so much the unrealized stories as their unconsummated relations, his and Leah's, that had left her desolate. Too busy bursting with his outsized passion for her, he had yet to make room to accommodate hers for him.

"You love me," Saul tried tentatively, then, pleased with the way the words rang in his ear: "You love me!" he roared, like a man trying to hail a departing ship.

Still sullen-eyed, Leah allowed the corners of her lips to curl.

"You might say," she proceeded formally, "I have certain . . . unprofessional feelings toward you. So sue me."

Then Saul experienced a pain, concentrated somewhere in his imagination, of more heroic proportions than any he was familiar with—which led him to conclude that it must have belonged to Leah. He was grateful that she still trusted him enough to let him try it on.

"Leah," he asked her, needing to connect the pain to its source: how could he have neglected the question for so long? "Leah, how did you die?"

He had supposed something like the fashionable consumption of the period, the febrile flush it would have brought to her cheeks, the limpid glaze to her eye. But the explanation was less poignantly histrionic.

"I had a messy death," she forthrightly informed him. It seemed that her appendix had burst, sloshing her organs in a poison marinade. A mistaken diagnosis had led to a prolonged and agonizing ordeal. Offhandedly she mentioned—her voice disembodied, the rocker still keeping cadence—that had she survived she would have been sterile anyway. It was her first and parting reference to the fact that her unfinished business might have involved more than just telling tales.

The vacated chair rocked a few times on its own before running down.

He was slumped in a chair in the dining room staring into the slough of his black bean soup, when Iris began to sing in his ear:

"I wish I was in Dixie, oy vay, oy vay—"

He motioned as if to swat a gnat, making her a face that showed how his defenses were broken down, which was all that Iris needed to know.

"Fellow fellows," she cleared her throat, calling attention by sounding a glass with her spoon, "what am I bid for this fine, if slightly tarnished, specimen of a king-sized Jewish leprechaun? He'll bring minutes of enjoyment, not to mention good luck, to the happy purchaser. All right, so he's damaged, but give him a tumble and he's good as new—a regular Jewish-American prince. And that's not all. Buy now and we'll throw in his quaint little cottage under a mushroom, where who knows but he keeps a hidden pot of shekels. You all know how to find his cottage—where was it you told us? First star on the right and straight on till morning?

Ladies, don't be shy. Who'll start the bidding?"

Keeping his head down, Saul asked in vain for some quarter. He was seconded by some of the colonists deploring his persecution, but Iris wasn't ready to relent.

Plumping herself down in the chair next to Saul, she hissed at him under her breath, "So your enflamed libido went into remission—Gottenyu. But think of the others suffering from the epidemic that you began." Then she was on her feet again, exhorting her audience not to all make their offers at once.

Saul wasn't so dull that he couldn't recognize the method in her cruelty, which was after all only the disguise that her good intentions wore. Guardian angel manqué, she was still looking out for him, trying to procure a proxy for his bed. Beyond humiliation, however, Saul was also beyond gratitude. Tugging at her sleeve, he asked in a whisper that she please refrain from doing him any favors. And when she didn't budge, he spoke up a little too loudly, surprised at the anger that had caused him to raise his voice. "There's not a woman on earth who can satisfy me."

He hadn't meant it to sound so much like a challenge.

In Prospero's Cell Saul collapsed on the daybed and wished he were dead. After an indefinite time the door opened, admitting a visitor and a chilly breeze, and he sat up like a shot to welcome Leah back. Though when had Leah ever needed to use the door?

Framed by the moonlit windows, his visitor appeared to be outfitted in shadows, from which she (Saul still hoped it was she) began the provocative act of extricating herself. She unwound her muffler like a long black bandage, revealing a perfect face, then released from under her stocking cap a wash of sable hair. She shed the shapeless greatcoat, exposing a dusky anatomy to which the residual shadows of her black lingerie still clung. She never bothered to remove her boots.

The flames in the grate crackled what sounded like a feeble applause as she crept into his bed. Fallen back on his elbows, Saul felt that he was being stalked. He would have covered his nostrils against the aphrodisiac of her tawny scent, had she not gripped his wrists so firmly, pressing him into the pillow.

"Helene?" he ventured, though who she once was seemed beside the point, the retiring artist having been transformed into what he now beheld.

"We drew straws," she breathed huskily, in a tone which—to Saul's thinking—was better suited to saying, "We drew blood."

He wanted to tell her he wasn't interested. He was injured, he was saving himself, was spoken for; he had a headache. But his straying hands would have proved him a hypocrite. As she nuzzled his neck and mopped his chest with her hair, he watched his mutinous fingers, in flight from his conscience, light upon her black-stockinged thighs. They fluttered along her flanks, tried to hide in the folds of her camisole, where, flushed out by her undulations, they were forced to seek obscurer warmths and depths.

Then the rest of him had hypnotically followed the lead of his hands. With his arms and hips, his tongue, he clove to her, burrowing wherever he could, as if to enter this fitful woman Saul had first to escape himself.

Clenching shut his eyes, he gave the woman he was embracing another face.

"I'm exploding!" he warned, feeling the blood run away from his brain as he shoved the waist of his long johns to his knees.

And a sweet-and-sour voice affirmed: "Bombs aweigh!"

When he raised his head to look beyond the artist's heaving shoulders, Saul was staring into the face he'd pictured in his blindness. Instantly he went limp beneath Helene, trying to signal with a faithless hand that this was all some kind of accident.

"What's the matter?" gasped Helene, rigid with panic, oblivious to the presence of the paranormal. "Is it your heart?" Putting an ear to that organ till she'd determined that it pounded like a pneumatic fist.

Saul's attention remained riveted to Leah, who sat in the rocking chair facing the daybed, looking on as serenely as a spectator at a recital. "So," she said, furrowing her brow in serious interest, "this is what it means to bomb in bed?"

Still pinned and wriggling in the vise of Helene's silken knees, Saul pleaded with the ghost, "Have a little mercy."

Leah shrugged it was out of her hands, while Helene, as if having heard her watchword, straightened herself with arms defiantly akimbo and pronounced, "I have no mercy." Then, the taskmistress of pleasure and pain, she gathered the mane of her hair into a topknot, leaned forward, and began to lash Saul across his bristly cheeks.

Between strokes he looked helplessly at Leah, who seemed to have scooted her chair even closer. "Lucky me," she chirped, her old amused self, "to have such a ringside seat."

"My naughty slave," admonished Helene, as Saul pulled a strand of her hair from his teeth, baring his other cheek in time to receive another mouthful. She promised that this was just the beginning, that no part of his body would go unstung by her punishing whip. As his head was snapped thus from side to side, Saul was made to look back and forth between the spirit and the flesh. In his extremity he sent up a prayer that he might be rid of them both, and when no answer was forthcoming, cried out, "Enough already!"

But that only spurred on Helene, who was busily working

her way down his torso. This was no occasion, Saul realized, for his old standby of passive surrender. Nobody's victim, he righted himself so violently that his sham persecutor, bucked off balance, tumbled onto the floor.

Saul started an apology, then thought better of it, afraid that she might be encouraged to renew her efforts. Risen to her feet, Helene accused him with a withering stare of spoiling her sport. Shaking off the indignity, she smoothed her whispering garment with a motion that was both a taunt and a caress. Then having displayed to its best advantage the Indian gift of her sensuous self, she put on again, along with her heavy greatcoat, her dramatic reticence. She gathered up the rest of her things and made for the studio door, snarling inaudibly but for a parting curse:

"Don't look for a second chance, you phony turd."

Saul could have assured her that missed opportunities were the name of his game.

The flames leaped as the door slammed, the rocker creaked—and there was Leah, never so opaque, with a hand to her mouth as if hiding her shock or her merriment. Assuming the latter, Saul asked beyond consolation, "You think it's funny?"

Leah hung her head in an improbable show of opprobrium. Saul responded, despite having been caught in flagrante, by taking on the air of an injured party.

"You win, Leah," he conceded, though what was the contest? "I'll leave here in a couple of days," he began, matter-of-factly unfolding the map of the rest of his life, "and take to wandering, probably flay myself from town to town, calling your name . . . " He was warming to the vision, fondly describing his advance toward a lonely death, when he couldn't help noticing, beyond the remarkable clarity of her rocking form, that she was gazing unchastely at his still-exposed lap.

Quickly he made to cover himself with the comforter, but even its thickness couldn't conceal his reawakened desire, which lifted the material like the ground above a magic bean.

Then she was standing and, with a slightly irritated shrug, had dropped her thin white shift. Fallen down around her ankles, it made a puddle out of which she stepped as onto a shore. Afraid to look directly at her nakedness, Saul continued to stare at the heap of shucked graveclothes, as if their absence of Leah were the real miracle.

"Saulie," she said tenderly to snap him out of it, "I'm here." And when he still couldn't bring himself to lift his head, she added, "Must I draw you a diagram?" Then, with an exasperated sigh, "Come on, kiddo, give a girl a thrill."

He shaded his eyes to gape at her incandescence, wanting to weep over the spilled ink of her blue-black hair. He almost wished that she might pull off her head again, wad up her face or do sleight of hand with her ears, but tonight she looked so perfectly intact. Nothing about her delicate parts hinted that they might be detachable. There was a palpability about her small-pored breasts, her sunken belly with its single blemish of a half-moon scar, risen above the bush at the juncture of her tapered thighs.

"Why are you doing this?" Saul wanted to know; because after Helene's counterfeit, here was the authentic cruelty, the ultimate look-but-you-cannot-touch. It was unusual torture, this Pyramus and Thisbe stuff, tom-peeping through a chink in the cosmic design. Then there was the assault on his senses by her chicken-stock-and-parsley fragrance, spiced tonight with a distinctly mortal musk. So full of her essence was Saul that it seemed like there was more of her inside him than out; as if he were only a breath away from becoming Leah Rosenthal's exclusive abode.

If she knelt on the daybed with less ferocity than had her predecessor, Saul was nonetheless afraid. He marveled at how the mattress was indented under her weight, at the shadow she cast when (in a motion suggesting the tutelage of experienced angels) she tossed her hair. Then he was shuddering uncontrollably, his jaw rattling like a telegraph, the circuits popping up and down his spine. He was grief-stricken over the insoluble problem of what to do with his hands.

"Don't be scared to feel me, boychikl," said Leah, warming her fingers against his lips, his cheeks, his streaming eyes. "I took a sabbatical."

In the morning, thickheaded and sluggish, Saul was unable to explain the gout of blood on his sheet. Puzzled, he examined himself for old wounds that might have hemorrhaged in the night—though when in his closet life had he incurred any wounds?

"Either I had a nosebleed or I slept with a virgin," he concluded, the latter alternative reminding him with a wince of his failure with Helene.

Surely a woman of her enigmatic nature would keep such a fiasco under wraps, he told himself. While on the other hand, her secrecy notwithstanding, there were those with diabolical methods of extracting information. Nothing was sacred in this venomous gossip mill. By now his impotence was probably common knowledge, announced in the Colony newsletter and distributed throughout the known world. Saul was glad to be leaving soon.

As an experiment in retreat, it had been about as successful as his performance in bed last night. What, for instance, beyond a damaged reputation, did he have to show for his month-long stay? Padding to his desk, Saul fingered the tattered pages of "Felix and the Angel," then banged his brow at the disgrace—that he should have allowed the atmosphere to seduce him into such active foolishness.

"Gevalt," he groaned, though not usually given to Yiddish expletives. "Who did I think I was, the fiddler on the bomb-shelter roof?" How could he have lost his integrity so thoroughly as to write this fluff? Not to say a whole bale of notes outlining equally ludicrous ideas.

With no reason to linger, Saul decided to make his way back to the hall. Outside, the weather had turned bitter cold again, and the oyster-gray sky promised more snow. Masking his face in his upturned collar, Saul moved from tree to tree like a cartoon spy. He skulked below the terrace watching the colonists depart for their studios. Among them were a party of women which included Consuela and Bonny—Helene was blessedly not around. They were accompanied by a newly arrived resident, a shambling young man who, judging from their flurries of laughter, seemed to be teasing them.

My replacement, thought Saul.

Assuming that the coast was clear, he slunk into the dining room. It was vacated by all but Iris, who was headquartered there as usual, identifiable by the sound of her grumbling behind an open *New York Times*.

Saul figured that if he continued his sub rosa operations, he could pocket some food and get away undetected. But as Iris's grumbling had ceased, he suspected that her antennae had already alerted her to his presence. So, with the more or less comforting thought that he had nothing left to lose, he decided to face the music. He got some coffee and, as the kitchen was no longer serving, someone's leftover plate of cold toast aswim in egg. He paused a moment to lament the nasty habits he'd cultivated over the weeks. Then pulling up a chair adjacent to a headline denouncing some international atrocity, Saul thought that he couldn't wait to get back to the world.

He read the headline aloud with emphatic interest, eliciting a nasal "D'you mind?" from Iris. Biting his tongue, he jabbed his fork at the fishy eye of a yet unbroken fried egg, thinking: Cyclops. Then unable to stand the suspense (Was it for a reckoning he'd come here in the first place?), Saul recited another headline, this one an EXTRA:

> FELLOW AT ARTISTS' COLONY FAILS TO DELIVER GOODS
> Suspicion of Writer's Block Syndrome, Absence of Lead in Pencil Cited as Clue."

Iris lowered her paper, slid her eyeglasses halfway down her nose, then pushed them abruptly back up again.

"Okay, so you're a fraud. So you built us all up to a mighty letdown. So Saul the Satyr, unmasked, turns out to be just another goat with a crumpled horn." It was evident that she'd begun to enjoy herself. "Look at it this way, it was probably pity that put the woman in your bed, and now you've made yourself more worthy of pity than ever. So you see, everything works out. It's not the end of the world."

"Guess that was wishful thinking on my part, eh?" Saul repined. He was unable, as always, to tell whether Iris had twisted the knife or withdrawn a thorn from his paw, concluding that her gift lay in the ability to do both at once.

She was clucking her tongue with a sound like a clock gone mad, when he sheepishly inquired, "Just for the record, does everyone know about last night?"

Iris pursed her lips to consider. "The news may not have spread to the cook and the maintenance crew yet."

Rather than try to plumb further the depths of her bottle-thick lenses, Saul gave himself up to gloom.

"Look at it this way," piped Iris; Saul groaned that he'd had enough of her perspective, "now you can act your age."

He thanked heaven for small mercies. But having bent his head the better to mourn the loss of his appetite, he was forced to look up again at a honking noise. Iris, full of surprises, having removed her glasses to reveal a pair of eyes like pink paramecia, was laughing fit to be tied.

"Look at you," she managed through her honking and wheezing. "A fugitive from a sideshow—the Rabbi of Borneo. He says kaddish after swallowing live toads." She hooted hysterically, pausing long enough to accommodate more revelation: "The Hunger Artist in the Henhouse!" Then she dried her eyes and recommenced to howl.

As butt of the joke, Saul set his jaw on principle, though the humor was not entirely lost on him. And while he wasn't quite up to laughing at himself, he let slip the ghost of a smile over Iris's uncharacteristic zaniness. So what if it was at his expense? It was somehow endearing, that she could care enough, however perversely, to take such joy in his company. If ever she ceased her guffawing, he thought he would ask her to please stay in touch.

In the bathroom mirror of his seldom slept-in suite above the dining room, Saul saw the catalyst for Iris's carrying on: his hair like a bird's nest, face lampblacked in stubble, straw leaking out of his joints. After a shave and a bath, a change of clothes, he reapproached the mirror, and judged that at least the external damage was not beyond repair. In fact, his misadventurous month had been all but erased from his person, except from around his tired eyes. They seemed, in their sunken state, to have absorbed some nameless knowledge which, thank God, was nowhere else in evidence.

Due to depart the next afternoon, he returned with mixed feelings to the seat of his procrastination. It was a cute little refuge all right, his studio, suitable for every type of dreaming, but now it seemed mostly appointed in bad memories. Seeing no reason to rekindle the fire—he wouldn't be hanging around—Saul turned up the thermostat to reduce the chill. He took down the most recent "tombstone" from its hook in the paneled wall. Then, under the name and dates of the previous tenant, above a knot like a bloodshot eye, he inscribed himself with a leaky ballpoint pen. It was a liberating act. Come the next cataclysm and Saul too, like those listed prior to the storm of the thirties, would have dissolved into a stain.

After that, he had but to toss his notebooks and dictionary into a sack (the typewriter belonged to the Colony), and his tracks were virtually covered. There was of course the daybed, which he ought to make up, and that curious book of stories that needed returning. Snatching it up, he fanned his face with the yellow pages, shaking his head in disbelief. His short-lived fascination for this sort of thing, which the title alone should have dampened, would cause him ever after to question his own taste. Then there was the tale of Felix and the angel, about which the less said the better. It prompted Saul to think twice about lighting the fire, about torching Prospero's Cell and sowing the ground with salt.

In the tree outside his windows, the snowy owl had resumed its voyeuristic observation. It was one very easily amused owl, Saul surmised. Taking a seat at his desk for old times' sake, he stared back into the winking *memento mori* of its face, and was reminded of the serious work that he'd abandoned. He sadly recalled the prophetic zeal out of which Felix was born, as if Saul Bozoff had been singled out to collaborate with the Lord Almighty. Then he began to feel the undeniable stirrings once again. He blamed the bird for trying to rouse him before he was ready; it wouldn't do at this late hour to spoil an otherwise perfect record of inertia. Gesturing obscenely at the owl, Saul was surprised to find that the hand which gave the finger also held his pen.

He wondered what he thought he was doing. Did he expect to redeem four weeks in an afternoon? The fact of the matter was that, with his term of residence over for all practical purposes, the pressure was off Saul to produce. So where was the harm in fooling around on the page just to see what, if anything, might turn up?

Then, while he felt he was in no hurry, while he shouted "Whoa!" to his galloping impulses, it started again: the keening of his blood, the musical traffic along his nerves. Arcade lights came on in his brain. And though he wouldn't exactly have called it inspiration, Saul had already hatched a fresh strategy.

In this one Felix, outwitting oblivion, reads the signs and takes to his cellar well before the end. He remains there for such a time in dank isolation—nibbling bouillon cubes and licking the condensation off stones—that he can no longer remember the world he descended from. Frustrated with trying, able only to picture ashes and umbrellas of flame, he decides to see what he's been missing at whatever cost. In the forlorn hope of jolting his memory he climbs up his ladder.

"And lo, what he discovered above," wrote Saul, following the flourishes of his pen like a planchette on a Ouija board, "was a neighborhood on top of a river bluff mercifully spared by the Lord, full of cunning old world Jews.

"From their wagons and stands they were peddling prayer shawls and siddurs, goofer dust and mojo hands. They were distilling sacramental moonshine and living on air. In their shops they bartered with the shvartzeh farmers, swapping for geese and strings of onions the unspeakable name of God. Their tzaddiks pulled rabbits from under their yarmelkes and gutted them on the spot; they prayed till the floodwaters parted at the corner of Winchester and North Main. Their young men spawned catfish in the ritual bath; they dove into the holds of sunken steamboats looking for mermaids, searched the sewers for antebellum gold. They chased their runaway brides down to Beale Street, where, themselves seduced by the tumbling dice, they stayed on to play ragtime klesmer music in the saloons. Families laden with baggage stumbled down gangplanks, exchanged mischievous winks on the levee, then knelt to kiss the cobblestones . . . "

When he paused to catch his breath and read what he'd written, Saul was heartsick and ashamed. Just when he'd thought himself immune, here was more of the stuff that had infected the rest of his story. As for Felix's surfacing from underground, pure shmaltz; might as well trot him out of a house that fell from the sky. Disappointed in himself, Saul took it out on his hero. With a resolute effort he dispatched Felix back down to the bottom of his ladder; he sealed up the cellar and sat on the lid, though it rose again, releasing hordes of wild Jewish daughters and horny cheder boys.

"The Gramophone" and "Aaron Makes a Match" first appeared in *The Eureka Review*; "The Book of Mordecai" in *Gayoso Street Review*; "Lazar Malkin Enters Heaven" in *The Greensboro Review*; and "Shimmele Fly-by-Night" in *HomeWords: An Anthology of Tennessee Writers*.

Grateful acknowledgment is made for permission to reprint the following copyrighted material:

"Aaron Makes a Match" and "The Book of Mordecai" from *Isaac and the Undertaker's Daughter* by Steve Stern are reprinted by permission of the publisher, Lost Roads Publishers. Copyright © 1983 by Steve Stern.

Excerpt from *Sweeney Astray* translated by Seamus Heaney. Copyright © 1984 by Seamus Heaney. Reprinted by permission of Farrar, Straus and Giroux Inc.

Excerpt from "When You Awake" by J. R. Robertson and Richard Manuel. © 1969 Canaan Music, Inc. (ASCAP). All rights reserved. Used by permission.

The author wishes to thank the MacDowell Foundation for their generous hospitality.